THE VOID'S LAMENT

OF MAGIC: BOOK THREE

T. ARIYANNA

PROLOGUE

18 Years Earlier

A small wisp of purple smoke tumbled over itself, getting tangled. The woman touched it wistfully with a finger, and it trembled at her touch. She sent a small burst of magic into it, calming the smoke. She smiled as it curled around her finger, hugging it tightly.

The smoke rushed from her finger, stretching to the stone wall before Theresa. It brushed against the brickwork, dust scattering in the air. It circled around Theresa's head, and she spun with the smoke in the dark room. The walls were bare in the small spaceShe stood near a plush chair that had a layer of dust over the cushions. Behind her, near the door, was a small wooden work desk. Papers were piled neatly next to a locked journal. Quills were lined neatly on the desk just beside a large candle. The smoke perched atop the unlit candle and billowed out and up. It looked like it was playing, pretending to be part of the candle. Theresa giggled, and the smoke shot toward her. It darted past her, and rested on the windowsill. Theresa wiggled her fingers in the smoke and looked through the dark stained glass. She liked to watch the people below, but couldn't stand the thought of others seeing her. It was her ritual to sit alone in this dark room at the edge of the Tower, watching and thinking.

"Why don't you just give it a body already, Theresa? Wouldn't it be better to finally have it come to life?" a man's voice said behind the woman.

She whirled around, cupping the smoke in her hands protectively. The man had sharp features, and eyes that shone with a dark green color. His metallic pupils gleamed at her. Though she knew her eyes looked the same, there was something different in his.

Something darker. He smiled at her, showing a row of perfect white teeth between his thin lips. His short brown hair framed his face, the small curls sticking out every which way. It only added to his charm.

A small creature peeked out from behind his legs. Its pale green skin showed a web of black veins beneath. It clung to the man's coat with thin fingers, standing on frail and shaking legs. Filthy clothes hung from its frame, skin clinging to bones. It stared at her with fathomless black eyes.

"Crestyss! I've told you not to sneak up on me like that. You know I haven't found the right body for my little one, nor can I make one for it on my own." She rubbed her thumb over the cowering smoke, and it nestled into the palm of her hands.

"So sentimental. Why do you care if the body is right? All that matters is that it fits. Or could it be that you do not want your demon to have its own body? Don't you think it would be nice to have another demon around, Grite?"

He glanced down at the creature at his side. It nodded its head wildly, shrinking away from Crestyss' gaze. It shuffled anxiously under his glare, until he looked back to Theresa.

Though Theresa and Crestyss had created the essences, the souls, of their demons together, they had not given them life at the same time. Crestyss had forced his essence into any body he could find until it bonded with one. Theresa had been determined to find the best body for her creation, knowing it deserved as much.

Crestyss crossed the room, his own demon close behind like a shadow. He placed one hand on her shoulder, and the other over her hands. The smoke shook within her grasp, and she pulled away from him. She dared not look in his eyes, knowing the spell they held.

"I must be getting back now. My pack has been expecting me for some time," she muttered, pushing past him.

"Those mutts again? Haven't you moved onto bigger and better things? What about me, my dear?"

She froze at his words, anger roiling in her chest. She nearly clenched her fists, reminding herself at the last second about the essence in her hands.

"For the last time, Crestyss, they are not mutts. And I'd advise you to remember that."

He scoffed at her, and she looked over her shoulder to find him rolling his eyes. The demon stared at the ground, kicking at a loose stone in the floor.

"And as for you, you know I shall always return, Crestyss," Theresa whispered sadly. His chuckle echoed behind Theresa as she closed the door behind her and leaned against it. Her essence was pressed to her chest, and it hummed at the embrace. The essence thrummed with the rapid beat of her heart, and she willed it to slow.

She heard a crash from within the room. Before she could investigate, Crestyss was shouting. Grite was whimpering behind the door, and there was a thud. Theresa knew Crestyss had thrown his creation.

She backed away from the door as quietly as possible. Theresa pulled a small leather sack from her pocket and slipped the smoke into it, then tucked it away.

She meandered throughout the tower to the ground floor, into the streets of Centric. It was a relief to be out of Crestyss' domain, like light had entered her world again. The day was coming to an end, the sun moving to kiss the horizon, and the constant traffic of pedestrians and carriages had dwindled to a trickle as the vendors and booths closed for the day. She nodded a greeting to those she passed, but avoided conversation. She kept her eyes fixed on the ground, following the paths laid out by the large pipes that lined the streets. They carried water and fuel to all the buildings, and most were grateful, but Theresa couldn't understand the complexity of it all. The streetlamps above glowed with a powerful flame that was constantly being fed by such pipes. Though she feared the dark, Crestyss' impression on the city was far more terrifying to her.

As she wandered the housing district of the inner ring, she passed a small house with a purple door, a heart shaped window set into it. She paused, wondering if she should pay her friend a visit. The chimney atop the flat roof showed no smoke billowing out of it. *She must still be out.* There was a twinge of pain in Theresa's chest, but she shook it away. The pain was replaced with longing, and she pushed herself to get home as quickly as possible.

The market quarter had gone dark. There were hardly any people to be found, and only half of the street lamps were lit. The streets were cluttered with unmanned carriages and parked automobiles. She was still in awe at the recent advances that Crestyss had implemented: open carriages that powered themselves along the streets on fat tires. There still weren't many to be found, but those that drove along the uneven streets rattled and spat out smog. Shop signs swung in the wind, creaking ominously. A chill went down Theresa's spine as she passed by an especially dark store. She glanced in the window, wondering what shop it could be, but she couldn't make out the wares. The only thing to be seen in the darkness was her own silhouette staring back at her eerily.

Shaking her head, she pulled away from the shop and went on her way. She felt the essence buzzing in her pocket, and she patted its satchel to sooth it.

A dark alley near the walls dividing the rings of Centric opened up and Theresa ducked inside. She felt the darkness as though it were a curtain closing on her, separating her from everything else.holding up a dim light in her hand, Theresa checked the contents of the alley. A small cart that was missing a wheel was leaned against the wall, broken and empty barrels atop it. She held her hand out, willing the light to spread onto the cart. A slick substance gleamed with her light, and the wood looked rotted. She scoffed at the carelessness of whoever had abandoned their trash, and at all those that saw but chose to ignore it. Her voice echoed in the alley, but no sounds came back to her. It was completely empty, not even worthy of homing rats. When she found no sign of life, she reached into her other pocket, her fingers gliding over the surface of a crystal ball.

She plucked it from her pocket and admired it. It was a perfect fit in her palm, no larger than an apple. A white light glowed from the inside, illuminating her face. *Crestyss won't notice a few dozen of these missing. He rarely leaves his Tower, and so has no need for them. As long as no one catches me, it'll be fine.*

Theresa waved her hand in front of the ball, concentrating on her home. The light in the ball dissipated and was replaced by an image of her castle, overshadowing the Loren Woods around it.

She shattered the ball on the ground and was quickly enveloped by gray smoke. Theresa breathed it in, enjoying the scent of home that it carried.

Theresa exhaled, standing before the grand doors of her castle. She raised her right hand. A soft blue glow emanated from the faint outline of a lightning bolt on her palm. The plaque beside the door shined, its dark blue light blending with Theresa's.

She touched her skin to the cold metal, and the light became blinding. She took to the gates that opened to greet her, and through the grand doors of her castle that swung open with elegance. The chandelier inside lit as she crossed the threshold, and it filled the room with warmth. Tapestries of rare and marvelous creatures fluttered at the rush of her magic, as though they were alive themselves. Empty suits of armor stood at attention, ready to storm the entire world should she ask it of them.

Theresa allowed herself to smile. Let the humans think what they want of her. She had never done them any harm, and they hadn't the courage to attack her, so it did not matter what they called her. So long as their fear outweighed their worry, she was safe here.

Her suits of armor sprang into an offensive stance as

footsteps entered through the doors open behind her. Theresa spun in place, horror plastered onto her face. Where she expected weapons and angry faces, she found a panting wolf with something slung over his back.

"My lady, I must ask for your help," the wolf said, bowing his head to her. His pitch-black fur glistened in the flickering light of the chandelier. His brown ears flicked at every noise that came from outside. Brown paws pattered the ground anxiously. He licked his muzzle, showing pointed teeth, stained dark red.

"Goyik, what is this? Why do you intrude unannounced?" Theresa snapped. Though Goyik's appearance had startled her, she was quick to assume the role of his leader.

In answer, the wolf shifted awkwardly. He leaned forward and slid something off of his back carefully. He took a step away from it, nose never leaving the stone floor.

The figure rolled over onto the ground, shedding the light blanket that had kept it covered. A small boy fell out of the blanket, shaking violently and dressed only in a tattered pair of pants. His skin was deathly pale. He looked as though he was nothing more than a skeleton wrapped in the thinnest layer of skin. He coughed, limbs rattling on the floor. Blood was matted in his hair and covered his fingers.

Goyik nudged the boy onto his side, and Theresa gasped. Covering most of the boy's back were long gashes, though it was impossible to tell what they were from. Blood trickled from the cuts, but there didn't seem to be much left in the poor boy's body.

Theresa ran to the boy's side and collapsed, looking pointedly at Goyik.

"It was not from one of mine, my lady. I swear it,"

Goyik said. "He was found wandering by himself, muttering something about a monster chasing after him. He passed out, and we brought him straight to you."

"It's a good thing you did, Goyik. I might yet be able to save the poor thing." Theresa scooped the boy into her arms carefully, mindful of his injuries. His face contorted with pain.

Theresa carried the boy down a hall to the left, marching through the corridors as they constantly changed. Her magic controlling the castle made it ever changing to fit her needs, and they willed into existence as she marched through them. She went straight to the infirmary, where she laid the dying boy on a bed. He curled in on himself slowly.

Theresa worked on the boy, using every ounce of magic she had to heal his back. The wounds remained despite her best efforts, and she groaned in annoyance. "What's going on? Why won't it work? These are nothing more than simple wounds."

"Perhaps it is too late for him, my lady. I did my best to bring him to you, but I failed."

"No, not yet, Goyik. I won't let this child die! There has to be something." Theresa threw her hands into the air, and her long nails snagged on the trim of her coat. Her leather satchel fell from her pocket, and the smoke of her essence spilled out. It writhed on the floor with immense energy. She picked the smoke up, and it only grew more restless the closer it came to the boy.

Theresa looked back and forth from her smoke to the boy. He was dying, she knew that much. Even if she could find a way to heal his wounds, there was no guarantee he would survive the night. A twinge of guilt ate at her insides, but she made up her mind.

Without a second thought, she carefully coaxed the smoke into the largest gash in the boy's flesh. It slithered in, licking at the edges of skin. It dissolved into the boy's body quickly, turning the blood it touched purple.

The boy contorted and screamed, his eyes flying open. He stared at Theresa, his eyes changing as the boy and the demon fought for dominance. Hazel eyes stared at Theresa first, the pupils clouded over, then turned pitch black. The boy let out another wail, digging his fingers into the bed. The black receded from his eyes, leaving his pupils clear. Theresa sat helpless as the boy and demon alike writhed in pain.

The fighting within the body ceased. The boy was left with one completely black eye, another with a brown iris amongst the dark. The boy went silent, and he fell still. Blood ran down his cheeks. Hands went limp, one of them falling from the bed. Theresa read an accusation in his expression as the lifeless boy stared her down.

Theresa fluttered her hands over the boy's wounds, searching for her essence, but it hadn't returned. She dug her fingers into the boy's flesh, trying to dig it out.

"No!" she screamed in rage. "Not my Cyllorian! Not when I was so close!" She slammed her hands onto the table, tears of sorrow and rage spilling. She stared at the boy's eyes, half human and half demon.

"I won't lose you." Theresa formed a small thorn on her finger with her magic, pressing it against the skin on her wrist. It broke through and slid into her vein.

"But, my lady, you know the risks of…"

"Exactly, Goyik. I *do* know the risks. And I shall gladly take them."

She pulled the magic from her blood, now in the shape of a needle. The magic in her turned her blood into string, one end hanging from the needle, the other laying on her arm. Though the two pieces were not physically connected, they moved in sync with each other.

Using the needle, she stitched the edges of the boy's wounds. Black sutures bound the skin, though the thread was red. With every stroke of the needle, she bound herself to the boy. The wounds healed instantly. Flesh grew from the stitches to fill in the empty spaces on the boy's back. Once he was whole again, the needle shattered in Theresa's hand, the sharp pieces of magic pricking her fingers. Her blood dripped onto the boy's back, soaking into the soft tissue. The drops formed a pattern of a star, and the spots shone just below the surface.

She glanced at her wrist, where she had dipped the needle into her blood. The hole was now the top point of a glowing red star just under her skin. Though it was a faint connection, it was still strong enough to bind her to the boy...to the demon...forever.

She stared at the boy, waiting. The connection wouldn't have taken if he was truly lost, but the suspense was driving her mad. She wanted to shake the child, to smack him, anything to wake him up. She gripped the fabric covering her legs, squeezing until her knuckles turned white, to relieve the tension welling up inside.

She raised her hand slowly toward the boy's face, and she wiped the tears of blood away with the tips of her fingers. The boy sputtered under her touch, blood dribbling from his mouth. He spasmed with coughs, grabbing onto the edge of the bed as he wretched.

"Cyllorian," Theresa breathed, leaning closer to the boy.

He turned his head to her slowly, confusion filling his

face. *"Who are you?"* he asked. *"Where am I? Where is my mother? What's going on?"*

He rolled away from Theresa. He fell onto his newly healed wounds and groaned in pain. He struggled to look at his back, his frail limbs failing to work.

"Shh, shh. It's alright now, dear. It'll take some getting used to, as you sort through the child's old memories. But you needn't worry about those. They will fade with time. All you need to know is that you are my son, Cyllorian. You don't remember what happened when you were just an essence, and explaining it now will only confuse you more. But you are safe here. You are home now."

Theresa laid her hand on the boy's face, caressing his cheek with her thumb. He was rigid under her touch, his eyes wide in shock, but he didn't pull away. His mouth moved slowly as he worked through the situation.

After a moment, his face relaxed and a smile spread across his face. *"Mother,"* he said simply, laying his hand over hers. He pressed his cheek into her hand and closed his eyes.

"Yes, my precious Cyllorian. That's right. No matter what anyone says, you are my son."

She watched the boy's calm face in wonder, fighting tears. She ignored the worried look Goyik was giving her, and the nagging feeling in the pit of her stomach that something wasn't right. She ignored all of it, so that she could feel happiness after all of her sins... just for once.

CHAPTER 1

Cyllorian

"Theresa's been gone a long time," Kaitlyn said as she paced the large gathering room.

Two months had already passed since Cy and Kait had rescued Arion from Crestyss, but the days had gone slowly. Almost immediately, Theresa had left the castle, taking everyone that Cy and Kait had gathered, ushering them back to their lands to declare war on Crestyss. She had given them express orders to remain at the castle and wait for her. Cy had been all too happy to oblige, and was glad that Arion had been to weak to argue. But they hadn't heard a word from her yet, and her return was looking less and less likely with each passing day.

Theresa had turned most of the first floor of her castle into one room meant for meetings as she was expecting many more to soon join them. Though the room was vast, Kaitlyn never strayed more than a few feet from where they sat.

Cyllorian knew just how much Kaitlyn wanted to explore and examine every inch of Theresa's castle. In the first week since bringing Arion back, when he had shut himself inside a bedroom and refused to come out, Kaitlyn had tried to wander the castle herself while Cy stood by Arion's room. Hours later, Cy had gone to look for her, and found her lost in a far corner of the castle. She had gotten lost in a secluded area of the castle that held only bare and boring bedrooms. Cyllorian hadn't even known how many beds the castle had held, and he shuddered at the thought of having to share space with so many people.

Even now, Kaitlyn would pause in her pacing to stare in wonder at the tapestries that covered the walls, set high out of reach. They depicted creatures of myth and legend, creatures that Cy had no answers for whenever Kaitlyn had asked about them. There was a beautiful mural of a sunset over an unknown horizon, and one of a darkened battleground. Between the paintings were tall stained glass windows with crystalline patterns. Their colors danced through the room as the day passed.

The paintings disappeared into darkness along the walls, the other end of the room too far to see. Cy wondered if this room was larger than the castle was from the outside. It took an hour just to walk from one end to the other. The large entrance doors of the castle stood ominously in the shadows, ever out of reach of the painted sunlight. Silver metal gleamed on its own, crisscrossed over the wood.

Cy remembered the first time Arion had left his room, he had found Cy and Kait in this room, and Arion had recited passages about the paintings. He had stood far from them, and his voice was rough with the effort to be heard. Cyllorian thought he had glanced tears in Kaitlyn's eyes then, but he too was in shock at the sight of Arion.

Kaitlyn's voice drew Cy's attention back to her. Her gaze was fixed on the floor again, were feet moving purposefully within the intricate lines of the rug that covered most of the floor.

"Do you think we should go after her? Or check on her, somehow?" she asked as she came to a halt. She didn't address either one of them in particular, but she looked directly at Cyllorian. She tapped the toe of her boot against the ground as she watched him, waiting for an answer.

Cyllorian found himself lost in her eyes, as he had every day since they had rescued Arion. It felt as though he was fighting for her, despite Kaitlyn's awkwardness when around the other boy. Even still, her attention was always divided between the two of them, and Cy could barely control his jealousy.

"She'll be fine. Didn't she say she would be gone this long? She had a lot of people to try to recruit," Cy said, turning away from her. Though he was at a disadvantage in their fight over Kait with his current body, he was thankful that it didn't give away his true feelings. He forced a deep breath into the metal of his chest, and he rattled when he let it out in a loud sigh. Though Kaitlyn already knew how he felt, he was terrified of what anyone else might think. Especially Arion.

"Are you really so sure she's even coming back?" Arion griped. He was laying sideways in a chair, and he bent backwards over the arm to stare at Cy. His dull green eyes showed no signs of emotion.

"Arion!" Cy sniped, staring him down. No matter how much force he put into his gaze, Arion remained unphased and uncaring.

"Think about it. She locked Cyllorian away in a box with no intentions of ever letting him back out, she never liked Kaitlyn. . . and the only reason she even came back for me was to kill me." Arion crossed his arms over his face, and spoke in a monotone. Despite his insistence that he was more Void than Mage, a twinge of sadness could be heard in his last sentence.

"Why the hell would you think something like that, kid?" Cy asked, looking for any chance to change the subject. He looked to Kaitlyn for help, but she was staring at the ground in disappointment.

"Because she said so. Don't you remember? You were there, just before I got my memory back."

"I seriously have no idea what you're talking about. She wasn't making any sense then. Besides, why would she want to kill her own son?" Cy argued. He was scaring himself by defending Theresa, but the last thing he wanted to do was fuel Arion's rage.

"If I had just gotten to you first, taken your life myself, we could have made it. That's what she said, when she was trying to destroy my old body before this one got to it. You must've blocked it out. I only remembered it a couple days ago myself."

"You're sure you're not just confusing it with something Crestyss or Grite might have said? That doesn't sound like Theresa."

"Sure it does. And that's why she left, to get away from us. And if we were made to believe she'd be coming back to give us direction, we'd stay here and never leave. After all that trying, it only took a couple words to get rid of us all." Arion cackled lightly under his breath, as though he genuinely found the whole situation humorous.

"That's not why she left. She went to build up our army

before shit gets even worse for us. She told us that it was only a matter of time before Crestyss tries to take over the world, or whatever it is he wants. Now can we just drop the subject?" Cy said between clenched teeth. He was gripping the arms of the chair hard enough for his claws to bite into the wood.

"Then why did the others have to leave at the exact same time, hm? Answer me that," Arion retorted, a smug smile spreading across his face.

"They had to report back to their homes, and talk them into joining the war."

"Let me guess, did *Theresa* tell you that?" Arion bit back, sitting upright in his chair. His movements were so stiff and quick that it looked inhuman. Cy sat back in his chair to put more distance between them. Kaitlyn moved to sit on the floor at Cy's side, grabbing onto the leg of the chair.

Arion's eyes followed her every move, and his mouth twitched into a sneer for a split second before clearing completely. He glared at Cyllorian, a storm rolling deep in his eyes, nearly out of sight.

"They told me themselves why they were leaving, that good enough for you, kid?" Cy leaned forward slowly, holding himself up on his knees. He narrowed his eyes, daring Arion to make a move. They had been getting in arguments nearly every day, some of them escalating into physical fights on rare occasions. Being locked in the castle together was clearly not helping either of their moods.

"Right, because Jayr is *so* trustworthy and Gil has all his wits about him. And what about Adoette, did *she* tell you, Cyllorian? She likes you more than the others, I'm sure she tells you all sorts of things, doesn't she?" Arion taunted, raising his eyebrows suggestively.

Kaitlyn shifted on the ground beside him, and Cy lost

his temper. *"She has Noma, remember? As annoying as the bug is, she's helpful to her. She doesn't have to say anything!"*

"No, no, you're right about that. Body language can tell a lot about how someone is feeling," Arion scoffed, turning away. He leaned forward, then pushed off. The chair fell back onto the floor, and he kicked his legs in the air, laughing quietly to himself.

He reached his hands toward the ceiling, and green lightning weaved through his fingers. He closed his fists, then flung his fingers out, sending the lightning all around him. It stretched up into the air, growing with every inch it progressed. With a click of his tongue, the lightning shattered and teal sparks shot out in every direction. They hovered in the air around them, surrounding them with stars.

The only time Arion ever looked alive— really alive— was when he used his magic. It lit up his eyes the way they used to, and Cy's essence twisted in the metal body.

Guilt flooded him, mixed with hope. As much as they fought, Cy held no resentment toward Arion. He cared more for him, worried about him more each day, trying his best to make up for his mistakes. But there was no changing his bitter nature, and he found himself squelching Arion's spirits if they got too high. He told himself it was jealousy, part of their rivalry for Kaitlyn, but he knew he couldn't justify himself forever.

"Just like you used to do, for me," Kaitlyn cooed, reaching out to touch a star. As the magic touched her finger, it burst into flame. Her veins just under her skin became luminous, spreading throughout her whole hand.

Cy snatched up the exploding star before her, snuffing it out. He swat them each down, one by one, gaining a murderous scowl from Arion. *"Careful. He's still getting used to his magic again."*

Cy glared back at Arion, continuing to free the air of the stars. The light in the boy's eyes was gone again, replaced by the distant expression of the Void.

Arion swung his arm out, and each star slowly fell to the ground and died. "I can control it just fine. Better than you," Arion snapped, grinding his teeth. A grim smile overtook Arion's expression, and he taunted, "At least the magic I have is my own, and not some pity gift!"

"That's enough! You guys have already used up your allotted fight for the day!" Kaitlyn yelled, getting to her feet. She stood between them with her arms outstretched and her eyes shut tight.

While Cy watched Arion carefully for any wrong move, Arion's focus was on Kaitlyn. Sorrow glinted in the boy's eyes, and Cy backed down out of guilt.

Could he really still be there? This is all I can think of to get him back, but he's fighting it. He doesn't want to come back, I can tell. Am I just going about this the wrong way? What else is there for me to do?

In the rare moment of peace, Cy took the opportunity to check on Arion. Arion had found himself in his old clothes easily, and was never once seen without his coat. Tome was tucked into the pocket, though Cy hadn't seen Arion open it even once in the past month. His eyes had regained their color, but not the light that used to define him. If it weren't for the white hair that Arion had been so determined to keep, Cy could've almost told himself none of it had ever happened.

No. He could never convince himself of that. No matter what he tried to force himself to believe, nothing ever felt right about Arion. Not anymore. The boy had only gotten thinner since they had retrieved him, and Cy couldn't remember the last time he had seen Arion eat. Or sleep. Dark circles ringed his eyes, and his hands shook violently most of the time.

His sanity was the most questionable thing about him. Cy had always been able to know everything going on inside the boy's head. Now that he was unable to, he was always on edge. Arion had been unpredictable just before his death, and he was sure he could have only gotten worse from there. The only question was... just how *much* worse?

"Can we get along now?" Kaitlyn asked, exasperated. Cy was broken out of his reverie. Arion was staring back at him with a longing in his eyes that mirrored his own.

"Yeah," he said quietly, lowering his head. His voice was lighter now, calmer. Cy nodded silently, watching Arion as the boy studied his hands. Kaitlyn sat down on the ground between them, letting out her breath.

"Finally. I swear, getting you two to behave is worse than pulling teeth!" Kaitlyn giggled awkwardly, trying her best to make a joke of the situation.

Arion cringed at the comment, and put his hand to his cheek. His jaw dropped slightly, and Cy could see that he was running his tongue over the surface of his teeth. Checking that they were all there.

He caught Cy watching him, and quickly stopped what he was doing. His hands dropped into his lap. Arion's demon body wasn't capable of changing fully, but he could still manifest a set of short, black claws. He'd made a habit of playing with them whenever he avoided Cy. The claws were out now, picking at a loose string on Arion's pants. His expression went blank. Like always, there was no telling what could possibly be going on in his head.

"We're not the only ones who have a shitty situation. We

keep forgetting that. Yeah, we're angsty teenagers with massive mental damage all cooped up together, but that's not the end of the world. If something happened to Theresa, or she couldn't get all the people she needs, that's it. Crestyss wins, and Lontorra is destroyed. He brainwashed all the Mages, and most of everyone else, too, for that matter. He's going to kill all the humans, then the species that sided against him, then the ones that tried to stay out of it completely. Without anyone left after that, who knows what he'll do next. Probably go terrorize the rest of the world. So either way, being stuck here is better than being dead," Cy said finally. His accidental speech replaced the silence, and it echoed in the room.

"We won't let him win," Kaitlyn said simply, smiling at him. Her eyes flashed fiercely, and her pupils narrowed into slits. Dragon eyes.

He smiled back, but Arion's wide eyes staring into the distance caught his attention. He hadn't responded to his speech in any way, and it worried Cy. A bitter comeback or sarcastic remark would have been better than nothing.

"Arion?" he prompted, leaning to the side to try to meet his gaze.

Arion's eyes darted to him for a moment, before he fell backwards onto the chair again.

"Don't tell me you've got absolutely nothing to say to that."

"Nothing at all. At least, nothing you want to hear."

Cy narrowed his eyes, knowing what conversation would follow if he pressed the issue. *"You're right about that, kid. I* don't *want to hear it. And I don't want you thinking it, either, you got that? Hey, I'm talking to you, stubborn brat!"*

"Yeah, yeah. I hear you. Selfish demon," Arion muttered under his breath, waving his hand in the air dismissively. His lips pulled up in a slight smile, but he avoided Cy's gaze.

"We don't even need her..." Arion whispered slowly. He drummed his fingers on the ground beside him, his mind working anxiously. "We can do it ourselves. Sneak in and kill him without a second thought. He's the only one that wants a fight out of all this, not his followers. If he's dead, there's no threat. We don't need an army, especially not one led by a woman that effectively didn't exist until a few months ago.

"Just the three of us, we can do it. Right, Cy? You and me, we can storm his Tower and kill Crestyss. Just you and me, Cy... like before." Arion turned to Cy and smiled.

Cy readied himself to talk Arion down, worried he had let his mind go too far again. But the smile on the boy's face wasn't cunning or sadistic. It was elated, hopeful as he gazed at Cy.

"I'm not so sure, kid. We barely made it out of there with more people fighting for us, I don't think less is the way to go here. You're not in the best of shape for a fight, either. You gotta get your strength back before we go on any wild adventures. Remember last time we got in over our head?" Cy chose his words carefully, and spoke slowly.

He watched Arion closely, testing him. The boy's face grew dark, tormented, and he looked back to the ceiling. His mouth moved minutely, but there was no sound.

Arion closed his eyes at the silence, and Cy watched him carefully. He knew he wasn't trying to sleep. Arion did everything he could to stay awake. His breathing quickened, and his hand fluttered to his head. He dug into his scalp with his black claws, and his white blood soaked his hair.

"Arion," Cy said softly. Arion's eyes shot open and he glanced at Cy. There was fear deep within them, but the boy hardened his resolve in seconds. He retracted the claws

and quickly lowered his hand, wiping the blood off on the side of the chair.

As Cy thought how to phrase his concerns, Arion jumped up from the fallen chair. "I'm going outside," he said pointedly. He marched past both of them before they could say anything. Kaitlyn reached for his hand as he passed, but he dodged her grasp easily.

The door shut behind them with a resounding *thud*. Kaitlyn dropped her head and played with the thin band on her finger. "What does he do when he goes out there?" she wondered aloud. "What if he's. . ."

"Tuft keeps an eye on him. If something happened to him, or because of him, he would tell us. Tuft won't tell me anything else," Cy answered, chasing her fears away.

She didn't respond. Her expression was uncertain as she spun the ring on her finger.

Cy wanted to comfort her, to reach out to her, but couldn't. Not only did he lack the proper words, he lacked the right. He sighed, and clawed at his head.

In the depressed silence between them, voices could be heard outside the doors. Cy jumped from his chair, stepping in front of Kaitlyn reflexively. She stood slowly, shaking out her arms as they covered with scales. Vyekrin grumbled from the roof in response, and waited. Her own talons extended, and poison dripped from them.

Cy gathered his dwindling magic, and opened the door violently with a sweep of his arm. The voices ceased as Theresa and her small army stood in shock at their lances.

"What do you think you're doing?" Theresa scolded as she marched into the room. The others followed her, and Cy could make out only a couple faces among the crowd. Gil stood on his own, looking as lost as ever and glaring at the small huddle of Draken on the other side of Theresa.

Jayr was obviously ignoring him as he pushed Kaliyah in a wheelchair.

Adoette was jumping up and down somewhere in the middle of the crowd, her flowered hair bouncing wildly. She finally pushed her way through to the front, and she beamed when she caught sight of Cy. She waved her arm in a wide arc over her head, while Noma buzzed around her head. Cy noticed the small blue buds that ringed her head were gone, leaving small red thorns in their place.

"Well, are you just going to stand there, or are you going to greet us?" Theresa asked impatiently. Cy realized he was still in an attacking stance, and shifted into a normal position.

Theresa looked around the vacant room as the swarm of creatures wandered into the castle. "Where is he?" she asked irritably.

"He's outside somewhere," Cy answered, defensive at her tone.

"And you're not concerned with keeping an eye on him because..?"

"He's with Tuft, so why should I care past that point? He can do whatever he wants. I'm not his babysitter." Cy crossed his arms and avoided her scowl. Kaitlyn had shed her scales for her preferred human form, and left him to meet their new comrades.

"You should know better than to let him go unsupervised. Goyik, come." With a snap of her fingers, her trusted wolf was at her side, appearing from within the throngs of people behind them.

"Yes, Lady Theresa?" he asked dutifully.

"Find Arion," she said shortly, his name clipping off of her tongue violently, as though she couldn't stand the taste of it. Goyik bowed gracefully, and charged back through the doors.

As they waited Goyik's return, Theresa motioned for her army to step forward. "We've had some new recruits that will be residing with us for short periods at a time. They will attend every meeting and memorize every possible strategy, then report back to their homes so that everyone will be prepared. We must be careful to not draw attention to ourselves. I have a barrier that can keep only so many magical creatures hidden at once, or else we would all be here. But we will just have to make do with what we have."

"Fine by me. Just one question. Do I have to learn all of their names?" Cy asked sarcastically. Over two dozen pairs of eyes turned to him. Most scowled at him, including those he knew. Only Gil smiled at his remark, covering his mouth to hide a laugh.

"It would be helpful, yes, not to mention polite. Acquaint yourselves with each other quickly while I get ready."

With that, Theresa left the group of mostly strangers to talk amongst themselves. Despite her words telling them to mingle, more than half of the army left to explore the castle. As the crowd dispersed, Cy realized their cavalry was smaller than expected, less than fifty. He understood why Theresa had made the entry such a grand room as all the bodies shuffled through toward a large staircase that had formed silently across from the door. All that was left were those that he knew, and half a dozen new faces. Two Droll, two Draken, and two Mages. Adoette was the first to disband from the group, flitting about the room as though it was her first time inside the castle.

Seeing as how none seemed inclined to start, Cy spoke

first in a monotone. *"Hi, I'm Cyllorian, and I'm a demon. Get your complaining, bickering, and judging out of the way now, you have three seconds... and time's up, who's next?"*

The Droll chattered amongst themselves, standing a short ways behind Gil. They were clearly older than him, one large and clearly male with his chest bare beneath a thick vest. The other had dominant curves to her body, and the scales along her shoulders seemed larger than normal. They seemed lost in their own world as they pointed to various aspects of the vast room.

Jayr was flanked by two males, similar in size. While Jayr scowled behind a nervous Kaliyah, the other two Draken were smiling idiotically. It was difficult to recognize them outside of their armor, but Cy was certain they were Orthros and Lane, their guards from their time on Mount Draken.

Most of them looked amongst themselves for help. The first to step forward were two Mages, whose eyes burned like fire around the silver pupils. They had thin black hair, and gray splotches on their skin. The oldest, a boy with a thin face and high cheekbones, said, "I am Hunter Vamyr, a Mage. This is my sister, Twila. Crestyss killed our parents many years ago and captured us. He held us captive near the ocean, away from everyone. He experimented on us, tortured us, and turned us into something we still don't understand yet. This is why we choose to fight."

Hunter held himself high, but Cy could see the responsibility of being the oldest weighing on his shoulders. He couldn't be much older than himself, but the haunted look on his face said that Hunter had been through much more torment than Cy could imagine.

His sister couldn't be older than twelve. She had her long hair tied into pigtails. Even restrained, it nearly reached down to her hips. Her long, light pink dress with a red floral pattern reached to her ankles, but left her arms bare. There were dark rings all along her arms, of both bruises and scars. Silver bracelets squeezed her wrists, and when she lifted her hand to wave enthusiastically, a drop of blood ran from underneath the bands. She wiped it away without a second thought, and rubbed the blood onto her dress. It was then Cy realized the dark flowers on her dress were smudges of blood, rather than a pattern. Despite this, her smile was bright and genuine in her heart shaped face.

"Vamyr's, come here a moment, would you?" Theresa called as she levitated a table near the middle of the room. The two turned to look at her, and nodded. Moving as a single unit, they left for Theresa.

Gil stepped up to Cy and Kaitlyn, reading the distress that was clear on their faces. "Theresa told us about them before she left to save them. She said Crestyss had been mixing their blood with that of ancient creatures, a type of demon that got their immortality from the blood of others, and had special control over strong, dark magic. *Other-worldly*, she called it. There was supposed to be four, but the two middle siblings had already passed away by she time we got there. And the little one, Twila, is the strong-est. Because her magic as a Mage wasn't fully developed, it was the most malleable, so Crestyss did the most to her. He had those bracelets made specifically to keep her under control, by sending magical charges straight into her blood."

Gil looked after the orphans as they helped Theresa to set the room up. Hunter was using thick black strands of magic to move the furniture. Twila stood with her hands clasped behind her, picking at the bands around her wrists.

Her smile was plastered to her face as she watched her brother. Blood dripped to the floor without her notice.

Kaitlyn stepped closer to Cy, and he turned to face her. She was fidgeting in her place, rubbing her arms. Though she had turned away from the group, her gaze was still fixed on one in particular; Kaliyah. The other girl was staring at her hands, refusing to lift her head. The unknown Droll and Draken had disappeared while Cy was distracted by the Mages, leaving them in an uncomfortable silence.

Cy racked his brain for anything he could say to break the tension, but nothing that came to mind sounded right. He knew what kind of trouble he'd be in with Theresa if he started a fight as soon as they arrived, but honestly, what else did she expect? *Does she even know about Kaliyah and Kaitlyn's fight?*

Just as the silence was becoming unbearable, the doors flew open once again, and Arion stumbled into the room. He caught himself on his hands and knees, whirling to glare at a triumphant Goyik. Tome fell to the floor right in front of him. "What was that for? I wasn't doing anything!" he snapped.

"My Lady asked me to fetch you, so I did."

"No need. I'm fine on my own," he grumbled as he picked himself off the floor. He stuffed Tome hurriedly into his coat, and marched into the room. He walked straight past the curious glances, his attention fixed on Theresa.

Cy stepped in his way, worried that Arion would lose control of his temper. *"Welcome back, kid. Meet our new friends, will ya?"* He grabbed onto Arion's sleeve tightly, forcing the boy to meet his stern gaze. Cy held his hand out toward Gil and continued hesitantly, *"They're-"*

"He," Gil piped up, his voice breaking. "I had my birthday while I was gone, so...he."

Cy nodded shortly, though a bit confused. *"Right, he's—"*

Arion let out a sigh, cutting off Cy, and glared over his shoulder at the three that were left. "I don't care who they are," he barked, and went to turn away.

With a groan, Cy grabbed Arion's wrist, but Arion writhed under the touch. He twisted desperately until his fingers touched Cy's arm, sending lightning straight into Cy's essence. Cy jumped back from the shock, releasing Arion. Just as Arion was turning away again, Cy thought he saw guilt in his eyes.

"Arion—" Theresa called, harsher than necessary.

With a stomp of his foot, Arion cut her off. The room filled with thick green smoke, leaving everyone but Cy in a coughing fit. When the smoke cleared, Arion was long gone.

"This definitely won't be a fun group bonding vacation," Cy groaned, staring at the last remnants of the smoke.

CHAPTER 2

Cyllorian

Sitting quietly wasn't something Cy was used to doing. It felt wrong, his body listless. He picked one metal claw at a seam in his leg. Once Arion had disappeared, Theresa announced a meeting for her army. Cy and Kait had been sent away with the guise of finding Arion, but Cy could recognize when he wasn't wanted. Cy had led them to a small room that Arion had adapted into one of his workspaces. He'd been disappointed when it had been reverted back upon Theresa's arrival a month ago, but Arion had never bothered to change it again. It looked more like a plush tea room now. Arion avoided the room, but Cy had noticed that Kait seemed comfortable here.

Kaitlyn stood at the wall opposite him. The paintings on the wall had mesmerized her as they moved, as though a breeze blew through them. One pictured a storm overtaking the castle, another held a field bursting with flowers. Cy watched them carefully. He had never noticed them moving before, but he had never been one to stop and smell the roses.

Cy glanced over his shoulder at the desk behind him. There was a thick book open on the desk, and he tried to force himself to focus on the words, but Kaitlyn's presence weighed on his shoulders. He couldn't leave her alone to get lost in the castle again, especially now that Theresa was back.

"This isn't like you," Kaitlyn said. Her voice was quiet, but missing some of its softness. Cy didn't think she was mad at him, but something in her tone made his essence roil painfully within him.

"She obviously doesn't want us there," Cy answered.

Kaitlyn turned to glare at him, her hands on her hips. "You're really just going to let Theresa come back like nothing happened and start waging a war? You really don't care?"

Cy grit his teeth, the metal at his temples grinding. *"Nope. Not at all."*

"You won't stand up to fight for Lontorra? For your home?" Cy shook his head wordlessly. "What about for Arion?" Kaitlyn snapped.

"This is for Arion. If we join in this war, he'll think he should, too. Theresa and Crestyss can drag each other to hell, for all I care. I just want Arion to stay out of this. He's been through enough," Cy blurted out.

Kaitlyn's gaze softened, and Cy looked away. It seemed the only time they ever talked, it was about Arion. He was the only thing they had in common. Cy couldn't shake the nerves he had whenever he and Kaitlyn were alone, his one-sided feelings hanging in the air between them like a dagger. One wrong move, and someone was bound to get hurt.

They hadn't been able to have a proper conversation since they rescued Arion.

"I've had bags packed all month, ready to go. I just need to convince Arion," Cy added in the awkward silence.

"What?" Kaitlyn asked.

"We don't need to stay here and wait around for Theresa, but I'm not itching for a fight like Arion is. Theresa isn't our problem. As soon as I can get Arion to understand that, we're leaving. All three of us, we're getting out and never coming back."

"That's not what Arion wants." Kaitlyn was quiet, and Cy couldn't make out her tone.

"I don't care what he wants. All that matters is that he's safe. If I get him away from all of this, he'll go back to normal. He'll stop acting like a Void and just be Arion again."

Like he had been called, Arion burst into the room. Green sparks flew from his boots as he stomped into the center. He stopped between Cy and Kait. Cy could see the mass of emotions roiling in his eyes, but Arion shook them away.

"That's quite the tantrum there. What did the door ever do to you?"

"Theresa's holding a war meeting, and you two are just enjoying the scenery?" Arion snapped. He threw his arm toward the paintings. Cy thought he saw the storm grow stronger, but a second later and it was back to normal.

"We weren't invited," Cy responded sharper than he intended. He shot a glance at Kaitlyn, she was staring at the ground, but she remained quiet. Cy couldn't be sure if she agreed with him, but at least she was taking his side for the moment.

Cy grit his teeth and tried to force himself to relax. It scared him to see Arion's magic leaking out of him like this, but he was doing his best to avoid fights between them. Especially when Kait was around.

Arion scoffed and shook his head. Without another word, he marched out of the room. Cy shot up to follow him. *"Where are you going?"*

Arion's stride never broke as Cy quickly caught up to him. He grabbed Arion by his coat. Even with metal skin, the crackling magic around Arion gave Cy shivers. Kait caught up quickly once Arion was stopped, though she kept her distance.

"To the meeting." Arion refused to look at Cy as he spoke.

"And what exactly do you plan to do? Theresa doesn't want us to be a part of this war, or whatever she's planning. Good, let's just leave it at that, and let the rest of them follow her to the grave, if that's what she's planning. All we have to do is ignore her for now, then the castle will be ours, just like before."

"You don't know what she's planning," Arion whispered.

His words struck deep in Cy, and he hesitated to respond. *"And you do?"* The question was cautious, prodding. Cy knew it was risky to try to get any information out of Arion since bringing him home, but there was something about his tone. It sounded like he was begging, and scared.

Arion's jaw tensed, his eyes darting wildly, looking for the answer. Without warning, he shook his head and ripped his coat from Cy's grip. Arion took off down the hall at full speed.

Cy chased after him immediately, Kaitlyn on his heels. *"Arion, just think about this for a second, and leave it alone!"* Cy called after him.

Arion found the meeting room before Cy could catch

him, and blew the doors open with magic. Cy came up behind him to see the large entry room with tables pushed along the walls. Theresa's army filled the tables, familiar and strange faces all staring at the open doors. The tables laid as bare as the large open floor in front of them all.

The army was separated by species, and Cy picked out those he recognized. Gil sat at the end of a line of Droll, his seat closest to the door and right next to Adoette. Across from them sat Jayr, Draken flanking him. At Theresa's own table sat Mages, including the Vamyr siblings. From here, Cy could count them all, and found Theresa had only brought thirty followers. She had representatives from each species.

Though this was supposed to be the lead of her army, with those that would report back home, Cy was shocked at the youth on most faces. Aside from Theresa, there was only one adult each from the Droll and Draken, and none among the other Mages. Cy had assumed Theresa would want adults, properly trained warriors. She had gathered children.

Theresa sat across from the door, sitting high in an ornate chair. Her hands were pressed flat to the table. She kept her shoulders high as she glared at Arion. It took only a second before the room filled with whispers. Theresa slowly raised her hand, and the chatter ceased. Raising from her chair, she looked pointedly at each member in the room. All except for the man sitting on her left, who reached a shaking hand out to rest on her arm. She ignored him and shifted so his hand would fall back to his lap.

He leaned back into his chair, looking exhausted. His thin white hair was plastered to his forehead. The dark circles under his eyes and the skin pulled tight on his thin body turned him into a skeleton. Despite his ivory skin, there were small flecks of pitch black splattered over him. If it weren't for his intense gaze on Arion, Cy might have thought the man had fainted. Something gnawed at the back of Cy's mind about the man, but he knew he had never seen him before.

"What, exactly, do you think you are going to accomplish by interrupting us?" Theresa called across the room. Her voice echoed throughout the room. No one else even dared breath as Arion squared his shoulders and approached her. Cy dug his claws into the doorframe, unsure if he should stop Arion or not. He didn't care what happened to Theresa, but he couldn't just stand by and watch Arion start a war right here.

As Arion neared the center of the room, Jayr stood abruptly. Arion stopped and glared at him. "At least one of these people are willing to fight. What about the rest of you? Are you ready to die for *her*?" Arion jabbed a finger in Theresa's direction while he looked around the room. Cy was glad to see that he had gotten his magic under control for this confrontation, though he was trembling. Most of the other members turned away from his gaze, but a few met him unflinchingly. Jayr stared him down, at the ready to tackle him.

"Has she even told you why you're here yet? What she wants you to do? Does she trust your loyalty enough to tell you?" Arion spat the questions out quickly, without waiting for answers. "Because *I know*. I know everything she's scheming, everything she's going to do to you!"

Arion paused. His head moved on a swivel around the room, waiting for a reaction. Cy looked as he did and saw blank stares and undying loyalty on most faces. Any that held doubt in their hearts refused to show it and lowered their heads. Theresa watched on with a smug smile glued to her face. Despite this, Cy could see her wide eyes watching Arion's every move like a hawk.

"You really haven't stopped to question why she has a bunch of teenagers on her war council? What experience or knowledge could you possibly offer her? What do you think you can do for her, other than sacrifice?"

The expressions around him started to turn incredulous, annoyed. With a shake of his head, Arion reached his hand into his coat. "Fine, then. I'll show you."

As soon as his hand disappeared inside his coat, Jayr lunged over the table. Arion's free hand shot out and caught Jayr by the chest. Spinning lightly on his feet, he turned Jayr over and pinned him to the ground. He leaned in close with bared teeth. "You can't even win against a wimp in a demon's body. What good will you be on a battlefield?" Arion taunted before letting him up.

Jayr bared his teeth and pushed Arion away. "You're only standing because Theresa ordered us not to fight within the castle," Jayr hissed.

Arion scoffed, ignoring Jayr. "So the one that was quick to start a fight can't even handle me. What about the rest of you? You think any of you can do better than him?"

Again, Arion looked at each face closely, but most were watching Jayr retreat to his seat, Theresa included. Jayr climbed back over the table. He sunk into his seat, muttering under his breath.

Cy groaned as he saw Arion find Gil's gaze. Finally finding his voice, Cy dared to speak up, *"Arion, that's enough. Let's just go."*

If I don't get control of Arion soon, we're never going to get out of here. The thought made Cy start to panic.

He reached out for Arion, but he sent a light shock back that rattled Cy. Cy yanked his hand away, making a pained sound on purpose, hoping it would get Arion's attention. Arion's gaze was still fixed on Gil; Cy wasn't even sure if Arion had been aware he had used magic.

"What about you? You're not even afraid of me like the others, are you?" Arion walked right up to Gil and smacked his hands on the table. Gil jumped back at the sound, his face flushing a deep purple.

Gil cracked a nervous smile. "Should I be?"

Arion scoffed again. He turned back to Theresa. "This one doesn't even know that I'm a Mage in a demon body, does he? And he's just ignorantly staying under the same roof as me. That's the only way he can look at me without fear, unlike the rest of them, right?"

Theresa simply turned her attention to Gil, though he didn't notice. "Actually, I did know that. I helped bring you back," Gil said sheepishly. Cy watched Gil in awe. There was no trace of the mischief and cocky attitude that Cy had known from him. And his eyes had never left Arion since they got here.

Arion turned back to Gil. He inched his face closer, but Gil held still. "Cy's a demon, too, and I'm not afraid of him. Why would I be afraid of you?"

Arion laughed, and Cy thought for a moment that the air might be clearing. He relaxed and pulled his claws from the stone doorway. A heavy sigh whirled through his body and he closed his eyes in relief. Kaitlyn grabbed the hem of his shirt, and he was suddenly back on high alert.

Arion reached across the table, grabbed Gil by his collar and dragged him over the table onto the floor. "If you aren't scared, it must mean you think you stand a fighting chance in this war Theresa wants, huh? Prove it."

Grabbing Gil by the collar again, Arion hoisted him onto his feet. He shoved him so there was a bit of distance between them. Gil put his hands up defensively. "Hold on, that's— that's definitely not what I meant," Gil stammered.

Arion swung a wide punch toward Gil, but he jumped back just in time. "What did you mean, then?"

Gil's face flushed again. He tripped over his tongue as he tried to formulate an answer. Arion didn't give him time and lunged forward. Gil grabbed his arm and side-stepped the attack. Arion sped up his attacks, but Gil continued to deflect the blows, only barely. Arion smiled as Gil held his own. It had only been a couple minutes, but Gil was already struggling.

Cy could see this quickly getting out of control, as Arion was desperate to prove a point. Cy put himself between Arion and Gil, forcing Arion to look at him for the first time. *"That's enough, Arion. He didn't do anything to you."*

Anger twisted Arion's expression and filled his eyes. After a long moment, there was recognition in his gaze, and he finally backed off.

Theresa spoke up over the heavy silence that had settled in the room, "For those inquiring about the exclusivity of this meeting, I hope you now have your answers. Only those that fully understand what we are trying to accomplish, or better put, what we are trying to prevent, can be allowed this information. For those that are unaware of Arion's situation, he was held captive by Crestyss for quite some time, and given a new body. We don't know the extent of the damage done to his mind, but I cannot take the chance that Crestyss has altered his perceptions of the world. He is to be kept under close supervision. Under no circumstances is he to be given any information regarding our plans. If in the future, he proves his allegiance, he may be trusted."

Sparks flew from Arion's fists, but Cy acted quickly. He wrapped one arm around Arion's waist, clamping the other hand over his mouth. He grit his teeth against the guilt in his stomach as thin trails of smoke slipped between his fingers. Arion stopped fighting him and relaxed, and Cy dispersed his magic before Arion fainted. He lifted his hand from Arion's mouth tentatively, but Arion didn't move. His eyes looked dazed, empty like a Void. Cy didn't know how long the spell would last, but he hoped he could get Arion far away before it let up.

"I hope, Cyllorian," Theresa began slowly, "that I can trust you to keep him out of trouble." Cy shivered at the threat in her words. He glanced around, wondering if anyone else had caught it. Most of them were talking amongst themselves, paying no attention to him. Behind him, Kaitlyn had gone slightly pale.

Damnit, Cy thought, *Theresa's going to have a closer eye on Arion after this stunt. How am I going to get him out now?*

Arion started to stir in Cy's grasp, shaking the daze from his head. Though he was coming back into himself, his anger wasn't returning. Cy looked for an excuse to take Arion away while he stared coldly at Theresa. He needed to get Arion away from Theresa to prevent another fight, but more importantly, he wanted to ask Arion what he had been yelling about.

"Now that you've thoroughly ruined this meeting, I think it's now your responsibility to escort everyone to their rooms for the day." At Theresa's words, everyone else stood up obediently and gathered near the door.

Arion scowled, but Cy cut him off before he could snap, *"Yes, we'll see them out."* Arion turned his scowl to Cy. There was a mix of confusion and betrayal in his eyes. Cy simply grabbed him by the wrist and led him from the room. Gil fell in line beside Kaitlyn close behind them. The rest followed a noticeable distance behind.

Once outside the room, Arion yanked his hand from Cy's grip. He put as much space between them as possible, leaning against the wall as they walked. Despite his attitude, he stayed with the group the whole way to the dormitory wing that had been set up for their visitors.

The empty halls opened suddenly into an intersection of large hallways with numerous doors on either side. Arion hung close to the corner, his back turned to everyone. Cy and Kaitlyn stood to the side and let the rest pass them to their rooms. Gil stood near Arion, and Cy gave him a curious glance that he didn't notice. His eyes were still fixed on Arion. Cy couldn't blame him for being wary of Arion after being attacked in the meeting.

A gasp sounded from the closest room. A female Draken stood in front of her open door, her hands covering her mouth. Cy jumped to her side, ready to ask what was wrong. Before he could get a single word out, she ran giddily into the room and threw herself onto the plush mattress that rested atop a bed of burning coals. A thin cloud of dark smoke spun on itself near the ceiling.

Around him, the halls filled with a chorus of similar gasps and cheers as everyone else ran excitedly into their rooms. Gil's eyes darted with curiosity, and he approached his own room tentatively. Cy and Kait followed, unsure of what they should expect. As soon as the door opened, Cy and Kait flinched away, throwing their hands over their heads.

Gil let out a loud whoop, and was gone. He jumped into the pool of water that filled his room floor to ceiling without spilling past the magic barrier in the door. He swam in slow circles around the room on his back. Cy hadn't even noticed what being out of the water for so long had done to him, but his scales slowly began to shine again where smooth blue skin had been. The webbing returned to his fingers.

The first Draken that had seen their room popped her head back into the hallway. "Tell Theresa thanks for us. It was so nice of her to do this after so long."

Cy looked around the hallways, peering into what rooms he could. Each one had been magically customized to fit the needs of each person. He had never known Theresa to be so thoughtful, especially if she hadn't done so in the first place.

Kaitlyn's voice broke Cy from his suspicions, "Where did Arion go?"

Cy looked back to the spot Arion had been standing. The wall he had occupied was empty, save for a slightly scorched handprint on the stones, still sparking with green magic.

* * *

Arion

ARION WAS aimless as he wandered the halls of the castle, well aware of the shifting of stones around him. More often than not, he allowed the castle to guide him where he needed to go. Now it had taken him to a small alcove he guessed was in a corner of the castle, a small circular room. The doorway shut behind him as he passed through, leaving only a small glassless window near the ceiling. Across from him was a large painted window, the abstract colors allowing light to spill into the room, but kept him hidden from view should anyone look from outside.

Not that anyone but him had been brave enough to defy Theresa's orders to remain in the castle at all times. Arion scoffed at the thought of Theresa's mindless army as he sat himself on the large ledge against the window. The glass felt warm even through Arion's coat, and he fought against a shiver. He was relying more and more on his magic to keep him going, cursing himself whenever he used it. He pressed his cheek against the glass, shutting his eyes for just a moment to rest himself.

But the moment lasted too long. Images formed on his eyelids... a knife glinting with thick, white blood... Grite's twisted smile, flesh hanging from his teeth... Crestyss' eyes glowing as flames at Arion.

Arion jolted awake, his fist flying into the window. Cracks formed beneath, and he felt tiny splinters digging into his hand. He rubbed over the wound, using magic to disintegrate the glass. His racing heart beat heavy in his ears and the air he sucked into his lungs scraped against his dry throat.

Turning his head to rest his cheek against the cold stones behind him, Arion held perfectly still as he tried to regain control of his breathing. It almost felt like drowning, but then, Arion knew exactly how that felt.

He shook the thought away from his mind. His dreams were already cursed with such terrible memories, he refused to let them torture him while he was awake.

Knowing that only a distraction would fully clear his mind, he reached into his coat for the book he'd been pouring himself over for months trying to decipher. The back of his hand brushed against Tome.

A pit formed in his stomach, and he pulled the spell

book from its place slowly. Laying it gently in his right hand, Arion ran his fingers over the lightning bold engraved in the lock. A spark flew from his fingertips, but there was no reaction from Tome. Not that he had expected or needed one; Tome hadn't been locked in months.

The cover opened effortlessly, just like any book. But inside, the pages were barren. No sign of the note left inside from a time when Theresa had cared for him, no spells or instructions. Not a single speck of ink to be found as Arion flipped through each and every page methodically. He stared at the inside of the back cover for a long time.

Tome thumped against the stones where the doorway had been, falling open as it hit the ground. Arion dropped his hand into his lap, holding his breath against the burning in his eyes and cheeks.

Once he had returned, Arion had found Tome nestled among his stuff that Cy had kept safe in his absence. Arion couldn't remember the last time he had seen words upon Tome's pages, even before he had gone. In his darkest time in the months leading up to that night, Tome had been left abandoned on a table in the library.

Now Tome had abandoned him.

Arion tried to think back, distinguish exactly where things had gone wrong, what bad choice had led him here. His immediate answer had always been his birth, but then, he had never been in charge of that.

It seemed as though the only decisions Arion had ever made had been the wrong ones. Freeing Cyllorian, visiting Centric, making an enemy of the village, even following Cy and Kait home when he didn't know any better.

Staring at Tome, Arion knew that it all started with that book brought by a small white owl.

As if on cue, the very same owl ducked through the small inside window and dropped to perch atop Tome's pages. It pecked curiously at the pages, twitching its head side to side.

With a flutter of its small wings, it launched itself at Arion. Obediently, he held his arm out for the owl to perch. "Not a very good birthday gift anymore, is it?" he mused aloud. Arion lifted his hand to pet the bird, but it pecked at his fingers until they retreated. "A bit rude, considering you barged in on me."

Snow flapped his wings twice, and the wall gave way into a passage yet again. Shocked at the castle responding to Snow, Arion sat frozen as he took off. Snow swooped to snatch Tome deftly in its small talons and took for the winding halls.

Unsure what else to do, Arion jumped from the edge and gave chase after him. He struggled to keep Snow in view, catching only glimpses of him as he rounded corners. It felt like the owl was simply teasing Arion, playing a game of keep-away.

Though the castle was ever-changing, Arion had spent more than enough time walking the halls that he had a good sense of direction within the castle. With every twist and turn, he could sense they were going to the back of the castle. The walls began to narrow into the emergency passages that ran behind the library. Arion smirked, knowing a dead end was near. No matter how many times he had ventured deep into the castle, these secret hallways never changed. Arion rounded the final corner, skidding to a stop as he turned to face Snow smugly.

The abrupt end to the hall was empty. There were no windows for Snow to escape from, no holes in the walls.

Nothing. Arion stepped forward, wondering if his lack of sleep had begun to cause hallucinations.

He stepped toward the far wall that was taunting him. He ran his hands over the brickwork, but the wall was solid. He cursed himself over this ghost chase, and fell against the wall beside him.

The stones crunched under his weight, dust falling to the ground. He pressed again, and the wall opened on a hinge like a door.

Inside was a small dark room Arion had never seen. It was sparsely furnished, even more so than all the useless empty rooms the castle held. A small bed laid in one corner, half-collapsed to the floor as one leg of the frame had rotted away. The mattress atop the frame was thin and discolored, and Arion guessed the putrid smell filling his nostrils was coming from there. Beside the bed was a tiny dresser, the two drawers ripped violently from the base. One drawer laid across the room, the other hung from the base, the front wall hanging loose.

In the far wall was another door set into the stone made of dark wood. Though the slats were spaced apart, there was no light shining through, not even from underneath. It looked like it had been sealed. Arion thought he could see the outlines of bricks behind the door.

Light flooded into the room suddenly, making Arion flinch. He immediately sought the source, and found what looked to be a stained glass window, though it was cloudier than all the others that filled the castle. Arion recognized the image blurred by the spilt light, but it looked wrong somehow. He knew the crescent moon that hung off centered above a barren horizon, its reflection wavering in the water below. A silhouette stood opposite the moon, nothing but a shadow against the glistening waves of the ocean.

It took a few seconds of studying, but Arion realized the image he saw was mirrored from the one in his memory. He knew the image by heart, could paint it perfectly with his eyes closed, *but it was wrong.*

The realization hit him, and he gasped. *A painting.* It wasn't a window set high into the wall... it was a painting that hung on the back wall of the library. A painting that had hidden a secret in the castle that Arion hadn't known about for years. He hadn't even thought of the possibility that there could be anything left for him to find, but he had spent so many days tucked away in the back corners of the library, never knowing how close he had been to its best kept secret.

"Theresa had it specially made," a rough voice sounded from beneath the painting. Arion's gaze dropped to the man sitting in a chair far too small for him. At first Arion thought it was simply the dusty air that made the man look so sickly, but he recognized him. He had sat beside Theresa in the meeting. He'd been so still then, Arion thought he could have been a figment of his imagination.

The man looked like a skeleton, one that had rotted away along with this room. His pale skin was stretched tight over thin arms. The clothes hung on him heavily, causing him to hunch over as he tried to balance on the too-small seat. His hair was white and thin, black specks of dirt all throughout. His eyes were hidden in his face, sunken into his sharp cheekbones. Thin lips were parted over yellowed teeth, and Arion could hear his thin breath whistling from his mouth. For a second, Arion could see Theresa in the sullen expression, but he blinked, and it was gone.

The man leaned against the back of the chair, the wood groaning in protest though it held his weight. He closed his eyes as a breath rattled out of him. He was clearly struggling to catch his breath, but it looked as though the man hadn't moved in decades. How could he, when he looked to be nothing but skin and bones?

In the brief moment, Arion noticed what the man was holding: Tome. He cradled the book in his long fingers, the spell book looking far too heavy for the man to carry. Arion carefully investigated the room again, but there was no sign of Snow or where he could have gone. The door to the library was sealed shut, the painting fixed to the wall. He would have noticed if Snow had tried to sneak past him to exit where Arion entered.

Arion's eyes fell on the man again, his attention pulled to his hair. The more he looked, the less the black splotches looked like dirt, and the more they looked like...

"Snow?" Arion asked, incredulous as he recognized the speckled pattern across the owl's wings. The man smiled and pulled a pristine white feather from his lap behind Tome.

"My real name is Seyano, and I'm your uncle." The man smiled warmly while Arion simply gaped at him.

Before Arion could wrap his head around the declaration, Seyano's smile slipped and he spoke again, his gravelly voice turning grim, "We need to talk about Theresa."

CHAPTER 3

Arion

"If you're going to tell me to trust her or follow her or anything like that, then I don't want to hear it," Arion snapped, turning back to face the secret door he had entered the hidden room through.

"I'm not," Seyano said, his voice rough and quiet. He coughed to clear his throat, his chest rattling. "I can't tell you how you should feel about Theresa. I know what she's done to you. But you don't know what's been done to her. I'm not asking for you to sympathize with her, but you need to understand."

Arion heard the creaking of wood and shuffling on the stone floor. He glanced over his shoulder to see that Seyano was now standing in the center of the small room, swaying slightly like a flower in the wind. In his outstretched hand was Tome.

Being careful of Seyano's weakened state, Arion took Tome and tucked it into his pocket. "Understand what exactly? I already know that she wants to destroy Lontorra. I found her journals."

Seyano gave a sad smile. "There are many things that are too painful to express with the written word."

Suddenly, Seyano's stance faltered. He fell forward and Arion darted forward to catch him. Seyano draped one arm across Arion's shoulders. Seyano was surprisingly taller than Arion and he had to hunch over to lean his weight on Arion.

Another coughing fit wracked through Seyano. Arion could feel his heartbeat stutter. "Sit down," Arion said softly.

Seyano nodded, still trying to clear his throat. Arion guided him to the chair painfully slowly, and helped him sit. The chair groaned under his weight.

Subtly, Arion sent a surge of magic from underfoot. It wrapped around the chairs legs, adding extra support.

Seyano wiped a hand across his mouth, and it came away with a thick white substance.

"Void blood?" Arion asked accusingly. "Did Theresa—"

Seyano raised a hand to stop Arion. He was breathing heavily as he leaned back in the chair. His white eyes stared straight up at the ceiling, entranced. Arion followed his gaze, but found nothing but cracked and dusty stones. It was concerning how easily Arion could see Seyano's ribs through his thin shirt as his chest heaved with the effort.

Arion's hands twitched at his side. He wanted to do something, anything to ease Seyano's obvious suffering. The strong attachment he felt immediately to his uncle, who had been hidden from him his entire life, surprised Arion. And with that attachment came just another reason to loathe Theresa.

"I was younger than Theresa by two years," Seyano

started suddenly. He had shifted his weight so that one arm was propped on the back of the chair. It was being used as a pillow for his head. Though his eyes were closed, Arion could still see his eyes darting back and forth beneath the thin black veins webbed across his eyelids.

"We were always inseparable. Theresa was more of a mother to me than our own parents. They took us all across Lontorra. Our parents were the strongest healers the land had ever seen, you know? We would spend weeks at a time in any one place, learning from the people. We made many friends, allies for later in life.

"Not long after I turned five, I grew very sick. It was an illness my parents had never seen themselves, but they knew of it. They said my own blood was poison to me. They tried everything they could, but I only grew weaker and weaker. No cure, no treatment, nothing ever worked. Eventually, they couldn't care for me any longer. They left me here in this castle, deciding it would be best to live what remained of my life in comfort, not on the road. Of course, they were still needed elsewhere, and they couldn't abandon those in need.

"Theresa, being the dutiful older sister she was, stayed with me. She vowed she'd be a better healer than either of our parents had ever been. She promised me she would find a way to cure me if it was the last thing she did. When they left, she cursed our parents.

"She cared for me all by herself, while still finding the strength to make money, which she would then barter for ingredients and food for us both. She managed to find a way to weaken the disease. It turns out, if you remove the poison from the body, the person can begin to heal. So she would drain me of blood until I was on the brink of death, and replace it as best as she could. But she could never remove all of the poison, nor find its source, so it would simply spread to the new blood. It was not a cure, but it kept me alive. I was kept hidden in this very room. For my own safety, Theresa said."

Seyano paused. A ragged breath shook his frame. His glassy eyes wandered over the contents of the room, as though searching for something. His hands were clasped tightly in his lap. When he pulled them apart, Arion recognized the fluffy plume of a snow white feather.

"One day she returned home absolutely ecstatic. She told me she had a present for me, and gave me this—" Seyano raised the feather into a ray of light. He chuckled meekly. "I thought she had finally gone mad. It was the first time I had laughed in such a long time, but she didn't think it was the least bit funny. She had used every coin she had to buy this for me, enough money to feed us for a month. When she said that, I was furious. *You can't starve just to get me a trinket,* I told her. But it wasn't a trinket. This simple feather had been imbued with a charm that would allow me to take on the body of a small owl.

"*If you aren't in your body, the poison can no longer harm you,* she said. She was so sure that I couldn't speak my doubt. At the time, I didn't even know if I had the strength to withstand the change. My options were to take on this new form and hope her theory was correct, or die trying. I quite liked my odds, regardless of the outcome, and I relented. I told myself it was sheer luck that it had worked. Or maybe it was the result of my sister's love and devotion. I survived the change, but I could still feel the poison pumping through my veins.

"I hadn't truly changed bodies, just what my body looked like. I changed my shape, and that was all. My blood was still poisoned, but I never told Theresa that. I've never told anyone, though I must admit I can't recall my last conversation with anyone besides my sister. My blood will always be a poison, no matter what form I take. It just so happens that whatever disease I have, owls are immune. Or at least, that's what it seems.

"Our parents never once visited. A few years after they left, we learned that they had been killed by humans. It hadn't been long since the feud between Mages and humans which pushed the Mages to reside solely in Centric. The humans that killed them had been from a village I remembered. Their children had been wrought with a painful rash that caused swelling in the throat and suffocation. My parents had saved an entire generation, and yet the humans murdered our parents simply for what they were. Despite Theresa's poor opinion of our parents, she hated humans even more. To her, they were nothing more than pawns, or cattle. They were fodder for her anger.

"It wasn't long before Crestyss got his hands on her. He was a spoiled prince in Centric. If he so much as looked at something for too long, it belonged to him. He decided my sister was a treasure to be coveted. She hadn't the status or power to deny him, but she had the wit to use Crestyss. He gave her whatever she wanted it, except for freedom. I did not see her often once he had a hold on her. She made sure I was well taken care of, and she would treat me whenever she could.

"Theresa never trusted Crestyss. She told me of his plans, of his early experiments. He terrified her, but she needed him. I knew the truth was that she had been too afraid to defy him. Theresa was the only one in his good graces, and when his parents died and he took over control of Lontorra, there was no hope for escape."

Seyano's hands clenched into fists on his knees. His knuckles cracked as the skin was spread taught over the bone until blood pooled in the creases. He didn't even seem to notice as he continued, a deep rage settling into his voice.

"Theresa had always expressed concerns about Crestyss' intentions, his plans that he kept secret. When she was twenty, she told me what he *did* to her and I—"

He stopped suddenly, his eyes flicking to Arion. Arion shifted awkwardly under the gaze, so full of guilt and regret. He hadn't realized how still he had been standing while Seyano talked, and his joints ached when he moved.

"She lost all faith after that day. Faith in others, and in the world. She hated the humans that would scorn all our parents had done for them. She raged at the unfairness of a world in which I had to suffer. She swore that she would destroy everything that had ever caused either of us pain."

With a groan, Seyano pushed himself onto his feet with more strength than he'd had earlier. He grabbed Arion by the shoulders, squeezing them tightly.

"I'm sorry, Arion. I wish I could tell you that there was a part of her that still loved you, but even I do not know Theresa anymore. I remember her crying to me when she had to leave you, but I think that choice might have taken the last of her humanity. I can't find any compassion left in her, not even for myself. I am still alive out of obligation. You are alive because I made the choice that she would not. I gave you your magic because Theresa would not, for fear of what Crestyss might do to you, and what you might do to her. Now I need you to use that magic against her. I can't reason with her, Arion. No one can. Theresa will not stop until Lontorra is wiped from existence."

* * *

ARION DROPPED his head into his hands with a sigh. The entire morning, Kait had been following him suspiciously, while Cy rested his magic.

"Please, Arion. I know it would be easy for you," Kait begged again. She was heavy as she leaned on his shoulder, but the weight was comforting more than anything. He could practically hear the sickeningly sweet smile in her voice, though he couldn't bring himself to believe it.

Lifting his head, Arion was met with Kait's crystal blue eyes, and they sparkled, just the way they always had. His chest tightened. A mix of guilt and a strong protectiveness washed over him, but there was something missing.

Kait tilted her head at him, and her single braid fell from her shoulder. His gaze was fixed to it as he said, "I just don't see why you can't just change it yourself."

Kait dropped herself to the floor beside him, leaning into him fully. "I told you, it's just not the same. I'm still getting used to changing, and I just want to feel better in my normal body. It'll only take a second, please?"

Kait grabbed at the braid and pulled it loose. The long hair flowed through her fingers, and she ran her other hand through the short, uneven hair on her other side. She had been pinning her hair tightly to her head so the odd length wouldn't be noticeable, but it was clear it had been bothering her for a while.

"I think it's about time for a new look," she said quietly.

She turned those sparkling eyes on him again, and Arion turned away. He was being selfish, he knew. He never wanted to drag Kait into this mess of his life, and ever since she had caught up in it, everything was changing. It was torture to him to think of taking something from her with his own hands.

Kait was lost in a daze as she ran her fingers through the long hair. Arion was surprised to see her smiling as she twirled a curl round and round her finger. "Are you sure you want it all short?"

The hair fell from her hands as she nodded her head. "It's just hair. It'll grow back out. Not a big deal at all."

Arion looked down at his own hands. He was glad to see they weren't shaking today, but it was only a matter of time. "And you want me to use magic."

It wasn't a question, but Kait beamed that brilliant smile at Arion like she always had. "Why not?"

Because Cy would be mad if I did. Because it's dangerous. What if he's right and I'm not in control? What if I—

"So will you cut it? Please?" Kaitlyn broke through the torrent of thoughts that crashed in his head. Arion nodded quickly, then stood. Across the room was a small desk with a chair. Arion pulled the chair out for Kait, then set his hand against the wall. A spider web of magic sprung from his fingertips, stripping the stone of their rough exterior. What was left behind was a large circle mirror set perfectly into the brickwork. Kaitlyn gasped, still awed by any and every display of magic, then giggled as she sat in the chair.

"I'm in your hands," she said, and closed her eyes.

That's what worries me.

Staring straight into the mirror, Arion raised his hands. They were shaking now, though from nerves or exhaustion, he couldn't tell. The serene, trusting look on Kaitlyn's face managed to calm Arion, and he reminded himself that he could never hurt her. Holding his breath, Arion focused on a small flame covering his hands. Green fire burst forth, lapping at his fingers. There was no feeling, no heat or burning, and Grite had made sure he knew that feeling all too well. His breath hissed out between his teeth as he plunged his flaming hands into Kaitlyn's hair.

She didn't even flinch. Not at the fire, and not at his touch. Even her hair was still intact. He started on the short side, running his fingers through the longer strands at the front to even it all out. Tufts of hair fell from her head, still smoking. They turned to ash before they even hit the floor. As he finished the first side, Kait reached her hand up to feel the difference for herself. Her hand brushed over his, still ablaze, and she squeezed it. "It feels better already." She smiled, but her eyes stayed closed.

Arion smiled with her, if only for a moment, before he carefully moved over to the long side. He gathered the hair in one hand, and cut across it with his fingers. It came away easily, and burnt up in his hands. A lump had formed in his throat, but he shoved it down as he evened out the second side with the first.

He had tried to leave what length he could without it standing out, and her bangs hung forward to frame her face, but the back length of her hair was nearly to her scalp. He lowered his hands when he was done. The guilt that had nestled in his chest had dissipated, and he felt steadier than he had in a long time.

Once Arion's hands had left her head, Kait's eyes shot open. Her hands were covering her face, and Arion couldn't help but worry about her reaction. He opened his mouth to ask her opinion, but the words were caught in his throat.

"It looks amazing!" she cheered. Her sudden outburst startled Arion. "I've never had my hair short, never! It's good to get a new look." Kait stood and leaned closer to the mirror while she played with her new hair.

Arion smiled with relief, until his eyes wandered to his

own reflection. He looked so pale that it scared himself. It was like he was looking at a ghost. Dark circles ringed his eyes, drowning out any light in them, and his cheeks were sunken deep into his face. His heavy coat hung loose on his frame, his collarbones jutting out dangerously from under his shirt. And the long white hair that matted against his head looked disgusting. He thought he could still see blood dried in it in places, though it had to be his imagination.

Looking at his own reflection, he couldn't help but think of Grite. He wondered if this body had ever looked any different from this, and based on the body that Grite had now, Arion doubted it.

But Arion wasn't a demon, and he wasn't a Void anymore, either. He had come back. In the past month, he had more or less accepted it, but now the reality was staring him straight in the face, and it terrified him.

With a surge of confidence Arion didn't know he still had, his hands flared into a green flame again. He ran his hands through his hair vigorously, angrily. Then he rubbed them over his face, though he doubted it could fix him so easily.

"Arion," Kait said quietly. There was something warm in her voice, though Arion couldn't place it. He opened his eyes slowly, afraid he would meet the eyes of the Void again.

Staring back at him were a pair of bright green eyes, shining as magic waved through them. The color chased away the circles, and a satisfying blush lay across his cheeks. Best of all, the grimy white hair was gone. In its place lay short, spiky, brown hair, only a little shorter than Kait's. It stood up defiantly, just like he remembered.

A laugh bubbled up, and Kaitlyn was upon him. Her fingers were dancing an inch away from his face, lightly touching his cheeks. When he didn't move away, she ran her hands through his hair slowly. A tear ran down her cheek, and her lips trembled. She started laughing excitedly, and messed his hair up further. Arion laughed with her, leaning into her touch.

The door swung open violently, and a crack rang throughout the room as it hit the wall. Arion jumped away from Kaitlyn, tripping over his own feet onto the floor. Her hands flew to her chest as she whirled to see the source of the sound.

Cy barreled down on them, his eyes darting between them frantically. He stopped merely a foot away from them, his chest heaving even though he didn't need to breathe. *"I felt your magic surge throughout the whole castle. It was so strong it woke me up! What are you doing?"* Cy laid into Arion, and the exultation he had been feeling only seconds before was quickly turning to anger.

Kait wasted no time, and tugged on Cy's arm. "Look, look! He fixed it!" She pointed to her head, and Cy tore his glare from Arion. He watched as Cy practically melted as soon as his attention had turned to Kaitlyn. Another wave of anger rushed through him as he started to compliment her on the change.

Cy was so engrossed in Kaitlyn that he barely spared another glance for Arion as he sat sprawled on the floor. He cooed over Kait's new hair while a bright blush spread across her cheeks. It felt as though they both forgot Arion was even there.

What about me? The thought surprised Arion. All the anger slowly began to drain from him as the realization washed over him.

Arion forced himself to calm down and take deep breaths. This wasn't jealousy. At least not over Kaitlyn.

Arion could clearly remember Cy calling them brothers, but he had been nothing but hostile toward him ever since they brought him back.

Despite the anger, Arion couldn't help but notice that the magic inside Cy was stuttering. He'd barely taken any time to rest in the month that they waited for Theresa, and his magic was running low.

With the strange courage still running through him, Arion brought himself to his feet. His sudden move got Cy's attention, but Arion didn't give him the chance to berate him. He grabbed Cy by the wrist and shocked him. Cy tried to jerk away, but he had no strength to fight. Ignoring Kait's unending questions, Arion pulled Cy from the room. Gil was waiting outside, but the entourage exiting the room stunned him into silence.

Arion swung Cy in front of him and shoved him into the room across the hall. Cy stumbled, but remained standing. Arion followed closely after and slammed the door shut behind him. A magic barrier went up over the door just as Kait started banging on the door. Her frantic yelling was muffled, but stopped shortly.

"What the hell are you doing? You finally ready to get your frustration out or something?" Cy snapped at him. He tried to sound tough, but it was clear he was struggling to stand.

Arion stepped up to him, tucked his hand under Cy's arms, and hoisted him to his full height. Resting his hand on Cy's chest, he muttered, "Yeah, I am."

With as much focus as he could muster, he sent a strong wave of magic into Cy.

In an instant, Cy's metal body shattered to pieces. The metal heart inside fell heavily and spun across the floor among the metal debris. All that was left was a humanoid shaped plume of smoke. It roiled in place while Cy gasped from the sudden shift.

"From now on, you can't move," Arion ordered. He rolled up his right sleeve, carefully controlling his breathing as he did. He had studied the spell all month, but actually attempting it was another feat entirely.

"What do you mean? What's going on, what are you doing?" It was the first time Arion had ever heard Cy when he wasn't being even a tiny bit cocky, but he couldn't dare lose his focus to tease him.

Slowly, Arion drew a small line along his wrist just below the visible veins. A cut opened up, and blood beaded along it. With a deep breath, Arion pinched at the wound. He grimaced at the pain as a small needle formed of his magic emerged from the cut, a small red string hanging from the end. It hung only a few inches, but Arion could feel it tugging at his wrist.

Arion shot a glare at Cy, and reiterated, "Hold. Still."

Cy didn't dare make a sound as Arion crouched to Cy's feet. He watched the smoke curl against the edges of Cy's being, studying the movements for a moment. All he had to do was follow the outline of Cy's body, like he was tracing his shadow, and the body should fill out perfectly. He took one final breath that rattled in his lungs before he finally brought the needle down on the inside of Cy's thigh. The smoke swarmed with every calculated stitch that Arion set into him. It solidified behind his trail, and began to pale. The red string stuck out stark against Cy's skin, the sutures at odd lengths and admittedly a little shaky.

A sweat broke out over Arion's brow before he had even finished one leg, and he fought to control his breathing as he reached Cy's hip. He paused for a moment, amazed at how well the spell was already taking shape. One foot had taken form in full, and his toes even had small black talons curling from them. The skin beneath his hand was rough, but solid. Another strong breath, and he set in again, following along his side toward his arm.

"*Why?*" Cy asked finally.

Arion spoke slowly through his concentration, "Time for an upgrade. The metal body was cool and all, but not always practical."

Silence settled over them again as Arion made his way along the arm, over the wrist, and traced out each finger. The talons that formed as he went threatened to scratch him, but he ignored them. Arion rounded back over the top of his arm, and he could feel Cy's gaze watching him closely.

"*You fixed your hair, too.*" Cy's words made Arion pause. He picked up the speed as he moved from shoulder to neck hoping Cy wouldn't notice.

He stitched along the ears carefully, following the small point on the end that the smoke was forming. "It was getting in the way," he replied simply.

Arion rounded Cy's head easily, his demon form being bald. One black eye watched Arion work as Cy's face spread from the stitches. Half of his chest had already formed, the smoke obscuring what was within, and Cy had to focus himself to steady his breathing, now that it was necessary again. It allowed Arion to work peacefully and swiftly now that he had gotten used to the way the needle moved, and the shape of Cy's body.

It wasn't until Arion had reached Cy's other hip that Cy had gained his composure to speak again. "*I wonder what Gil thinks of your new haircut,*" he teased.

Arion choked on his breath at the mention of Gil. The

sudden pain in his chest made his hand jerk, and the needle was now stuck into Cy's newly forming flesh just inside his hip bone.

"Ouch!" Cy yelped, accusation clear in his tone. He jerked his head down to gape at the needle sticking into him. *"You stabbed me!"*

Arion plucked the needle from Cy, but there was a clear tear in the skin as it finished forming unevenly. "I told you to be careful." After examining the small string hanging from the needle, Arion set back to sewing Cy's body.

"You said to hold still, not hold my tongue," Cy quipped.

Now moving down his thigh, Arion ignored Cy so he could focus solely on the stitching directly in front of him, and not Cy's body that was coming into place right beside him. Cy coughed to hide a laugh, but didn't dare chide Arion any further.

With a tight chest and slight dizziness setting in, Arion held his breath for the final stretch. He finished Cy's second leg and met his first stitch, though it wasn't without difficulty. His sutures had evened out by the end, and they looked nearly perfect compared to the beginning. Once the string crossed over itself, Arion burned the needle and string in his hand. The cut in his arm had been slowly dripping blood along the floor, but that was caught up in the flames as well. A thin scar lay across his wrist.

Going backwards over the work that Arion had done, a small ball of flame burned away the string in Cy until there was almost no trace left. All but the small scar on his hip.

Arion fell back onto the floor, heaving air into his lungs. He flung a hand out toward a closet in the corner. The motion made him lose his balance, and he lay on the floor, his magic and energy both exhausted. He heard Cy shuffling through the clothing, though Arion wasn't completely sure there would be anything to fit him.

His breathing finally slowed, and he made a decision. "You can have her," he gasped out.

Cy stopped suddenly, the room going quiet. *"What?"* he asked, an air of faked innocence on the single word.

"I think it was always you. I missed Kaitlyn, and I love her. But not the way you do. It's gone now that you're not in my head. Everything's just been so confusing that I couldn't tell. I know things can't go back to what they were, but they can be better than they've been. We don't have to fight. I want it to be better."

Arion's thoughts came out in a rush. He didn't even know his feelings until they poured out of him, but as they left his mouth, they took with them an incredible weight from his chest.

Raising his right hand to show off the scar he could feel forming, he mumbled, "We're connected now, so we have to get along." The words sounded slurred to his own ears. They were so quiet he couldn't even be sure Cy heard him, but he didn't have the strength to say them again.

The sound of footsteps stopped right beside Arion, and he opened his eyes to see Cy standing above him, fully clothed and appearing as a human rather than a demon. His skin was a shade darker than Arion's. Purple eyes, like his smoke, sat atop high cheeks and thin lips. His hair was darker than Arion's, too, and shorter. It laid obediently against his head, unlike Arion's. Surprisingly, his ears still looked pointed. One hand was outstretched to help Arion up, his nails black but rounded, not talons, the other tucked into a pocket.

He looks right at home. The thought fluttered through

Arion's mind for only a second before the exhaustion wiped it away.

Arion took it and allowed Cy to pull him to his feet. They were closer in height now— Cy was taller by only a few inches. Standing next to him, Arion could see the resemblance between them, Cy's voice calling them brothers rang in his ears. Arion reached for the door, but Cy's words cut him off.

"Thank you, Arion."

He turned back to Cy, but a lump clogged his throat and kept him from speaking.

With his magic running sparse, the barrier on the door had faded. Kait and Gil must have heard them talking, because the door swung open just in front of them. Kait stood with her jaw dropped as she studied Cy. Her eyes darted a few times to Arion, but it was clear where her priority was now. She didn't even seem to notice as Arion slipped past her through the door and slunk down the hall.

Gil seemed to read the air just as well as Arion, and followed along beside him. Arion could feel his gaze on him, and Cy's words came back to him. He still didn't know what he meant by that, and he didn't think he wanted to find out.

"That was pretty impressive," Gil said, breaking the silence. He sounded proud. Arion had no idea why, but his words sent a warmth through Arion that rolled his stomach and burned his cheeks. He didn't have the strength left to speak, so he simply smiled in agreement.

Chapter 4

Arion

"I don't think I did too bad against you the other day. You remember, in the meeting room? Yeah, you were fast, but I was keeping up with you. Better than Jayr, at least. I can't tell you how great it was to see that look of defeat on his face. And he's so much bigger than you, too! But I'm not much of a close combat fighter, myself. Now, if you give me a crossbow, I'll hit every time, guaranteed."

Gil's voice had long turned into a senseless droning in Arion's ears. It was equally impressive and annoying that any person could talk as much as he did. Not to mention that he had been able to keep up with Arion trekking through the woods, all while yammering on and on.

The fresh air had reinvigorated Arion long enough for them to put a good amount of distance between them and the castle, but it couldn't stave off the exhaustion forever. When he felt himself running on fumes, he allowed himself to stop at a large tree with pines that withstood the chill in the air. Ignoring Gil's enthralling description of the crystals that the Droll mined for trading, Arion spoke, a bit harsher than intended. "Why are you here?"

Gil finally stopped talking, his mouth hanging open as he was cut off mid-sentence. His tongue clicked in his mouth, and his gaze shifted away awkwardly. "Well, you know, Cy came and got me, asked for help. Now Theresa has this big plan and all." He shuffled his feet beneath him, running his hands over the small scales that remained atop his head. Arion narrowed his eyes, feeling as though Gil was avoiding his question.

Arion tried his question again, not leaving room for Gil to give a poor answer. "So, are you here for Cy, or for Theresa?" he asked slowly. There was something about Gil that was hard to read, maybe due to his relaxed demeanor. And Arion was far too impatient to just let him run his course.

Gil chuckled, and it sounded strained. He still wouldn't meet Arion's eyes. His light blue skin darkened in his cheeks. He looked like he wanted to turn and run. A small, mischievous grin crept onto Arion's face. *Got him.*

"I'm not sure about Theresa's plan, but we've all been sensing war in the air for a while now, so I think I'd rather be on Theresa's side than Crestyss'. I don't really want to fight, but the Droll owe her a lot. Cy was the one going around looking for someone to help resurrect you, or heal you, even if Theresa was the one that told him where to go. I was the one that volunteered for that, after all. So, I guess technically, if I'm here for anyone, then I guess I'm here for you. At least, that's why I came in the first place."

Gil chattered on in a rush. As he spoke, he only got faster and faster, his voice shaking nervously.

Arion couldn't help but be taken aback. He thought he had prepared himself for whatever answer Gil could have given, even if he had denied either affiliation. But he had never been an option himself, especially not one that he would have ever guessed a stranger would make.

"What?" Arion snapped. The sudden outburst drew Gil's attention back to Arion, and his cheeks darkened even further.

"Don't get me wrong, Cy is cool and all. And I saw Theresa try to kill you before, even if she didn't know it was you, so I know she's not innocent. I just think that—"

Arion cut him off sharply. "That's not what I meant! Who are you spying on me for?" He slammed his fist into the tree behind him, but only managed to cut himself on the bark. It healed before he even had a chance to wince at the sudden twinge of pain.

Gil's face paled as the accusation hit him. "I... I..." Gil stuttered for a moment. His head dropped, but Arion could still see his eyes darting around furiously. "I'm not spying on you."

"Like I'd believe that. Theresa is just waiting for an excuse to get rid of me for good, and Cy hasn't trusted me for a second before today. Which one of them asked you to keep tabs on me?" Arion spat. He took a heavy step forward, the anger driving him.

"I swear, I'm here right now because I want to be, not because someone asked me to." Gil raised his head. His jaw was set tight and his eyes were stern. He stared Arion down without fear, or guilt.

Arion scoffed. "And why should I believe you? What other reason could you possibly have for following me everywhere? Don't think I haven't noticed that you're constantly watching me, too. You're not nearly as subtle as you think you are."

The color returned to Gil's face. Everything from his

chin to his ears turned violet. His lips pursed into a thin line. He was stuck stiff as a board, but his eyes flashed around furiously, looking at everything except for Arion.

The sudden shift in attitude struck Arion, and he backed himself to the tree. He put his hand behind him, desperately trying to find any magic left in him. He didn't know what to think of Gil's reaction, unable to predict what might happen next.

"Intruder! Intruder!" Tuft yelled as he launched himself from a small tree, landing perfectly in-between Arion and Gil. He locked eyes with Arion for only a second, before bolting back into the throng of trees.

He didn't even spare a final glance for Gil, Arion simply took off after Tuft. He was regretting how much he had neglected his health in the past month. He just had to hope his body wouldn't give out on him after expending so much magic on Cy.

The run was short before Tuft buried himself in thick brush a few feet away from a large tree that had been felled, creating a small shelter at its base. Arion was grateful for the short run, but worried that the intruder had gotten so close to the castle in the first place. Arion tucked in close to Tuft, leaning into him to rest. He could feel a low growl in Tuft's chest, though it was inaudible. Gil dropped close to Arion, and there was no space for him to shift away. He shot a curious glance at Gil, but his attention was focused straight ahead, scanning for danger.

Tuft's glare was fixated on the shadows beneath the fallen tree, and something moved underneath.

"Animal?" Arion breathed, and Tuft shook his head once, slowly. "Crestyss?"

A grunt sounded from Tuft's throat, and Arion tensed. Though his memories had returned, the body he inhabited had a mind of its own. A thick fear settled in the pit of his stomach. He felt like he might throw up. Fists clenched at his sides, he bit his tongue until he tasted blood. The bitter tang in his mouth, and the warmth as he swallowed, chased away the fear. He readied himself to attack first, but a quick movement under the tree stalled him. Something shot out from under the tree just to disappear as quickly. Something thin and green and almost slimy.

A tail. A very familiar tail.

Arion's body deflated at the sight, a mix of relief and disappointment washing over him. Tuft and Gil both turned to look at him suspiciously. "Is there only one?" he asked Tuft. After a long moment, Tuft nodded slowly.

With a huff, Arion struggled to his feet. "I'll handle this." He left their hiding place quickly, ignoring the hands and teeth that reached for him. It only took a few strides before he was standing against the shadows under the tree. "Get out!" he barked.

He was met with laughter, and the gritty cackle that haunted his nightmares even now. *Well, now, is that really how you should greet a visitor?*

Grite's voice wafted from under the tree, though it was almost unrecognizable. Most of the time that Arion had heard him, he had a higher, nasally voice, something that grated against the nerves with a single word. Now it was slightly deeper, and more relaxed.

It was almost *normal.*

"I see you've made yourself right comfortable in there, huh?" Thick talons dug into the felled tree across from Arion, and Grite slowly hoisted himself up on the other side. He leaned against the tree heavily, though he made it look effortless. Despite the maniacal grin plastered to his dirty face, Arion could see his shoulders trembling, and his

chest heaving unevenly. He was covered in dirt and blood, shreds of clothing hung on his frail frame.

"Why are *you* here?" Arion snapped, ignoring Grite's taunts.

"*Ah that—*" Grite held up a finger, then dragged his hands across his forehead. Most of the dirt scrubbed loose, but one spot remained. He pointed at it with one chipped talon. "*Crestyss tried to kill me,*" he said simply. He laid his arm across the tree and rested his head on it, slumping his shoulders forward to hide the strain in them.

Arion didn't dare believe him, but curiosity gnawed at him. "Why would he do that?"

Grite's gaze followed Gil and Tuft as they emerged from the brush to stand on either side of Arion, though they stayed a few steps away from Grite. He was still a demon, after all.

"*Because I failed, and you got away.*" He shrugged his shoulders. The words were passive, but there was deep loathing rooted in his voice.

"You failed him many times, as far as I remember. Why try to kill you now?"

A smile slithered across Grite's face, and Arion shivered. That smile had been plastered to his eyelids for so long, it was all he could see if he dared to close his eyes. Now it was here, real and right in front of him yet again.

But he didn't feel threatened. Was it because he had his magic? Because he wasn't alone?

"*You've learned quite a few things since I last saw you. Good,*" Grite hissed, a hint of his old voice slipping through his teeth.

Arion wanted to ask him what he meant, but Tuft shot upright and turned his attention to their left, toward the castle. Within seconds, he had dropped himself to the ground, his tail tucked beneath him. "Theresa," he whimpered.

Just as he spoke her name, Theresa emerged gracefully from the shadows, a small army trailing behind her. Goyik was at her side, snarling at Grite. Snow was perched sleepily on her shoulder. In the mass of people, Arion could see Cy and Kait trying to push their way forward. Tuft crawled a few feet away from Theresa, and Arion caught sight of Gil standing behind him.

Theresa snapped her fingers. Jayr and another Draken sprung into action, tearing the fallen tree away from Grite. He stumbled backward at the sudden attack, and fell to the ground. The two Draken bore down on him.

A strange feeling fluttered in Arion's chest. There was a hint of fear, almost like a memory. And there was pity as he looked at Grite. He was barely standing, and yet he had dragged himself here. The swell of emotions compelled Arion. There was more to Grite than he understood, and Arion needed to know what it was.

"Back off!" Arion yelled, lunging for Jayr. He managed to yank him away, and the other Draken paused. Grite was emitting a long stream of curses, some of them from another language. He gingerly shifted his weight to one side. Everyone gasped at the sight of Grite's leg. Most of his thigh was missing, a large hole blown straight through it. Through the shreds of cloth barely covering him, Arion recognized the hole in his chest that he had given him.

Theresa was unfazed. "Kill it," she ordered. The two Draken started forward again. Arion grabbed their arms and found the last bit of magic he had left. Their bodies spasmed as he shocked them, and they fell back. Arion quickly put himself between them and Grite. He stared down Theresa defiantly.

"I found him. He's mine," Arion snapped.

Gil knelt beside Grite. He couldn't seem to take his eyes off of the gaping wound in Grite's leg. At a loss for what to do, his hands fluttered nervously in the air around the demon.

Responding to the challenge, Theresa walked until she was inches from Arion. "Get out of the way, or die along with that thing."

Jayr had already recovered and was standing defensively behind Theresa.

Arion raised his jaw. "He has information on Crestyss and his plans. Or are you too concerned with what he might have to say about you?"

Grite snickered behind him, and Arion wanted nothing more than to kick him. He held his ground, resolving himself to get him later, should he actually manage to save him now.

Theresa glared with disgust at Grite over Arion's shoulder. "If my information is correct, didn't he torture you endlessly? Why would you want to spare such a vile creature?" Theresa tried a sickly sweet voice, but it only made Arion's blood boil.

"I would consider what you've done to me to be the same," he spat back.

Grite erupted into a strained chorus of laughter behind him, and Theresa sneered at the both of them. She opened her mouth, ready to shout, but stopped as Kait dragged Cy to stand at Arion's side. Kait grabbed his hand and squeezed it reassuringly. Cy stood next to Arion, but his murderous glare was fixed on Grite, who simply waved teasingly at him. Theresa studied Cy for a moment. She clearly hadn't seen his new body yet, or at least, hadn't bothered to notice.

Arion smiled smugly with the support. "If you really think this pathetic excuse for a demon looks all that intimidating, I really think you ought to reconsider this war idea of yours," Arion chided. Grite's laughter ended with a snort, but he didn't protest.

Theresa was obviously feeling the pressure of the situation. She was supposed to be in charge, and she even had an audience with her, but she was being defied by teenagers. She squared her shoulders and turned with a wave of her cloak. "You have a week to retrieve any useful information from it. If you still refuse to listen to me then, I'll throw you into the dungeons next to it."

She waved her hand above her head, and her entourage followed her out of the woods, back toward the castle.

Arion's knees buckled under him. His hand slipped from Kait's, but he was caught by Cy before he hit the ground. Shaking the exhaustion from his head, he turned back to assess the situation he had gotten himself into.

Grite was leaning back on his hands, a smug grin aimed at the sky. Gil was half standing next to him. His gaze raked over Arion again and again. Kaitlyn's face popped up in front of Arion, and he jumped back.

"Are you alright? What happened?" she asked. Her fingers grazed his face, catching beads of sweat that had formed.

He grabbed her hand tightly, and held her close for a moment. Then he turned to Cy, who was also studying his condition, and nodded once. Cy helped him climb to his feet. Arion swayed momentarily and held onto Cy's arm for stability. "I'm fine," Arion huffed. "Just running on embers. The creation spell took just about everything I had." Cy flinched beside him. Arion squeezed tighter on Cy's arm, and felt him relax.

Despite his original worries, Arion had already gotten used to Cy's new body. He'd seen him in so many bodies before, but with just a glance he could tell that this was Cyllorian, truly him as he was meant to be. He allowed himself a proud moment for his craftsmanship before Cy brought his attention back to the issue at hand.

"So, you saved him so I could do the honors of killing this bitch, right? I can't think of any other reason why we would stand up for..." Cy ended his sentence with an obscene gesture toward Grite. Grite flashed a wide, toothy grin back at him that quickly turned into a sneer.

"Don't use that tone with me," Grite quipped. His voice was rough with something Arion couldn't place. *"Just because you have that fancy new body doesn't mean you're actually any different from me, you know."*

A thickness hung in the air with Grite's words. The silence was deafening, and Arion braced himself for Cy's anger he was sure would come. Slowly, Cy grabbed Arion's hand that held him, and passed it to Kaitlyn. He crossed the short distance between him and Grite excruciatingly slowly. For a second, Arion wondered if he should warn Gil to get away.

Cy's hand shot out toward Grite, but the other demon didn't even blink an eye at the movement. He simply stared at the hand offered to him. *"I know,"* Cy admitted as he waited for Grite.

Grite's smile slipped from his face. The two demons stared at each other, a silent conversation happening between them. Grite snatched Cy's hand, gripping so tight as he was pulled up that his talons dug into the back of Cy's hand.

"Well, as long as you know, then it's fine." Grite's voice was a swirl of smug and serious as he spoke. He glanced

down at their hands still joined, a question in his eyes. Cy squeezed until his green skin turned pale, a plume of purple smoke furling out from his fingertips. It curled around Grite's wrist, and he hissed. He tried to pry his hand away, but Cy's grip didn't falter. The smoke slithered along his arm, down to his leg. It filled the empty space in his leg, licking at the edges of his wound like fire.

Finally, Cy released Grite and he staggered back, catching himself on his bad leg. It held his weight as though nothing was wrong, and the smoke flared a bright purple.

"We're not carrying you back. You'll walk to the dungeons on your own."

It was the first time Arion had seen Grite truly lost for words. He wrenched his gaze away from Cy to inspect the magic keeping his leg together, testing the limits carefully.

"It won't last for long, so let's go," Cy barked an order, then snapped twice. A thick rope of smoke tied Grite's hands together in front of him, the other end in Cy's possession. Grite let out a quick growl, but seemed to think better of it.

Cy turned back to Arion, who was surprised at the effort it took just to keep standing. All the sleepless nights and starved days were finally catching up with him, and he kicked himself for letting himself get so weak. He let Cy grab him under the arm, leaning his whole weight on his brother as he led them back toward the castle. Gil fell in line beside Arion quickly, walking so close that Arion was sure he would trip over him. Kait walked on the other side of Cy, throwing cautious glances over her shoulder at Grite, who was dutifully following behind them.

The closer they grew to the castle, the more of Arion's strength seemed to return. They crossed through the double doors into the cobbled entryway, and a surge of magic flooded into Arion. He gasped for breath at the rush, able to stand on his own again. Cy let him go and gave him space to breathe. Arion glared at Gil as he hovered uncomfortably close, looking like he expected Arion to fall over at any moment.

Arion brushed past Gil toward the far corner of the room. The stones rattled as he grew near, shifting out of the way and crumbling to dust to form a large doorway. A winding set of stairs delved into darkness, and Arion plunged in without hesitation. Shuffling footsteps followed him.

Small lanterns sprouted from the walls as he passed, illuminating the path ahead. At the bottom, the stairway opened up straight into a room filled with iron-barred cells. Choosing the closest one, Arion opened the door for Grite.

Grite turned up his nose and walked himself to the cell. Stopping just inside the door, he tilted his head back to Arion. *"You're enjoying this a little too much, don't you think?"* he teased.

"Not nearly enough, actually." Arion nodded to Cy. The smoke binding Grite's hands and filling his wound disappeared, and he collapsed forward into the cell. "Get your rest. We only have a week with Grite, after all. Well, you do."

Arion slammed the door and left the cell without a second glance. He could hear Grite dragging himself across the stones, but he ignored him.

Cy grabbed Arion's shoulder as he tried to pass back up the stairs. *"I'm on your side, even if I don't know what you're thinking right now. But Theresa is right. We can't afford to keep him around for long. We have no idea why he's here or what he wants. We could be playing right into their trap—*" Cy whispered hastily, his eyes never leaving Grite as he writhed on the small bed.

"It's not a trap," Arion cut Cy off, speaking with as much confidence as possible. "He wants to kill Crestyss as much as the rest of us, maybe even more than Theresa herself. He's not here for us, but he's not here for Crestyss, either. He's here for himself. This is probably the first decision he's ever made on his own."

Arion spared a glance for the creature now asleep in the cell, his limbs spilling over the edges of the bed. He dared to think Grite looked peaceful in sleep.

Knowing it wouldn't last long, Arion left in search of even a sliver of peace for himself.

Chapter 5

Cyllorian

Arion's words hung in the air long after he dissolved into the darkness of the stairs. Cy stood, unable to take his eyes off the demon sleeping in the cell. If Grite really was solely here for himself, it only made Cy trust him less. He doubted Grite would have any sense of loyalty. Cy wanted to believe Arion, but he couldn't think of any good that could come from having Grite around.

Gil was the first to recover, bounding up the steps two at a time. Kaitlyn watched him run up the stairs, giggling under her breath.

With a final glance at Grite, Cy held his hand out for Kait to ascend the stairs first. She took the offering, climbing at a steady pace. A solemn silence fell as the dimly lit stairway engulfed them, only the rhythmic *thuds* of their footsteps echoing along the walls. Cy watched

Kait's short hair bounce atop her head as they went, mesmerizing him.

Since Theresa's arrival, Cy and Kait hadn't spent much time together. Even before, she had always been fretting over Arion. When they were alone together, Cy was always painfully aware of Kaitlyn. The vibrant expressions on her face... how she would still reach to fidget with her braids, and blush when she remembered they were gone... and sometimes that her body would shift without her realizing, tinting her skin color or adding features like scales or feathers. The change would always startle her, and she'd shake herself to return to normal.

Her fingers were twisting around a ribbon tied at the hem of her shirt. Cy could tell she was deep in thought. As they walked, waves of color washed through her hair slowly, turning it shades of blue. Without thinking, Cy reached for a lock of hair that looked like the morning sky.

"Do you think he'll be all right?" Kait's small voice drifted down to Cy, and he flinched.

Pulling his hand away slowly, Cy berated himself for being careless. *Arion,* he thought. *Of course she's thinking of Arion.*

Cy shook his head, willing the acidic taste of jealousy away. Despite what Arion had told him, it said nothing of how Kaitlyn felt. *"We're doing all we can for him, but you know how the kid is. As long as he can get some sleep, he'll see another day,"* Cy replied, hoping his jealousy couldn't be heard.

Kaitlyn stopped, and Cy had to catch himself before he ran into her. "I meant Grite," she said slowly, a question in her voice.

A wave of embarrassment washed over Cy at his

assumptions, and he dropped his head to hide his blush. *"Why would you care about him?"*

"Did you see him? I know I worry about Arion a lot, but...all those wounds. And Grite's weaker and thinner than Arion, too. How could Crestyss treat him like that? Even if this is a trap, maybe we can convince him that it's better with us. Maybe he'll switch sides. If we show him that it's safe here, he'll come around."

"I'm sure Grite knows what kind of person Crestyss is. Don't forget, he tortured Arion."

Kaitlyn nodded slowly as she turned back to the stairs. In the distance, light could be seen, and voices were wafting down to them. Their pace quickened as they neared the exit.

"He probably learned from experience," Kaitlyn growled. Her protectiveness was charming. Cy only hoped it never got her into trouble.

The foyer was bustling with people, members of Theresa's army. A few turned to Cy and Kait as they emerged, their voices lowering into hushed whispers. Kait paid them no mind. Her attention was focused on the large double doors that led back outside. One was propped open, a strong breeze blowing in. Unsure what else to do, Cy followed close behind Kait as she approached the doors.

Gil rushed in through the open door, nearly crashing into Kaitlyn. Cy grabbed her and pulled her back into him quickly. He could feel her heart beating fast against his chest, and he held his breath to keep himself calm. Aware that he was holding her too closely, Cy released Kaitlyn and stepped back. She turned her face away from him, and Cy cursed himself.

Just as he passed them, Gil stopped and turned around.

He rubbed his hand along his head and asked shyly, "Do you know where Arion went?"

His voice was quiet, his cheeks a light purple color. It was the first time Gil had ever been unable to look Cy in the eyes, his gaze fixed on the open doorway.

"He should be sleeping," Kaitlyn answered, a hint of a threat for Gil not to disturb him.

Gil shrugged apologetically. "He's not in his room."

Kaitlyn groaned, but Cy answered before she could complain, *"Try the library. He likes to hide in there."*

"Thanks," Gil chirped awkwardly with a smile. With a wave, he turned and jogged out of the room, gaining nearly everyone's attention. Kaitlyn stared after him with her head tilted. The attention gathered around them dissolved into hushed conversations, most of them echoes of Theresa's concerns.

"Did you want to check on Vyekrin?" Cy asked as Kait leaned toward the door once more. She whirled on him, her eyes wide and her cheeks bright. Her mouth flapped open and closed like a fish.

Cy smirked, chuckling under his breath. *"Arion's not the only one that's been sneaking out of the castle."*

"How did you know?" she hissed at him. She stepped closer and lowered her head. Her eyes darted around, but no one was paying any attention to them anymore. Cy stifled another laugh as Kait's cheeks began to shimmer with scales. He hoped she couldn't hear his heart racing.

"It's not exactly easy to hide a thirty foot dragon. Especially since he prefers to be on your shoulder over anywhere else."

Kait pursed her lips into a flat line. Her eyes darted around the room suspiciously, then grabbed Cy by the wrist. "Come on," she said simply and pulled him through the open door. They took a sharp left turn once outside, toward the abandoned gardens.

She led Cy around the long side of the castle, ducking between the walls and a row of tall hedges that lunged toward the sky like spikes. Small colored flowers sprung from the vines that wove their way up the castle wall. They danced in a breeze that shouldn't have been able to reach them. Large leaves reached to touch them as they went. Cy gazed down at Kait's hand wrapped around his wrist. His fingers ached to intertwine with hers, but he held himself back.

The hedges ended at the lip of a small pond. It shimmered teal under the sun, crystal clear with an array of plants within. Across the pond, the garden was filled with all kinds of flora, from bushes made of red, spindly vines covered in thorns to deep purple flowers dusted with glowing pollen big enough that you could lay inside and use a petal as a blanket.

"I found some books in the library about the garden. Theresa was studying all of these plants for medicine. She used to be a healer, but I don't think she ever found what she was looking for."

Kaitlyn had slowed her pace until she was standing in front of a small dock that reached out into the pond. Letting Cy's hand drop from hers, she stepped out and reached into the water. A bout of green and yellow seaweed wrapped around her fingers.

Cy started toward her, but was stopped as a loud *thud* sounded against the wall right next to him. He whirled around to find the wall was empty, save for a bit of dirt falling off and a patch of crushed vines. He had expected to see Vyekrin, his protectiveness rivaling Kaitlyn's, but he was nowhere to be seen. Cy craned his head every which way.

Kait laughed behind him. "Arion's also not the only one learning new tricks," Kait quipped smugly. As she spoke, the light in front of Cy roiled. Patches of blue scales appeared and spread until all of Vyekrin was visible, clung to the wall. His face was inches from Cy, and his breath ruffled Cy's hair as the dragon let out a breathy laugh of his own.

Impressed, demon? Vyekrin's voice resounded in Cy's head.

Shaking his head absently, Cy could only think to say, *"Very."*

Vyekrin laughed again and descended from the wall to curl around the pond where Kait sat, his tail wrapping possessively around her.

Kait leaned back against him, her eyes closing peacefully. "We need a favor, Vye. Grite was found in the woods, and we're worried he might have been followed. Can you take us up to check the woods?"

We cannot venture beyond the veil.

"I know. I just want a better view to see if anything's coming." Kaitlyn gently lifted her hand from the water, swaying it side to side to loosen the tangled seaweed that clung to her. Tiny shimmering scales had covered her hand. They disappeared as she shook her hand, leaving no trace of scale nor water. "Please, Vyekrin. He might not seem like it, but Arion is... he's scared, Vye. But he needs to rest, so if there's anything we can to help him, we must."

Cy was taken aback by Kait's bluntness. *So she's noticed it, too,* he thought. It wasn't simply his own paranoia. There was something going on with Arion.

Vyekrin bowed low to the ground and stretched his

wings out in front, offering his back to her. She climbed up with ease, settling herself on the dragon's back as though it was the only place she belonged. Her hand reached out for Cy, and he thought he could see a bit of mischief within her smile. "Are you coming?"

Cy remembered the last time he had flown with Vyekrin, and he didn't want to risk his brand-new beating heart. But Kaitlyn's outstretched hand was far too enticing to reject. Swallowing a lump in his throat, he grabbed hold of her and let her help him onto the dragon's back behind her. Vyekrin rumbled with laughter beneath him as he shuffled his weight forward and back. He didn't want to sit too close to Kaitlyn, but he wasn't brave enough to go through the flight without holding onto her.

Hold on tight, demon. Vyekrin's voice boomed in Cy's head, his amusement dancing in the few words.

Before Cy could respond, Vyekrin jumped toward the castle. He landed gently on the wall despite his size and began to scale the brickwork up toward the sky. Despite all his efforts to be careful around Kaitlyn, Cy instantly wrapped his arms around her waist. His heels dug into Vye's side, though he doubted the dragon even noticed. Burying his face in Kaitlyn's shoulder, he prayed the castle could hold Vyekrin's weight and they wouldn't plummet to their deaths.

He held his breath as they ascended, oddly enjoying the way his body begged for air. Vyekrin leapt forward and righted himself atop the roof. Cy's grip around Kaitlyn slipped. He caught himself quickly, but not before he was forced to stare straight down to the ground. His stomach flipped. Nausea was not a feeling he missed while in his metal body.

Vyekrin took to the sky before Cy could change his

mind, the beat of his large wings breaking through the whooshing of wind in Cy's ears. He clung to Kaitlyn once more, and he felt her tilt her head away from, allowing him to press his forehead to her shoulder. Cy felt his blush be ripped away by the wind.

Nearly vertical again, Vyekrin climbed the sky toward the clouds. Cy's ears popped painfully as they went, another sensation he had forgotten about. Even when he had been with Arion, he was aware of Arion's body, but could not feel it himself.

While Cy held on for his life, now that he had to fear for it, Kaitlyn had one arm stretched toward the clouds. She was yelling loudly as Vyekrin made a large circle around the castle.

"I thought this was a scouting mission, not a joy ride!" Cy screamed as loud as he could, his voice muffled by Kait's shoulder. Without a response, Cy dared to peek over Kait's shoulder. She reached forward and patted Vyekrin three times.

Immediately, Vyekrin slowed and coasted just below the clouds. His nose dipped and he lowered himself gently, leveling out a hundred feet above the treetops. Kaitlyn leaned back into Cy, her head thumping into his own shoulder.

"Aren't you going to help look?" she teased. She pulled forward with a giggle, but she didn't make any attempts to separate them.

The wind was no longer threatening to rip Cy from the dragon's back, and his stomach settled in its rightful place. Carefully, he pried his stiff arms from around Kaitlyn's waist. Resting one on Kait's shoulder, and the other gripping Vye, Cy tilted over to watch the ground.

Though the trees were dense, from this high up the

woods looked like swaths of fabric pieced together haphazardly. The sun was nearly touching the tree line. The woods were striped light and dark from the light thrown across them.

The empty spaces below showed patches of wildflowers, specks of woodland animals preparing for nightfall. Swarms of birds flew beneath them, diving for the trees for shelter. The woods were calm, undisturbed by the rest of the world outside.

Despite the fear of flying, being in the air was peaceful. No sounds could reach them and the world below felt so far away. For a second, Cy wondered if they could simply fly until there was nothing left. Far on the horizon, the ocean sparkled enticingly.

Vye turned to sweep back along the woods, and Centric came into view. The Towers stood proudly, lit like beacons for all Mages. But not for Cyllorian.

Never for a demon.

His heart twisted, and he turned back to Kaitlyn. She was scanning the ground dutifully. Cy shivered from the wind, colder than on the ground. Kaitlyn's bare arms were now covered in thick scales, protecting her. Cy wasn't sure if she even knew she had shifted.

He glanced at his own hand on her shoulder, the pale but human skin stark in contrast to the scales creeping up her neck. Slowly, he shifted his skin to match hers, purple scales covering his arm. They spread across his shoulders, up his neck, and thinned out across his face. His eyes teared as they changed, and his vision adapted with them.

Everything seemed to be crystal clear, details sharp even in the distance. His focus grazed over the edge of the trees, and he could even see the faint shimmer of the barrier Theresa had raised. Even with heightened vision, there was nothing to be seen.

"I think it's clear."

Kaitlyn twisted to meet him, and froze, obviously caught off guard by his appearance. She quickly looked down at herself, and only then seemed to notice she had changed. She shook her head, muttering to herself, but didn't return to normal.

"You sounded disappointed," Kait pressed.

Cy looked down at the castle. *"I just hope Arion's right about Grite. Even if he can be trusted, this can't be easy for him. You know he's still having nightmares, don't you?"*

Kait followed his gaze. When she spoke, she sounded on the verge of tears. "I've been trying to find something to help. Theresa has so many medical books, but there's too many to get through. And her handwriting isn't exactly the neatest."

"I didn't know you were good with medicines."

Kait shrugged her shoulders. "I've never tried before now. But I was a good student. And now, it's hard to explain, but I understand things better. If I touch something, or someone, it's like I can *feel* what, or who, they are. Or what they're feeling. It must be part of being a shifter."

She spoke without hesitation or concern. It had barely been a few months since her life had been shaken with the news that she wasn't human, but she had adapted to her new life with such ease.

Vyekrin turned again, heading back to the castle. Cy watched Kaitlyn stare longingly after her old village as it came and went from sight, though she kept her body forward.

Cy wanted to comfort her, but he didn't know the words. On top of the drastic shift to her reality, they were immediately headed for war. He couldn't tell her that things would turn out well, or that she had chosen the right path. And he couldn't bring himself to ask her to leave, either, as selfish as he knew it was. Whatever choices might give him a chance, he hoped she'd make them.

The sun dipped out of sight, the sky painted with streaks of red and violet. Vye lowered himself, sweeping around the castle to land effortlessly near the gardens where they had departed.

Cy disembarked wordlessly while Kaitlyn praised Vyekrin for the ride. Lost in guilt and indecision, Cy waited for Kaitlyn on a stone bench between two tall cacti with spindly vines covered in long orange thistles. He plucked one and watched as the plant bled thick clear goop.

"Well, you survived another ride. I might make a frequent flyer of you yet, Cy," Kaitlyn joked as she joined him.

Cy didn't respond or look up. Kaitlyn bent over until she was in his vision, a half-smile across her face. She chuckled, then said, "Maybe not."

A silence fell over them as Kait righted herself on the bench. Behind them, Vyekrin could be heard settling himself against the castle, the brickwork groaning in protest.

The pond nearby opened into a stream that flowed past them, the water splashing onto the shore. A chorus of small birds could be heard from a nearby tree, and there was a whistle coming from a fern with expansive leaves.

Turning over the thorn in his hand, Cy spoke nervously to break the silence, *"Do you know what these do?"* He used the thorn as a wand to point to the cacti behind them.

Kaitlyn studied them quietly for a moment. "Not a lot, actually. The stuff inside the vines is good for itching and burning. If you dry out the vines, they can be used for strong ropes. And the cactus itself is edible as long as you peel the skin. Why do you ask?"

"Just testing your memory," Cy teased. He flicked the thistle into the water, and it disappeared in the current. The air had gone still, hushing the garden. Darkness was falling upon them. Cy had long traded his dragon eyes and skin for human, and it was getting harder to see as night drew closer. Before the day was gone entirely, Cy reached into his pocket, and brought its contents out in front of him.

Noticing immediately, Kaitlyn asked, "Is that...your heart?"

Cradling the small trinket in his hands, Cy ran his thumb over the intricate metalwork of the locket that held his essence only days before. He nodded slowly, his voice caught in his throat.

"I thought your body was destroyed. I saw the pieces of it in the room after Arion fixed you."

"Not everything," Cy answered carefully, worried his voice might crack from his nerves.

Inching her hand out, Kaitlyn asked, "Do you mind if I look at it?"

Cy lowered the heart into her hands swiftly so she wouldn't notice that he was shaking. He waited while she turned it over in her hands a few times, her fingers picking out the small details. The latch clicked and the heart opened, but there was nothing inside. She closed it carefully, and held it out for Cy to take.

Without a word, Cy stood from the bench and turned to leave. Kait jumped up behind him, grabbing his sleeve. "Your heart?"

Taking a deep breath, Cy faced her. He cupped her

hand with his own, but still didn't retrieve the heart. *"Do you remember what I told you? It was made for you."*

"But Arion gave it to you," Kait interjected. Her voice was getting shrill, but Cy couldn't place the emotion behind it. Nervousness? Guilt? Jealousy?

Cy closed her fingers over the locket and closed the distance between them. He lifted a hand to caress her cheek, though he couldn't meet her gaze. He took a shaky breath and whispered, *"And I'm giving it to you. My heart has always been yours."*

He leaned forward to kiss her forehead. Before she could respond, Cy turned on his heel and retreated into the castle.

CHAPTER 6

Arion

Tome laid on the cold stones of the library before Arion's feet. Knees pulled up to his chest, arms around himself, Arion stared at Tome. A cold draft wafted from under the hidden door beside him, and he pulled his coat tighter. He'd never noticed the gap in the stones, but it had become all he could see since the room had been opened.

He thought of what Seyano had told him, of his and Theresa's childhood, their parents and his illness. That turning into an owl was the only reason he had survived this long, with blood that poisoned him with every beat of his heart. The countless procedures Theresa had used to try to cure him, or at least prolong his life. Shifting his gaze to the faint light seeping from the cracks under the door, Arion could almost hear the cries of pain shut behind it.

"Are you in here?" Gil's voice echoed throughout the library, bouncing ominously off the numerous shelves throughout the room. Arion dropped his head onto his knees. A groan escaped his lips, and he immediately regretted it as it echoed back. Footsteps approached, and it wasn't long before Gil's head popped up around the shelf that hid Arion tucked in the back corner.

Gil smiled softly as he sat himself next to Arion, uncomfortably close in the small space. "Why are you hiding all the way back here? And why didn't you just go to bed? Aren't you tired?"

Arion glared at him without lifting his head. "Unbearably so," he muttered through gritted teeth.

Seeming deep in thought, Gil leaned his head back and turned his gaze to the painted ceiling. "I guess it is still a bit bright out to sleep. I'm definitely not used to this much light. Lorile never gets as bright as the surface does, but I think I'm adjusting pretty well. That amazing room helps, too!" Gil turned back to Arion, a bright smile stretching his face.

His gaze slipped from Arion to Tome, his smile slipping as well. His eyes widened in wonder. "Is that...is that your spell book?" Gil whispered excitedly.

Stretching his legs out on either side of Tome, Arion pursed his lips and nodded curtly. He was thankful that Gil's attention was on something other than himself, for once.

"I've never actually seen one before. Most adults don't use them, I think. I know Theresa doesn't." Gil reached out a hand slowly, and ran a finger over the raised ornate design along the edge.

"Because Theresa doesn't have much magic left," Arion hissed. He had been able to sense it in her, how weak her magic had grown. He saw it in the dullness of her eyes, and in the way she surrounded herself with power instead of relying on her own. He had read it for himself in a hidden journal, that his birth had drained her.

Even back then, she had blamed him for her misfortunes.

Bitterness had been festering inside him for so long, it was nearly impossible to keep his anger in check. Between the exhaustion and his lack of care regarding Gil, his guard had fallen.

It was the first time Arion had witnessed Gil speechless, and he watched him closely. It wasn't intentional, but this would be a test of allegiance.

Gil nodded slowly after a while. "I've noticed that she doesn't use as much magic as she used to, and not as much as other Mages. But I didn't know a Mage could *lose* their magic."

"Mages can lose a lot of things," Arion said solemnly. He watched Tome carefully, though it lay lifeless under Gil's touch.

Gil looked between Arion and Tome in silence for a moment. "May I?" he asked softly. His eyes were serious as he studied Arion, waiting for his reply.

Throwing his hand into the air haphazardly, Arion scoffed. "Knock yourself out."

Gil picked up Tome gently and set it across his lap. With a deep breath, he lifted the heavy cover. His jaw fell slack, the air whooshing out of his chest.

A blank page stared back at Gil, devoid of any ink. He turned another page, but was only met with white. Another and another, Gil flipped through the pages quickly until he reached the back cover. Not a single speck of ink could be found within Tome.

"What happened?" Gil asked. Somehow, he found

himself right at the root of the problem, skipping the obvious questions that Arion couldn't answer.

Not that this question was any easier to explain. Arion shook his head, too tired even for sarcasm. "I don't know. I don't know what happened or when, but Tome is...done with me."

Gil flipped his thumb through the pages, deep in thought. "Have you tried?"

"Tried what exactly?" Arion snapped. He snatched Tome back from Gil and tucked it into his coat. "Do you think if I knew how to fix it, I would just sit here doing nothing? Do you think I don't want things to get better? Do you think I enjoy being like this?"

Arion's words came out in a rush, leaving his chest tight with pain. His tired eyes stung, fists clenched tight enough at his sides that he felt his fingertips going numb. Tiny sparks flew from the cracks in his fists, disintegrating before they touched the floor.

There wasn't a hint of fear in Gil's eyes as they swept over Arion. His usual smile was replaced with a deep frown, his wide eyes glimmering with the threat of tears of his own. "Do you *want* to get better? Or do you want it all to be over?"

The words hit Arion like a slap in the face, and he twisted himself away from Gil. "What is that supposed to mean?" Arion growled under his breath.

There was a long moment of silence, and Arion hoped Gil would finally leave him alone. Instead, he spoke slowly... carefully. "Cyllorian said you gave up once before, to save him and Kaitlyn. You made Cy a new body, and helped fix Kaitlyn, but what about you? What have you done to try to fix yourself, after everything?"

Arion snorted. "So you think I need fixing, too. Is it that obvious I'm broken?"

"Yes, it is," Gil responded with no hesitation, and Arion snorted again. "It was obvious when Cy was broken, and Kaitlyn. We're not made perfect, and we're not *meant* to be perfect. We all need fixing sometimes. But if you keep denying it and rejecting help when it's available, you'll never get better."

"And how, exactly, do you suggest I fix myself?" Arion whirled back on Gil before he noticed the tears rolling down his cheeks. He scrubbed them away with his sleeve, refusing to meet Gil's gaze.

"For starters, I think some sleep would help," Gil offered quietly.

A deep chorus of laughter erupted from Arion, one that burned in his chest and brought more tears to his eyes. "If only it was that easy," he scoffed, catching his breath.

Gil waited until the echoes of Arion's laughter faded before he spoke again, giving Arion a moment to clean his face of the tears that wouldn't stop. "Why don't you try? I'll stay here with you, so no one wakes you up. I can find a book to read while I wait."

Arion lifted his eyebrows incredulously at Gil, who was now looking at the floor. A deep blush had spread across his cheeks.

Arion shook his head, not wanting to think too deeply into it. He pulled a small soft cover book from an inside coat pocket. The cover featured spiraling towers in the distance and a strange suit of armor in the center. He dropped it onto Gil's lap, then laid himself down along the wall. Hiking his coat up to cover his eyes, he muttered, "Try this one. It's quite the interesting read."

"I know this one, but it's been so long since I've read it.

I don't really remember it." Arion could hear Gil flipping through the pages, then he started to read aloud.

"Once there was a time when the land was engulfed in darkness. It was so fraught with evil that nothing could grow, and light could not reach them. The people suffered, and pleaded with the deities above to spare them from such a fate.

"Their cries reached the gods, and they delivered unto the people an army made of light itself that would save them from evil. But the army was hidden so that darkness could not taint it. Only a true hero, a soul born of righteousness, could find and lead the army.

"Many searched for the army, but none prevailed for years. Until one day..."

Exhaustion washed over Arion while Gil read, forcing him to sleep.

* * *

It was cold in the library when Arion awoke. The setting sun projected red and purple splotches along the painted ceiling through the arched windows. The tall shelves blocked some of the light, creating odd shapes that climbed higher as the sun sank lower.

Arion laid still for a moment in utter disbelief. He had been asleep for hours, and not a single nightmare struck him. He shot upright and shook the numbness from his hands. He smacked himself on the leg and winced at the slight twinge of pain. He wasn't dreaming now, though he still couldn't trust that his issue was resolved so suddenly.

His legs lined up with Gil's and a wave of embarrassment came over Arion. True to his word, Gil was still here. He must think Arion's dramatics after waking up were odd. Arion didn't want to face him or explain himself. Gritting his teeth, he thought it better to just get it over with, and turned around.

Gil had taken a thick book from a nearby shelf and was using it as a pillow, his head leaned back onto a shelf at what looked like an uncomfortable angle. His hands were resting in his lap, one hand still holding open the book Arion had given him. Arion slipped it out of his fingers carefully.

Gil wrapped his arms around himself and shivered as Arion took the book. His face was twisted in discomfort, though he didn't look like he'd awaken that easily. Arion paused a moment before leaving, then made a decision with a groan.

Quickly, Arion slipped his coat from his shoulders and laid it atop Gil. Gil clutched the coat to himself and shifted in his sleep, slowly laying down until he was curled in a ball on the floor. Arion felt his face heat up watching the other boy wriggle in his slumber. Arion shook off the confusion, along with whatever strange feeling had begun to writhe in his stomach, and looked absently into the empty library.

There was no reason to be embarrassed about his excitement from sleeping, but there was still the conversation they had just before taking a nap. Angry at himself for letting his guard fall so far, Arion stood and left the library as quietly as possible.

Once outside, Arion waved his hand in front of the wall across from the library's double doors. The stones crumbled away, leaving a small doorway with steep stairs descending into darkness. He took the stairs two at a time, the lamps along the wall struggling to keep up with his pace. The stairs let out in the dungeons, just across from Grite's cell.

The demon was lounging in his cot, one talon digging a pattern into a stone brick beside him. His damaged leg was thrown leisurely over the other, bouncing in the air to inaudible music. *"Well, you sure took your sweet time coming back to see me. Didn't Theresa say you only had a week before I'm—"*

To finish his sentence, he lifted his talon from the wall and slowly traced a line across his neck, a gagging sound coming from deep in his throat.

Chairs lined the wall between the cells. Arion grabbed one and dragged it directly in front of Grite's cell, ignoring how the loud scraping sound made Grite cringe. "I was busy," Arion said shortly, clearly leaving no room for a discussion on the subject.

Of course, Grite ignored that. He eyed Arion up and down, a sly smile twisting up one corner of his mouth. *"Looks like someone got a good chunk of beauty sleep, huh? Who helped you with that? Cy, or that Droll?"*

Arion flinched away. With his coat missing, there was nothing to hide behind now. "What are you talking about?" he spat.

Grite's face fell suddenly, all teasing gone from his expression. A darkness swept over his eyes as he stared at Arion. *"You're not the only one with nightmares around here. Not anymore."*

A lump formed in Arion's throat at Grite's words, and he struggled to swallow it. The last person he wanted to know about his nightmares was Grite, terrified of what the treacherous demon would do with any information.

Slapping his hands down on his knees, Arion changed the subject. "Why are you here?"

Grite let out a loud huff, a visible plume of dusty air

escaping his nose, and said simply, *"I told you. I want to kill Crestyss."*

"How exactly do you plan to do that? What do you want from me?"

At that, Grite's eyes went wide. *"I was hoping you had a plan ready. Self-destructive murder missions do seem to be your specialty, after all."*

Arion's fists clenched on his lap. He couldn't argue with Grite, especially since he had spoken with genuine surprise.

And Grite wasn't wrong.

"It's not a full plan. Just an idea, right now."

Grite flung himself forward, coming to full attention. He struggled to cross his legs. He spread his hands out on the bed in front of them, leaning his whole weight on them. Though the demon couldn't weigh much, his arms shook underneath him. *"Let's hear it."*

Arion studied Grite for a long moment. Not once yet had he asked to be let go, or even tried to bargain for his life. As soon as Arion had confirmed they were thinking the same thing, he was eager and ready. He couldn't believe that this could possibly be the same demon that had tortured him just a month ago, had chased him down to kill him.

Now that he had to speak his plan out loud, Arion realized just how awful it was. "We sneak into his Tower at night, and kill him."

"And?" Grite asked expectantly after a few minutes of silence.

"That's all I've got."

"What?! You're supposed to have a month's worth of a head start on this plan, and you have nothing? Of course, we're going

to have to sneak in, but what else? Do you just expect us to walk in there?"

"I wasn't planning on taking *you* of all people with me!" Arion snapped back, throwing up his arms in exasperation. His face was growing warm again, though he knew this was from frustration.

"Of course you weren't, you were going to go alone and off yourself in the process, right? Believe it or not, but I'd rather not die. If I did I would have just let Crestyss do it instead of dragging myself through the woods," Grite snarled. *"You're going to have to come up with a new plan."*

"I don't know what else you were expecting," Arion grumbled.

Grite's eyes were following the book still in Arion's grip as he waved his hands around. *"What's that?"* he asked.

Arion narrowed his eyes, irritated at the change of subject. He tossed the book through the cell bars, and it landed directly in front of Grite. "It's just an old folk tale. As old as Lontorra itself, some say."

Grite grabbed it roughly, his talons piercing the binding of the book. Arion winced at the mistreatment, but Grite's sneer as he studied the cover kept him quiet. Without looking up, Grite tossed it back through the bars. *"A righteous tale of how the world was cleansed by an immortal army made by gods. Said army was laid to rest beneath the promised land until they were needed again. So, you know this story, too?"*

Arion opened his mouth to answer, but something in Grite's tone made him hesitate. Grite was staring down at his talons, a small shred of the book caught on his thumb.

"Yes, I do," Arion affirmed. Grite looked at him then. It felt as though he were trying to speak to Arion through his gaze.

"We really are on the same page then. Aren't we?" Grite nodded to the book in Arion's hand.

"So it is real?"

"Crestyss and Theresa both believe it. They always have. This was their plan to take over all of Lontorra when they were on the same side. What do you think you're here for?"

Arion sputtered, "What does that mean?"

Grite's face twisted in disgust, and he leaned back against the wall. It looked as though he were retreating. His mouth twisted as he said, *"Crestyss made you for a reason. He used Theresa for her body and magic, and forced her to give birth to you. He knew that the mix of his and Theresa's magic would give him something powerful enough to lead the army. And that's where you came in. Why do you think he wanted your memories to come back so badly before? Without your memories, you had no magic. And without magic, you were of no use to him. Same as me."*

A wave of hatred and grief washed over Arion, and his head dropped as he tried to process what Grite said. He had every reason to lie to him, and Arion had no reason to trust him. But every word Grite said had settled in a hollow pit in his chest, filling him with all the explanations he had been lacking his entire life.

"How did you survive?" Arion asked quietly.

"What?"

"You said Crestyss tried to kill you. He shot you in the head with that magic gun, right? How could you have survived that?"

There was a long pause as Grite returned Arion's determined stare. If he couldn't answer, then he couldn't be trusted. And Arion wanted nothing more than to be able to trust this demon right now.

"When I caught you and bit you, you had started to remem-

ber. Your magic was coming back, but only a little. It was in your blood. I returned to present it to Crestyss, but it wasn't good enough. He shot me. But I kept just enough of your blood for myself, and used it to keep me alive, yet just barely. I had to wait for his guards to clean up my body and toss me outside before I could make a run for it."

Grite was staring behind Arion now, lost in thought. He was running his talons back and forth along the grooves in the wall beside him. It looked like he didn't even know he was doing it. His eyes were glossed over, and his hurt leg hung off the bed, swinging. Arion couldn't help but think it would fall off at any moment.

There was nothing Arion could think to say in response. Grite's words about how Crestyss had "made" Arion filled in so many gaps in Arion's knowledge, and gave clear solutions to the questions that had been flooding his mind. As terrible as it all was, he desperately wanted it to be true. He just wanted to understand.

Grite startled Arion when he spoke up again. *"What do you think could possibly possess a man to dress the way Crestyss does?"* Arion stared blankly at Grite, caught completely off guard by the total shift in conversation and tone. Grite cocked his head and continued, sounding desperate now, *"Don't you remember? The long shirts that hung like dresses and those pants— Ugh, those pants. It gave so much information that no one needed, or even wanted to imagine. I just don't know how he expected to rule a whole country wearing such tight clothes that left him looking more overstuffed than a straw doll!"*

Grite ended his rant by rolling half off the bed. He hung upside down, dragging his knuckles along the floor. His eyes were rolling in his head, over and over. Arion worried they'd pop out.

Arion burst out laughing. The fit wracked him so much, he struggled to stay in his chair, doubled over on himself with laughter. Grite's cackles echoed his own, and Arion couldn't help but think of Crestyss strutting through the dungeon halls. No longer a fearsome ruler, but a stuck up prince fussing over his appearance.

"Is that why he was always late to the dungeons? Did it just take him *that* long to get dressed each day?" Arion remarked through bouts of chuckles.

Grite snorted, then there was a loud *thud*. Arion looked up to see Grite had fallen completely out of bed and was rolling on the floor, holding his stomach. *"You have no idea!"* he bellowed. *"Those were the days he dressed quickly. You didn't even see him when he had to make a public appearance, sheesh!"*

They lost themselves in their laughter, the sounds filling the dungeons so much that they hadn't even heard the sound of footsteps descending the stairs.

"What joke did I miss? I'm a little jealous I didn't get to hear it," Gil mused from behind Arion.

Arion choked on his laughter. Gil's presence scared him. He whirled in his chair to see Gil standing far too close, his eyes still bleary from his nap.

Arion's coat was draped neatly over one arm. He held it out to Arion, "Thanks. I didn't realize the library got so cold in the evening."

A sleepy smile spread over Gil's face. Without meeting his gaze, Arion took his coat. He was immensely aware of Grite's eyes focused on him. Through the corner of his eye, he thought he caught a glimpse of a smug grin on Grite.

"What do you want?" Arion barked, sounding harsher than he meant.

Busy rubbing the sleep from his eyes, Gil didn't seem to

notice Arion's tone, or at least was unbothered. "Huh?" he muttered, his voice thick as he spoke through a yawn. "There's a party tomorrow night."

"Who decided now was a good time for a party?" Arion blurted.

Gil beamed, now fully awake. "Mine. I'm sure the Draken don't mind having war meetings every day, but I'm getting bored. Cy seemed on board when I passed him on my way here. We need to lighten up around her. And you're coming."

Arion balked at Gil's declaration. In the cell, Grite quipped, *"Sounds like a date."*

Chapter 7

Arion

The echoing sounds of footsteps sent a lump into Arion's throat. Grite fell silent mid-sentence, his eyebrows raising as he stared expectantly at the stairs across from his cell. Arion dropped his head, gripping the folded coat in his lap tightly.

"You really did come back for him, huh?" Grite mused aloud as the footsteps grew closer. Grite had been restless in his cell while he and Arion talked, and was now laying backwards in his bed with his legs propped up along the wall. Some time in the past hour, he had broken off a piece from the wall, and was now tossing it in the air and catching it like a ball.

Gil stepped up beside Arion with no hesitation. "Well, yeah. It's already midnight. Everyone else is already there, well, everyone our age. Are you ready? Or were you still talking?"

Before Arion could protest, Grite spoke up, *"Oh please,*

by all means, take him. Don't let me hog him all night." He let out a low chuckle, and Arion shot him a glare.

Gil jumped back up, energized. "Great! Let's head up." Gil grabbed Arion's arm, and he flinched away. Though he didn't release Arion entirely, Gil loosened his grip. With a small tug of encouragement, Arion relented and stood from his seat.

Grite didn't say a word as they left for the stairs, but Arion could feel his gaze prickling the back of his neck. Firmly pulling his arm from Gil's grasp, Arion threw his coat back over his shoulders.

"You really like that coat, don't you? I can see why; it suits you," Gil prodded, ignoring the tension in the air.

Arion studied Gil through the corner of his eye as they ascended. "Why are you so adamant about me coming? I'm only going to ruin it. No one wants me there," Arion snapped.

Gil's face scrunched up in thought. He turned to face Arion head on. "Well, I think it's obvious I want you there. And Cy and Kait, too. Why wouldn't they? As far as everyone else, well...you've been going out of your way to make them dislike you. I don't know why you're trying to be so scary, but maybe this can be a chance to change their minds."

There was no point arguing with Gil when he was right. Arion pursed his lips. He was starting to hate how easily Gil could see through him, and he didn't have the energy to prove him wrong. It didn't matter if one person was unphased by him, as long as the rest left him alone.

In response to Arion's silence, Gil changed the subject to ramble about what they had done to prepare for the party. Arion let him drone on past the point of listening. The stairs seemed endless, and Arion realized the castle was taking them straight to the party. The murmur of distant voices could be heard above them. Arion shoved his fists into his pockets. His gaze automatically drifted to the ground as they emerged, and the voices stopped. The weight of at least a dozen eyes fell on Arion's shoulders.

Desperately trying to avoid the gazes, Arion finally noticed Gil standing proudly in the room. Though he had complained about the cold before, his arms were bare. Gil was thinner than Arion had originally thought, his turquoise shirt tight over his chest. Lean muscles stood out through the fabric, and over his arms. He wore black pants that cut off a few inches above his ankles, showing off his pale blue skin between the fabric and his short black boots. A thick silver band wrapped in strands of leather was around his wrist. A matching silver chain hung around his neck, a sharply-cut glue crystal rested in the middle of his chest. There was a faint light glimmering inside of it.

Arion had gotten used to seeing Gil thanks to his constant presence, but this outfit threw Arion off. He felt his cheeks flush, and wrenched his eyes away. *I'm not dressed for this, I shouldn't be here.* He told himself the heat that had filled him was embarrassment.

"Cy, I got him!" Gil called out beside him, making Arion jump. Before Arion could berate Gil for bringing even more attention to them, Cy emerged from the crowd.

Cy had found himself a pair of loose black slacks and gray undershirt, and a deep purple vest that lay unbuttoned. Cy's eyes were wide. *"Wow, good job. What did you bribe him with?"* Cy joked. Arion was ready to snap at him, but was cut off by Cy patting him on the shoulder. Cy had put himself squarely in front of Arion, and he noticed that he was blocked from most everyone's gaze. They all soon returned to their hushed conversations.

Arion's eyes fell on Kait as she trailed behind Cy. She was dressed similarly, with black pants and a shining blue blouse held close to her figure with a small white corset. Her face was dotted with shimmering blue scales, her hair spiked up and glowing white in the otherwise dim room.

Kait blushed lightly, turning the scales on her cheeks purple, and held up her arms to show a rainbow of scales glimmering in the low light. "I thought I should start practicing," she said sheepishly.

With a bit of a forced smile, Arion praised her. "It looks like it's coming easily to you now."

"If we're taking time to brag a bit, look at what I did. I decorated most of the room myself." Cy puffed up his chest, one hand smugly on his hip while the other waved toward the room.

It was a long oval room, with the far wall filled with large stained-glass windows depicting the moon and stars. Along the walls were diamond shaped sconces holding large purple flames. They danced along to a soft melody of strings that hung tangible in the air like banners descending from smoke that clung to the ceiling. Arion watched the music trail along them slowly, sounding more like a lullaby than anything. The smoke curled in one big circle around the room, fluffy and billowing. A faint glow could be seen deep in them.

The whole room made Arion want to take a nap.

Across the room, one of the flames started to die. A pixie appeared from the smoke and flitted straight to Cy's ear. She whispered something, gesturing to the dying flame. Arion leaned around Cy to see the Kindling girl was watching it with worry, as though it were alive.

Cy lifted his hand like he wanted to shoo the pixie away, but stopped himself. With a huff, he said, *"I'll go fix it. Tell Adoette it's fine. Nothing's wrong. It's just a lot of magic to keep going at once."*

The pixie crossed her arms and stomped her foot in the air. She stuck her tongue out at Cy, then quickly flitted back over to the Kindling.

"Be right back," Cy said with a wave, then followed.

Kait watched as he left. She picked at the hem of her corset nervously, though Arion didn't think she was aware she was doing it. Her gaze scanned over the crowd. A few people were still watching them, and they averted their gaze as she caught them. She turned back to Arion with a smile. Arion could tell it was strained, though he couldn't tell if it was because of Cy, or all the attention on them.

"I'm fine, Kait. You can go. Not like I'm going to be left alone with him around, anyway," Arion offered, jutting a thumb toward Gil.

Gil made a sound like he was offended, but Arion could see the corners of his mouth turning up.

Kait's face dropped, now filled with guilt. "Are you sure? I didn't mean to..."

Kait was lost for words, looking between Gil and Arion inquisitively.

It was a relief to see the care in her eyes, and it only confirmed Arion's feelings, or lack thereof, even farther. With a deep breath, Arion forced a gentle smile and reassured her, "I know, Kait. It's all right. I promise, I'm fine."

She met Arion's gaze, and he felt just like he had the first time she had approached him. He felt safe, and cared for, and so appreciative for everything that Kaitlyn had done for him, and so much more.

But there were no more romantic feelings left when he looked at Kaitlyn. There was a strong protectiveness, which he had mistaken for love earlier. As long as she was his friend, his family, he would be happy.

A warm and genuine smile spread over Kait's face slowly. Her eyes glistened with the threat of tears. Bouncing once on her toes, she flung herself at Arion and wrapped him in a tight hug that stole Arion's breath.

Shocked at first, there was a long moment before Arion could return the embrace. He held her tight, digging his fingers into her shoulders as he squeezed. He buried his face in her shoulder.

"I love you, Arion. You know that, right?" Kait's whisper sent a chill down Arion's spine. A warmth deep inside him welled up, replacing the cold. His eyes ached with the sting of tears, and he was glad his face was covered.

Afraid his voice would give him away, he nodded against her. Her grip tightened for a moment, then she slowly released him. Her hands lingered on his shoulders, forcing him to look at her.

"Be good, Arion. Try to have some fun, okay?" Kait asserted, shaking Arion lightly.

Still unsure of himself, Arion simply nodded. With a flash of a toothy grin, Kait turned back to the crowd, satisfied. Arion watched her approach Cy and Adoette, and the Kindling wrapped Kaitlyn in another hug. The two girls swayed while Cy attempted to coax the fire back to full volume. Watching Cy wave his hands around aimlessly at the flame made Arion chuckle, and helped to calm him down. Arion made a big show of scrutinizing the decorations of the room.

"*Fun* she says. Sure," Arion said mischievously.

"What are you— Hey!" Gil started, but Arion strutted toward the middle of the room before he could finish. He ignored the eyes that followed him. Gil was close behind him, question after question spilling from his mouth, but Arion wasn't listening.

Once in the center Arion stopped and looked over the room again, a plan forming in his mind. He closed his eyes, took in a deep breath, then stomped his left foot onto the ground as hard as he could.

Magic shot out from him in a wave, silencing the whole room. Cautiously, Arion opened his eyes to watch his vision take shape. Every flame snuffed out, the strings burned and crackled, the smoke faded into the stones. To his left, the wall gave way to a large alcove in the shape of a half-dome. Instruments made of light green crystal formed within, producing a fast melody that buzzed through the floor. From the ceiling rained stars of all sizes that floated through the air as though they were dancing to the music.

Around the room were stunned expressions and dropped jaws. Across the room, Cy looked furious. Arion turned away from him to stop from laughing. A chorus of murmurs rose in the room slowly as some began to sway with the loud music, and others played with the stars.

From behind him, Gil yelped. Arion whirled quickly to see Gil sprawled back along the floor, patting his arms frantically as the stars bumped into him. One fell gracefully onto the tip of his nose, and he froze. His eyes crossed as he stared at the star like it was a vicious beast about to eat him.

Suddenly he looked back to Arion, desperation clear in his eyes. "Help," he pleaded, his voice cracking.

Arion immediately doubled over with laughter, unable to contain himself. After a few stunned seconds, others joined in with him, though none matched his volume. Tears pricked the corners of his eyes.

"It won't hurt you," Arion said through his laughter. With a slight wave of his hand, the star was caught in a breeze and carried off into the room. Arion held a hand out to Gil. His face was deep purple, and he took Arion's hand with a pout. Gil's hand was warm in Arion's. It settled him as he pulled Gil to his feet. Gil held tightly to Arion even after returning to his feet, and Arion was too distracted by the party to let go.

While Arion helped Gil stand, everyone else had entertained themselves. Some were playing catch with the stars, while others watched the crystal band play. Most were dancing, having paired up with those they had been talking with. Among the crowd were Kait and Adoette, jumping and swaying out of tune with the music. Cy was standing nearby, his tender gaze fixed to Kait.

The steady beat hummed beneath Arion's feet, and the newfound excitement in the air was reaching Arion. He didn't fight it, as it filled him with the same carefree feeling. The sensation was brand new to him, and it felt like a breath of air after months, years of drowning.

Gil's grip tightened on Arion's hand, drawing his attention. Giddiness bubbled up in Arion, and he felt his body moving on its own. He turned to face Gil, a mischievous smile on his face, and he grabbed Gil's other hand. Gil stumbled as Arion pulled him toward the crowd. "Wh- what are you doing?" Gil asked, now having to shout over the cacophony of music and exuberant voices.

"What Kaitlyn told me to. Having fun!" Arion yelled back. He locked hands with Gil, and before he could question him further, Arion spun them both as fast as he could. Gil struggled to keep up with Arion, nearly tripping. Arion kept him upright and slowed his pace, laughing at Gil's exasperation. He closed his eyes against the dizziness, letting himself slip into the childish joy that had been so sorely absent in his life.

"What is going on here?" Theresa's voice bellowed through the room. Arion froze at the sound, his grip tightening on Gil's hands, and the music ceased with him. The crowd parted as everyone retreated to the walls. The stars dropped to the floor, though they still glowed dimly.

Theresa stood just inside the room, a few adults gathered behind her. She surveyed the room with disapproval. The way they had stopped, Arion was hidden behind Gil, and for once, he shrunk away from Theresa. He felt more vulnerable than he could ever remember being and couldn't muster the strength to face her.

"I thought so much better of all of you," Theresa's words cut through the air like a knife, her distaste dripping like poison. "The fate of Lontorra rests on you, and here you are, frolicking like children. How immature—"

The tower shook violently, cutting off Theresa's tirade. The crystal instruments shattered, shards exploding into the room. Screams rang out as the tower shook again. The windows cracked and fell away, tearing the wall down with it. Outside, a ring of trees surrounding the castle were aflame. Fireballs heaved into the walls. Another tremor rumbled through the castle.

The castle was being attacked. They had been found.

Arion found his voice among the cries of terror. "Get to the dungeons! Now!" He released Gil's hands and swept his arms toward the door where Theresa stood immobile. A gust of air swept up from behind him, pushing everyone in the right direction. The panicked teenagers stampeded out the doors. Arion shoved his way through the crowd out into the hallway. The balcony just outside fell away, changing into a wide staircase plummeting into the depths of the castle. Pressing himself into the wall to avoid the mass of people, Arion sent a surge of magic throughout the castle, willing anyone left to descend as well.

Cy, Kait and Gil brought up the rear of the mob, urging everyone forward as fast as possible. Gil grabbed Arion, and Arion let him pull him as they ran down the stairs. Another quake, and the crowd stumbled forward as a whole, most able to keep their footing. Those that fell were quickly hefted up and dragged by those unwilling to slow down.

They reached the dungeons in time for another attack, and the ceiling above them groaned in protest. Dust rained down on them as the hordes of people swarmed the middle of the room.

Arion pushed them aside as he ran to Grite's cell to unlock it. Theresa's voice, shrill and pained, cut over the panicked chorus of voices, "What are you doing? That *thing* brought Crestyss here, and you're trying to release it?"

Ignoring Theresa's scolding, Arion quickly grabbed the metal of the door. It melted away in his hands, and the door swung open. He lunged for Grite to drag him out, but Cy and Gil rushed in before he could. They hoisted the wounded demon onto their shoulders.

"Where are we going, kid?" Cy asked frantically.

Arion looked to the only wall that hadn't turned into stairs for those fleeing the castle. He crashed into it and pressed both hands to the cold stones. With a shove and magic, the wall collapsed. Behind it was a dark tunnel carved into the dirt.

The crowd rushed for the tunnel without any direction. The adults, mostly Mages, led the charge. They held their hands up, illuminating the way forward with magic in their palms.

Cy and Gil, carrying Grite, brought up the rear of the mob, and Arion waited for them. Once they passed him, Arion stepped into the tunnel. With a wave of his hand, the stone wall rebuilt itself behind them.

The sounds of the attack were muffled in the tunnel, and the fear quickly subsided into confusion. Questions filled the air as they all trudged through the winding mess of tunnels. Before long, Arion could no longer hear the destruction of the castle.

They spent hours wandering the tunnels. It felt like they were going in circles. The crowd had slowed significantly when it had gone quiet, and began to complain quietly amongst themselves soon after. They clearly couldn't return to the castle, but there was not telling where they were going.

The hallway suddenly gave way to a large room with a low dirt ceiling, roots emerging like hands to grab them. One wall lay bare, while the other three were filled with doorways leading to a maze of catacombs. The mass of about thirty people huddled at the entrance, too scared to go into the room.

More questions and concerns erupted from the crowd, and Theresa stepped forward into the room. "Calm down, everyone, please." She spoke softly, forcing the masses to be quiet so they could hear her. "We will be safe here, I promise. This labyrinth cannot be found so easily, and is hidden with strong magic. The castle may have been found by Crestyss due to negligence, but I can guarantee that he will never find us here."

Theresa's promises did little to quell the crowd, and everything to rekindle the rage within Arion. He bypassed the crowd and placed himself squarely in front of the barren wall. "I think they deserve more of an explanation than that, Theresa."

All eyes turned to him, and he placed his hand on the wall. Theresa's eyes narrowed. "Don't try to turn the blame from anyone but yourself," Theresa deflected. "It's obvious that Crestyss only found us because of the *stray* you brought into my castle."

"Your castle?" Arion scoffed, falling for Theresa's taunts. "And who was it that got us here in the first place? Who commanded the castle to guide us to safety? I didn't see you doing anything to protect those loyal to you. And Crestyss isn't here for Grite. He's been missing for a month — who knows how long he spent in the woods without any of us knowing. Crestyss would have attacked then, before we even knew about Grite. But you've left the castle plenty of times since you began to recruit your army. He could have been tracking *you*. And I think it's time your army knew exactly what they had signed up for."

Arion's magic ripped through the dirt wall like lightning. The smell of scorched soil filled the room. Looking behind him, Arion puffed with pride as his fears unfolded before him.

Beyond the wall lay a seemingly endless room, filled with what looked like suits of armor. There were no gaps at the joints, no way to adorn the metal, and no holes in the faces for eyes. They were bodies, like Cy's had been, made completely of metal and ready to host a soul.

"Tell me, Theresa," Arion prodded. "Who are these for?"

CHAPTER 8

Cyllorian

Whispers sprang from the crowd in a fury. Cy twisted himself to see around the writhing mass of bodies that blocked the way. He couldn't force his way through with Grite on his shoulder, and he didn't dare release him. Despite Arion's odd trust in the other demon, there was no denying he was dangerous.

"What is it? What's in there?" Gil asked, also stretching to his full height. Grite flinched at Gil's voice, lowering his head.

Cy opened his mouth to interrogate Grite, but was cut off by Kaitlyn changing into her dragon form and climbing the wall beside them. Vyekrin emerged from the folds of her blouse onto her shoulder, smoke furling from his nostrils.

"They— they look like you, Cy," Kait choked out. Her face paled as she examined the room ahead of them.

With a shake of her head, she jumped back to the

ground. Vyekrin leapt from her shoulder to watch the scene unfold from a higher perch. Kaitlyn stumbled over her words as she spoke quickly, clarifying, "Not like you do now— like before. There's hundreds of metal bodies without faces. It's not armor for everyone, it's new bodies."

Theresa's mocking tone cut out over the crowd. "And what am I supposed to know about these? They look more like those things that *you* make, Arion. Wasn't Cyllorian in something just like this until recently?"

Cy clenched his jaw. Near the back of the crowd, he saw a familiar pair of silhouettes. Pulling Grite and Gil along with him, Cy grabbed at the two Draken too afraid to approach the action. *"Lane. Orthros. Hold him."* Cy thrust Grite into their arms before any of them could protest and pushed his way into the crowd.

"You just tried to say this was your castle!" Arion yelled, his voice echoing overhead. "You knew about these tunnels even if you didn't build them yourself. You didn't even pretend to look surprised when you saw these. You're planning to turn everyone here into your own Void army, and I can prove it!"

Cy shoved the last of the Mages from his way to see Arion holding a small book in Theresa's face. She scowled at it for a moment before erupting into hysterics. Arion visibly shrunk away, struggling to hold his ground. The onlookers glanced at each other for guidance, but everyone was stunned into silence.

Once Theresa could breathe again, she said,, "You think you understand me because of a silly children's book? A bedtime story that all of Lontorra knows by heart. It's nothing more than a fairytale." Theresa snatched the book from Arion's hands. She held it out toward her followers, encouraging them to laugh with her. A few started to chuckle, but most remained silent.

Arion stumbled at the sudden movement, barely catching himself from falling. Cy stepped forward to help, but the sheer rage on Arion's face stopped him.

"If it's only a fairytale, then why does the Void army even exist?" Arion snarled. Theresa turned back to him, daggers in her eyes. "There's truth in every story. You and Crestyss have been fighting over this one for a long time. I told you Grite had valuable information." Arion smirked. Cy could see his fists were shaking at his sides, magic sparking from them.

Theresa whirled back to the crowd. Her eyes were frantic, wild as they landed on something far away. The panic was gone in an instant. Her features turned sharp and cold like ice, and Cy thought he could see the slimmest glimmer of magic left in her eyes.

Cy took the opportunity he was given and stepped away from the crowd. He held his hand out for Arion, pleading with him, *"Arion, stop. That's enough. If you lose control of your magic, Crestyss will find us. Let's just grab Grite and leave, then Crestyss will follow us. He'll leave the castle alone."*

The overflowing magic in Arion's hands stopped dead. His face dropped, and the shaking moved from his hands to his legs. A choking noise escaped Arion's mouth while he looked back and forth between Cy and Theresa. Cy could only imagine the victorious look on Theresa's face, but he ignored her. He didn't care about her; he was doing this for Arion's sake.

"What are you...Why? Why are you on her side? You see them, too, Cy! Look at them!" Arion flung his hand out toward the metal army. His control broke, and a bolt of magic flew from his hand. It collided with one of the bodies, tearing a hole through the shoulder. Thick dust plumed up from within the body.

Cy grabbed Arion by his shoulders and shook him. He leaned toward Arion and whispered, *"I don't care about Theresa or her damn army! I care about you and you're scaring me right now! You have to calm down."*

"You don't get it," Arion hissed back.

Kaitlyn had rushed to join them. She pulled on Cy's coat, begging them not to fight. Her voice was drowned out as Theresa addressed the audience, "Even the ever-loyal demon doesn't believe him. He is nothing but an irrational, uncontrollable child lashing out."

Cy spun to face Theresa, knocking Kaitlyn back as he did. The rage fell from him as soon as it had risen, now replaced by guilt. He turned to apologize to Kaitlyn, but she wasn't paying attention to him.

"Arion!" she yelled. She reached out for him, but the room filled with a thin cloud of green smoke that didn't quite cover his escape through one of the many doorways. Her hand clamped down on Cy's wrist and she pulled him in the pursuit of Arion. She was still in her dragon form, and didn't notice her claws digging into Cy's arm. He grit his teeth against the sting and pushed to keep up with her.

They rounded the corner into the doorway Arion had taken and found a small circular room with even more pathways spaced every few feet apart. There was no light in any direction, and no sign that Arion had been here at all.

Kaitlyn threw down Cy's arm, and he staggered with the force. She paced in a huff from doorway to doorway, staring down into each. "What were you thinking? He already thinks you're on Theresa's side and the first thing you say to him is *stop*? How did you expect him to react? On top of that, he's been trying to tell us for weeks that Theresa's up to something, and now he has proof, and you still don't even listen to him. What the hell were you trying to accomplish, Cyllorian?"

Cy stood stunned at her outburst, searching for any explanation. *"I told you, I don't want him involved in this. What else am I supposed to do, let him throw his life away for Theresa?"* he said finally. He dropped his head, breathing heavily. His shaking hands at his side came into view, his real hands made of flesh and bone, and his gut twisted. He snarled under his breath at himself.

With a grand wave of her arm, Kait turned back toward him. "Are you at least going to help look for him, or just let him get lost in the tunnels?"

Cy was spared from answering by Gil turning the corner to join them in the small room. He was nearly dragging Grite along behind him, and the demon was protesting through gasps for air. Once in the room, Gil dropped him with a groan. Grite promptly collapsed against the wall, sliding down into a sitting position.

"Where did he go?" Gil asked in a rush.

"We don't know," Kait answered. She waved at Cy again, and it felt like a slap in the face. "Thanks to *someone*, he's probably halfway across Lontorra by now."

Stepping forward, Cy opened his mouth to defend himself. A sharp pain shot up his right arm, and his knees buckled beneath him. He clawed at his sleeve, blood soaking into the material. Etched into his inner arm was a crude arrow pointing up. As he stared, letters were scratched below it; H...E...then a line that dragged nearly to his elbow.

"What is that?" Kait squeaked in Cy's ear. She was

perched right beside him. Her fingers danced hesitantly around the wound.

Arion's words from before sounded in Cy's mind. *We're connected.*

"We have to get to the surface. Arion's in trouble."

It was Gil's turn to examine the tunnels. He popped his head into each one, pressed his ear to the dirt wall, and sniffed the air. "Gil, what are you—" Kait started to ask, but Gil raised a hand to cut her off.

Remembering the labyrinth of tunnels leading to Lorile, Cy left Gil to his methods. He ignored the pain in his arm, and reached out toward Grite. A tendril of smoke rose from his fingers and weaved its way through and around Grite's leg. It filled the wound and held tight like a bandage.

"What's this for?" Grite snipped, staring at his leg with disdain.

Cy raised his eyebrow at him. *"Would you rather stay down here with Theresa?"*

Grite looked at him for a long minute. His nails dug into the side of the wall, and he hauled himself to his feet, breath coming shallow through gritted teeth. He shifted his weight gradually onto his hurt leg and huffed in approval. *"I guess this will do."*

"It better. It takes more magic than I'm really willing to spend on you."

Before Cy could change his mind, Gil spoke up from the furthest right tunnel. "Let's go," he barked, and darted down the dark tunnel.

Kait followed next with Cy close behind her. She was gradually picking up speed to keep up with Gil. It took Cy a minute to notice, but she had made herself taller to quicken her pace. Grite's labored footsteps could be heard behind them, but he was still stumbling as he went.

"*A little help?*" Grite snarled as he tripped over his own feet again. Cy touched his hand to the wall, and the ceiling burst into light above them, moving in waves of purple, blue and white like water flowing above them. Kaitlyn's gasp echoed along the hall, though her pace never faltered as she watched the lights above her.

The tunnel quickly turned into a twisting slope taking them upward. They ducked and weaved to avoid the growing vines that hung well into the tunnel. Pouring light could be seen ahead nearby, outlining the rough shape of a door.

Gil shoved his way through the door. They all spilled out into a small clearing ringed with small, young trees. The flowers filling the field were all painted red with the light from the woods burning around the castle. A low whirring sound could be heard in the air, though there was no wind to make a noise of any sort.

Behind them, whole trees began to snap, and they rushed forward blindly into the open. A grinding roar sounded that pierced their ears. They panicked and covered their ears, spinning to find the culprit.

Barreling over the trees was a large metal dragon made from scraps, gears and mechanics. With a sound of scraping metal, it spread its large wings slowly and with obvious strain. A coiling snakelike metal body followed behind, crushing the trees into the ground. It roared again, its body jerking in pain. Arion dangled from its mouth by his leg. He was desperately stabbing at the metal scales that lined the creature's neck with a long spear.

"It's about time!" Arion yelled. The beast roiled as

Arion pried away two of its scales. It shook its head like a wild animal, and Arion screamed in pain himself.

"Arion!" Kait and Gil yelled at the same time. Kaitlyn looked more dragon than human, now with a mouth full of pointed teeth that she bared at the beast. It hadn't seemed to notice any of them yet as it wrestled with a less than cooperative Arion.

"What is that thing?" she yelled as blue scales covered her entire body.

"Crestyss' pet. You didn't think Arion got his crafting ability from Theresa, did you?" Grite answered ominously. His attempt at a joke fell flat at the fear in his voice.

Cy let himself shift back to his demon form, thick talons growing from his fingertips. He moved to follow Kait as she charged for the dragon.

Gil grabbed his arm and stopped him. "I need to fight," he begged.

"What are you going to do? Just stay here."

Gil yanked him back sharply. "You have magic now, so make me a crossbow. I'm not just going to sit back and watch!" he growled. His knuckles were white on Cy's sleeve.

Cy closed his eyes and focused. He could feel the smoke unfurling from his palms. It stretched and formed, gaining weight in his hands. Within seconds, a large crossbow was nestled in his hands, black paint swirling along it like smoke. Prying his arm from Gil's grip, he replaced it with the crossbow.

He left Gil staring at the new weapon and ran to help Kaitlyn, who was already halfway up the monster's back. She left holes in the metal, acid dripping from them as they ate away at it.

"Where are the bolts?!" Gil yelled behind him, rage clear in his strained voice.

"Just pull it!" Cy called back. He was already upon the beast and couldn't risk turning back. He climbed on top and started ripping the scales from its body. If he could get inside and find whatever was at its core, he could easily shut this thing down.

A sharp whistle rent the air, and the beast reared back from the impact of a large bolt being buried deep into its neck just below its jaw. Arion tried to reach for it, but the dragon swung its head again, throwing him high into the air. He twisted wildly to try to right himself, but the dragon caught him easily as he descended, its teeth latching onto Arion's left shoulder. He screamed again, and lightning raced throughout the dragon's body. It screeched at the magic, and with more speed than Cy thought it had, the dragon launched itself into the air.

Cy was quickly thrown from its tail as it took to the sky. He barely managed to catch himself among the scales and pieces he had torn from its body. He rolled on the ground to stare at the beast in the air. Kaitlyn had one hand latched onto the arm of its wing. With the other, she was cutting the leather to ribbons. Over and over, she slashed at it, the layers peeling away.

"Kaitlyn!" Cy yelled as the dragon rose higher and higher into the sky, growing unsteady on its damaged wing.

The creature lurched forward once it reached its peak, just as Kaitlyn was reaching across to its other wing. She fell from its back, a piece of metal still stuck to her claws. She rolled in the sky and tried to shake the metal from her hand.

Cy used his magic to create a dense cloud of smoke as

large as he could, and threw it up to meet her as she fell. It slowed her descent, and Cy was able to catch her easily before she hit the ground. The beast roared again, and it dipped in the sky momentarily, before it caught itself raggedly. The rising sun glinted perfectly off the metal, allowing the creature to nearly disappear in the sky.

Gil helped Cy set Kaitlyn down. They all took off after the weakened dragon. Even Grite did his best to keep up. "Where is it taking him? Isn't Talgrin the other direction?" Gil asked as they ran.

Cy examined the land before them and chuckled victoriously. *"To its own doom. The stupid thing is headed for the Wasteland."*

Vyekrin sprung from Kaitlyn's shoulder, growing as he soared through the air. His body cut them off, but Kaitlyn climbed onto his back immediately. Gil followedimmediately and Cy pushed Grite up while Gil pulled him. Once Cy was on, Vyekrin lunged forward. He wove through the sparse trees easily, and Cy noticed he wasn't at his full size. He was grateful Vyekrin wasn't flying; they couldn't risk being seen by Crestyss or his monster.

It had been unclear how long they had spent in the tunnels in their escape, but as they found themselves already reaching the edge of the woods, and as the sun bled the horizon red as it rose, Cy was surprised that they had lost the whole night. He was thankful for the wind blowing the smoke from the fire away from them, so that he could keep his eye on the metal beast that flew clumsily in large spirals. He almost thought he could see green sparks coming from it, but doubted that his vision could get that precise.

The lush forest gave way to barren fields of mud and grass. Rolling hills blocked the horizon, as well as the sun.

Even the air here felt thicker with smog, and Cy could taste rust on the wind as he ran. Before them sprung the mounds of discarded junk; the Wastelands. Bile rose in Cy's throat as he thought of the last time he was here, but he forced the memories from his mind. He had no reason to fear the Wasteland dwellers any longer.

The beast stalled as it flew over the first wall made from debris. There was a grinding sound that drove Vyekrin to a halt. He writhed at the noise, and covered them all with his wings. It did little to dull the noise, and they all protected their ears. Through the gap in Vye's wings, Cy could see the damaged dragon was curling in on itself midair, like a snake readying to strike. Arion was caught in its grip, and it didn't look like he was moving.

Cy slipped from Vye's back, and hit the ground hard. The sound had stopped, but left a ringing in his ears. Glancing around to check on the others, he saw that Vyekrin had shrunk himself again, and was crawling toward Kaitlyn along the ground, wobbling unsteadily. Cy was disappointed they no longer had a ride, but thought it was better not to terrify the Wastelanders with another dragon.

Kaitlyn looked the most shaken, half of her body devoid of scales. Grite was a little ways behind them. Cy had half expected him to run the first chance he got. What surprised him the most was Gil standing in the center of them all, a trickle of blood coming from his ear and the crossbow raised to fire. Blood dripped from the tip of whatever Gil had loaded, and Cy didn't get a chance to make clear sense of it before Gil sent it flying toward the beast. He lowered the crossbow to his side slowly, clenching his jaw.

It was a long moment as they all watched the projectile

dissolve into the stretching light of the sun. Cy held his breath, and he could hear nothing through the ringing in his ears.

The sky lit green with lightning spewing from the cracks in the beast. It reared its head and let loose a scream of metal ripping through itself. Cy shielded himself from the blinding light, but didn't dare take his eyes off of Arion as the creature's grip fell slack, though it didn't release him. It hung motionless in the air a moment, then fell backward over itself, plummeting into the heart of the Wasteland. The air filled with distant screams.

By the time the light had faded, Gil was gone. Cy could see him far ahead, running into the winding paths. Kaitlyn passed Cy, and he launched himself into a sprint.

Gil was nowhere to be seen as he reached the entrance to the Wastelands. Cy grumbled under his breath, and jumped to scale the walls. Metal and garbage dislodged beneath his claws, but he refused to be slowed down. He leapt to the top and surveyed the winding paths laid out.

The ground trembled beneath him, nearly shaking him from his perch. He dropped to a crouch and dug his talons into the largest object in the wall, a wide and curved slab of metal that crunched underfoot. Behind him, Kaitlyn was holding on to the edge of the wall, a fire in her eyes.

"It's fallen," she said gravely as she hoisted herself up and over to stand beside Cy. The center of the Wastelands was now filled with smoke and dust, the inner walls destroyed. Within the cloud loomed the shadowy figure of the slain beast.

Cyllorian

Cy scanned ahead for the quickest path, and saw Gil pushing his way toward the smoke, tearing through the weakest walls he could find. Cy readied himself to jump down. But Kaitlyn simply pounced atop the next wall, and the next, running along them and ignoring the structure entirely. Cy allowed himself time to grin before he followed, though he stopped to help Gil atop the walls as well.

It took them only seconds to reach the disaster area where walls had been taken out with the dragon's impact. The blinding dust had already begun to scatter, and Cy could see the great beast twisted upon itself, the edges of each piece of metal warped and charred. The wing that wasn't pinned under itself was flapping meekly and sporadically, and its tail was twitching back and forth. Despite this, the body was already swarmed with scavengers picking it apart like vultures. They ran around it, crazed, arms full of random pieces from the corpse. There were so many voices shouting over each other that Cy couldn't even hear himself think. They even looked ready to trample each other as they flocked to the far reaches, where the metal was mostly untouched by claw and magic.

Gil bound from the wall toward the crowd. Before Cy could question him, he saw why. Arion was laying as far from the chaos as he could get, curled on himself to avoid the crowd. He was gripping his wounded shoulder, but his head was hung, and Cy couldn't see his face.

Cy hurried to follow Gil, Kaitlyn right behind him. Gil reached him first, and gingerly shook Arion by the shoulder. He stirred, lifting his head, though his eyes wouldn't focus. He fell forward, and Gil caught him. He gathered Arion onto his lap and wrapped his arms tight around him, all the while glaring at the unruly crowd before them. Kaitlyn stepped forward as a shield, and Cy took his opportunity to assess Arion.

One leg was completely bare and filled with holes. His coat was drenched in blood from the bite to his shoulder. Cy was just glad he hadn't lost either limb. Arion had been saved by the demon body Crestyss had put him into. The wounds had already begun to stitch themselves back together, albeit slowly. He hovered his hand just above Arion's leg, using his own magic to aid in the healing.

Arion jerked away in shock, clutching at Gil's arms that held him. He looked between the two of them, his face paler than Cy had ever seen. *"Hold still, kid, just let me help,"* Cy coaxed, inching his hand forward.

Arion's breathing hitched as he forced himself to relax, giving a shaky nod, though his grip didn't loosen. Cy went back to healing his leg, and Arion groaned at the pain. He ignored the riotous crowd behind him, sure that Kaitlyn would have them handled. Grite was panting heavily behind him, but Cy paid him no mind. He hadn't much time to practice his magic yet, and he couldn't risk screwing up.

"It's you!" A voice apart from all the rest sounded behind Cy, and the dread that followed drained the magic from him.

Cy turned to face the voice to find a boy not much younger than himself, one arm filled with scraps, and the other pointing past him at Arion, eyes wide and a smile spread across his face. He tossed his haul aside and dove back into the crowd, pulling on anyone he could reach to get their attention, waving his arms wildly as he spoke.

Arion slowly untangled himself from Gil and stood cautiously on his freshly healed leg. Gil held his undamaged arm to keep Arion steady, as Cy could see his legs shaking. His chest was rising and falling rapidly, though there was no emotion betrayed on his face.

Some of the crowd had turned to examine them, though most were too focused on their scavenging. Pulling Gil with him, Arion pushed through the crowd to face the creature that had attacked him, its body still writhing against the parasites that had swarmed it. Cy flanked Arion across from Gil to keep him safe from the crowd. They stopped just before the beast's head. The available eye had already been plucked from its socket, leaving a gaping hole revealing thick wires wound together like rope. A long, winding tongue lolled out through gaps where teeth had been extracted. Hot air washed over their legs from its mouth, as though it was still struggling to breathe.

Grimacing, Arion placed his left hand atop the beast's head. One final contained shock wracked through its body, and the creature lay still. Now the whole of the Wasteland was watching Arion. Those that had still been touching the beast recoiled as Arion's magic reached them.

The boy from before returned to their sides, carrying something large wrapped meticulously in cloth. He hurriedly unwrapped it and offered it to Arion without a word.

Arion took it from him, and rolled it over in his hands until the features became clear. Arion stroked the top of it fondly, magic sparking from his fingertips. Within seconds, a light was emanating from within, and its eyes opened.

Orion sprung upward as though nothing had happened. The small metal owl Arion had made for surveillance had no perception of the time that had passed, or the misfortunes that had befallen Arion. All it knew was that it was reunited with its creator.

Orion perched itself atop Arion's shoulder, nuzzling closer to him. A small smile was on Arion's face, but only for a moment. Seriousness overtook him as he turned toward the crowd, now fully engaged in him.

"A war is coming that will shake all of Lontorra. I know you have all been cast aside by this land, but we have a plan to reclaim it," Arion announced into the silence. Murmurs arose around them, the scavengers converging back onto themselves.

"Arion, this isn't our fight!" Cy shot incredulously. He spoke sharper than he meant, and a twang of guilt swept over him. It was his carelessness, his crass way of speaking that had gotten them here in the first place, and here he still defied Arion.

Arion didn't seem to notice, or at least didn't react to Cy's tone. Cy had expected Arion to get angry again, but his eyes were steady with confidence. "We live here, too, Cyllorian. Crestyss and Theresa, they don't want to take over Lontorra, they want to destroy it. We can't let them."

Cy groaned, but Arion held firm. No one else was arguing with Arion, only Cy was standing firm on his opinion. It was obvious there was no changing Arion's mind, especially now that he was out of Theresa's control. *"Fine, but we do this together. So, what's this great plan of yours?"*

Arion smiled in relief, but he didn't speak. He simply turned away from the group, locked eyes with a weary Grite, and let slip a mischievous grin.

Arion sat cross-legged, hunched over a heap of twisted metal he had confiscated from the scavengers. It hadn't taken long for the Wastelanders to clean up the fallen dragon. They cleared a large space for Arion to begin his work. Many of the scavengers had left to rebuild their walls, while a group of them hung around to observe Arion working under the guise of helping. The sun was no overhead, keeping them warm despite the chill in the air.

Gil sat beside him, obediently providing bits and pieces from the various piles surrounding them. A crowd had gathered to watch as Arion worked meticulously, using his magic to forge a hulking body of...

"What is this thing again?" Cy asked, leaning over Arion's shoulder. The bloodstained and battered coat remained draped over him, and Cy searched the skin beneath for any hint of the wound that had once been. Arion had actually asked Cy for help healing himself, but Cy didn't fully trust his magic's capabilities just yet.

"A vehicle," Arion answered simply. His words were short as he focused on his project, but Cy could sense a hint of excitement in his voice as he layered metal sheets over wires and tubing.

Cy nodded his head slowly, though he knew Arion wasn't actually paying any attention to him. *"I just want to make sure I got this all right, so tell me the plan one more time."* Cy did his best to sound cheerful, or optimistic, or even just *polite* with his request. He wasn't so sure it worked.

Arion sighed and handed a long tube back to Gil, and turned to face Cy. "We need a place to lay low while we figure out how to ambush Crestyss before the war happens. And if I'm right, we have a week, or two if we're lucky. Theresa is going to move fast, especially now that the army isn't a secret anymore. We won't be found in the human village, but we don't have days to get there, so I'm making something to get us there faster. We can't risk being seen on Vyekrin."

"Do you really think we'll be able to just walk in there and the humans will help us? And we don't exactly have anything that can storm the Towers," Cy couldn't help the challenge in his voice. *"These guys don't want to fight either. We can just wait here with the Wastelanders until this stupid fight is over. I'm sure they'd love it, they pretty much worship you."*

Arion's face fell at Cy's response, and Cy waited for the fight to start. With a deep breath, Arion said with strained calmness, "I don't know if it will work, but I saw something in a book that could do the trick. And if we don't stop this, they're going to destroy everyone and everything. It doesn't matter which one of them wins, Cy. Crestyss wants to rule the world, and Theresa wants to crush it. Can you really just sit by and let that happen?"

"Why are you so intent on making this our fight? Tell me, what has this world done for you that you want to protect it so badly?" Cy snapped. Though he had told himself he was on

Arion's side, he couldn't deny how dangerous it was. *"We don't have to do this. You* don't *have to do this, Arion. I'm not going to let you get hurt again!"*

"I know I don't have to, but I *want* to. I'm not running away anymore, Cy. I– I can't run and ignore what's going on. After what Crestyss did to me, and what Theresa did, I can't just let this go. I'm not fighting for either of them, or for Lontorra. I'm fighting for us, and for myself."

Everyone was silent at Arion's speech. He kept his head down, and Cy could see his face turning red. *"Arion."* Cy broke the silence and waited until Arion lifted his head to meet Cy's gaze.

"If I think this is going too far, getting too dangerous, I will drag you out. I don't care how, but I'll find a way to get us out of Lontorra, and I won't look back. You understand, kid?"

Arion smiled slowly. It reached his eyes and made them gleam. "Yeah, I understand."

Murmurs rose from the crowd watching their conversation, whispers of fear and worry flooded Cy's ears.

Arion went back to his work, and Cy didn't dare press his luck. It had been so long since they had been on the same page. It felt like a miracle that they had come to an agreement, despite Cy having to relent on his own feelings on the issue.

Before he could drown himself in his words any further, Kaitlyn joined them. As she skipped up to meet them, she bumped into Cy. The blush that rose to his face was immediately lost as he realized she used that as an excuse to grab his arm and squeeze as hard as she could, her talons threatening to pierce him. She must have thought they were fighting again. Cy couldn't blame her, it was the only thing they had done for so long.

"I'm not sure what you're making, but is there

anything we can find for you?" Her chipper voice broke through the tension in the air. Her hand flexed on Cy's arm in a threat. He knew better than to argue.

Glancing over the piles he had already gathered, Cy watched as Arion's mind worked. Arion listed things off as he rummaged through the nearest piles, "We need something for seats, but not chairs. Something long and curved, like a saddle. Two of them. And a large cart, but it can't be made of wood. And as many wheels as you can find."

"Leave it to us!" Kaitlyn chirped, and diligently pulled Cy as she turned toward the catacombs of the Wasteland.

Cy watched over his shoulder as he was led off to see Arion right back to focusing on his work. "Where does this go?" Gil asked, holding up the tube he had retrieved for Arion before Cy had interrupted him.

Arion lifted the frame he had built to show a mostly hollow shell, holes near the bottom of the half circle. "It needs to come out from under here, pointed this way." He guided Gil to the right placement, and welded it in place with another tube while Gil held it steady.

"He does seem to at least be learning what teamwork is," Cy muttered in awe. His comment gained him a pinch from Kaitlyn as she yanked him to quicken his pace.

As they dived into the winding paths, they passed a smaller crowd that was fascinated with Grite, who was enjoying frightening the kids with the hole in his leg as he stuck his arm through it grotesquely.

Kait was silent as she released Cy's arm and started digging through the walls that had been felled already. Cy watched her pick through the rubble, her mouth set in a pout. He walked to the next pile and started searching as well. *"You're mad at me,"* Cy prodded.

Halting abruptly, Kaitlyn threw the twisted pole she

was holding at Cy. "Of course, I'm mad! Look where we are, what happened to Arion! He wouldn't have run off and gotten hurt like that if you could just... You can see he's getting better, you said it yourself just now. He's working with Gil, when just a week ago, he was trying to fight him. He smiled last night, Cy, actually smiled. He *laughed*. And all you can do is doubt and question him. You were the one that told me you're brothers, and I know siblings fight, but this is too much, Cyllorian! If you really want him to get better, you have to help him, not fight him!"

Kaitlyn yelled until she was short of breath. She struggled to control herself, looking ready to yell again any second. Cy stood in silence, too afraid to speak and risk interrupting her. Once she had finally got her breathing under control, there were tears in her eyes. She puffed her chest up again, reached back into the pile beside her, and grabbed whatever her hand met first. She threw it at Cy, barely missing his legs.

"Say something, Cy!" she yelled, and fell to the ground, scrubbing at her eyes. "What was all of this for if you don't even want him here now?"

Guilt washed over Cy. He had never stopped to think how he was affecting others aside from Arion. He didn't know Kait could get so mad at him for Arion's sake. He thought she had understood him wanting to protect Arion, had agreed with him.

Cy dropped to the ground across from Kait. He drew in the loose dirt with the small scrap of metal he had been holding, unable to meet Kait's eyes.

"I do want him here. Just not everything else. I'm tired of him acting like a Void all the time, like nothing matters to him— like he's still trapped and being tortured. I'm tired of Theresa and her damned war she's so hell bent on waging. And I'm tired of Arion

getting caught up in everyone else's bullshit, mine included! I'd rather we all just built a boat and got lost at sea than stay here and deal with all of this. I thought you knew that?"

Cy's thoughts and anger boiled out of him, and once he started he couldn't stop himself from unleashing everything he hadn't even known he'd been holding. *"I want him to be free of Theresa, free of fear. Free of me. But if I don't have him then...what do I have? I'm nothing but a worthless demon."*

Cy leaned back and chucked the metal over the wall as hard as he could. He watched it raise and fall, dipping behind another wall further away. He heard the resounded clang as the metal struck something, and he released the breath he had been holding. A whisper trickled over from Kaitlyn, and Cy's head snapped forward to stare at her.

"What did you say?" he breathed.

Kaitlyn cleared her throat and kicked at the debris spilled out along the ground. "You have me," she said again, only barely louder than the first time.

Her face was flushed, and she rushed to continue, "And Gil's here on our side, and even Grite. I don't know why you even think Arion is going anywhere. If he wanted to leave, I'm sure he would have already. He *does* care about you, Cy, I can tell. You just have to try to get along better."

Behind her, green lightning flashed, and a crowd cheered. Kaitlyn whirled to see what was happening. Sparks rose into the air again, spreading out in a small circle before falling to the ground. More cheering and laughter rose from the crowd that Arion was showing off to.

While Kaitlyn was distracted, Cy stood and stepped up to her. *"We better get back to work. You heard him; we don't have much time."* He held his hand out to her as she turned back to him. She puffed her cheeks up at him but took his hand and let him pull her to her feet.

As soon as she was up, she let go of him and went back to digging back through her pile, grumbling incoherently under her breath. Her hair changed colors in waves of red and orange as she dug, deliberately tossing things over her shoulder for Cy to dodge.

"I'll try harder. I promise," Cy assured before returning to his own search.

Whirling on him with narrowed eyes, Kait snapped, "You better. I'm watching you two."

Cy chuckled as he dug through the trash before him. *"I wouldn't have it any other way,"* he teased.

Kaitlyn didn't answer, and he dared to glance over at her. There was a dark look on her face as she stood with what looked like a knife in her hand.

"Arion's right, we can't just leave," Kaitlyn said suddenly. Her gaze had drifted away from the knife in her hand. "If Crestyss and Theresa really do start a war, what then? They both hate humans, Cy. My home will be destroyed. My dad will–" Her voice hitched in her throat.

"He'll be killed, Cy. So many people will die. Have you really not been thinking of anyone else?"

Cy froze at her question. His stomach roiled with guilt as the realization hit him. He had told himself over and over that he had Arion and Kait's best interest at heart, but he knew how selfish he was. All he wanted was to hide them away from the world for himself. He had completely forgotten what Kaitlyn had given up to stay with them. She had been so good at hiding her pain, that Cy had never noticed.

Or Cy had just been that bad at paying attention to the

people around him. He wondered if he'd ever be anything other than a selfish demon.

The sun rose high in the sky and began its descent before Kaitlyn and Cy had scoured the most accessible piles of scrap. They had managed to find a small metal wheelbarrow that was missing one side, a few curved pieces that Arion could weld together into seats, and three wheels of two different sizes. They returned to Arion's worksite to find him mingling among the scavengers while they showed off their own smaller creations.

Cy froze when he saw Arion laughing lightheartedly with the boy that retrieved Orion for him. The bird was hopping from boy to boy, cooing as it played. Gil was hovering nearby. Cy watched as he grabbed Arion's shoulder lightly to steady him as Orion made him stumble.

"Coming?" Kaitlyn called from ahead, gaining Cy's and the crowd's attention. Cy nodded and brought the wheelbarrow forward to show their haul.

"We found everything," Kaitlyn announced cheerily, no sign of their fight earlier that day. Arion rummaged through their findings, nodding approvingly. Sometime while they had been gone, Arion had fixed his clothes, most likely with magic, and Cy was shocked to see more color in his face underneath the grime and dirt that had covered him while he worked.

"How is everything coming?" Cy asked awkwardly, reminding himself of his promise.

Arion looked up from the new parts and smirked. "See for yourself," he said with a grand wave of his arm. The mob of people parted at his gesture to reveal a large two wheeled bicycle, its body bulbous and rounded near the wheels, but slim and long in-between. The handles rose high and stretched back to cradle the space where someone would sit. Welded to the side was what looked like a wheelbarrow with a seat surrounded by walls and a small extra wheel.

Cy tilted his head in confusion, biting his tongue. He knew what a bike was, and this certainly looked similar, but there was something off, something missing. Being extra careful to control his tone, Cy asked, *"Arion, where are the pedals?"*

Arion chuckled at the question, as did most of the scavengers. "I call it a magicycle. They run on magic, and go faster than you can imagine. You and I are going to power them."

"Them?" Cy looked back to Arion now, and saw just how alight his eyes were with excitement at his creation.

Arion nodded back toward the crowd. They had shifted again to show most of the body of another bicycle, this one clearly taller even without the wheels attached yet. Arion took the cart from Cy and began fixing the largest wheel to the front of the bike.

"Well, Cy. Are you ready for a ride?"

CHAPTER 10

Arion

Wind rushed through Arion's hair and pulled at the skin of his face. He leaned forward into the force of it, and felt Gil tighten against him. Arion glanced over his shoulder. Gil had his face buried in Arion's back, his face green. He whimpered again as the bike they rode bounced over a stick in their path.

In the car attached to their bike, Grite had his eyes closed, and he was slumped over. Arion wasn't sure if he was simply exhausted from the day, or if he had passed out. Arion nudged Grite with his foot. Grite groaned and slid down further into the sidecar.

Behind them rode Cy with Kait hanging onto him loosely, one hand raised in the air. He could only barely make out Cy's voice yelling something to Kaitlyn, but her smile said she didn't care. She had changed her hair to shoulder-length so it could fly around her.

It hadn't even been an hour and the ruins of Arion's childhood home crept up over the horizon. They would come to the village soon. A lump formed in Arion's throat. He still didn't know what he could say to sway the villagers, if he could even convince them that he really was alive after the incident. He was thankful that Grite was completely unrecognizable compared to the last time he had been in the village.

Arion leaned to the side, guiding the bicycle to the right. Magic sparked from the wheels as he hit another branch, and Gil yelped behind him. He squeezed tighter around Arion, his fingers digging into his chest. Arion took a deep breath and bent forward, pushing the vehicle to go faster. Cy yelled a curse at him, but Arion was sure he would keep up.

The stone walls of the village rose up from the ground like a tomb, encapsulating everything within it. Arion slowed the bike to a stop before they would be seen by any wandering near the walls.

Cy pulled up beside him and immediately disembarked. He threw the helmet he had demanded to the ground and kicked the bike. Kait reclined on the bike, her hair sticking up wildly and a manic grin plastered to her face.

"That was fun!" she exclaimed. "Flying is still better. No clouds down here." She giggled as her eyes followed Cy as he paced in large circles around all of them, breathing heavily.

Arion released the handles and fell back into Gil, but he didn't let go. Arion kept himself from snapping at Gil to let go. He could feel Gil trembling against his back. One leg shook against the side of the bike, rattling the frame against the tire.

Instead, he turned to Grite, praying the demon was still alive. "Hey, get up."

Arion smacked Grite's arm and the demon startled awake. *"What?"* he barked.

"Easy," Cy snapped. *"You're lucky we didn't just tie you up and drag you here on the back of the bikes. Watch yourself."*

"We're here. Time to get to work." Arion reached for Gil's hands around his waist, holding his breath. He gently pried them from his shirt and slid off the bike and out of Gil's grasp. Kait was at their side with her hand on Gil's shoulder.

"So," Cy began through an exaggerated sigh *"What's next? Because we better be done with these things."* Cy kicked his bike again, harder now that Kait wasn't on it. It shifted where it stood, but the three wheels kept the thing from toppling.

"The scavengers are going to follow with their own carts, bringing loads of parts. They have their own cars, but they're not going to be as fast as us. Our job is to gain the trust of the village before they get here," Arion answered, setting off toward the village. A score of footsteps followed close behind him.

It was Kaitlyn's turn to speak up, worry clear in her voice, "Do you know what you're going to tell them, Arion? That we're here to save the world? It might not be that easy, not after what happened last time."

Where Cy had been incredulous and challenging, Kaitlyn concerned. She was looking at the village with remorse and longing. Arion felt guilty for everything he had put Kait through.

Grite cut into the conversation before Arion could answer. *"If I can forgive and forget, they should have no problem doing the same."* He beat his fist over his chest, but it made no sound. The torn shirt he wore pressed into the hole in his chest.

Arion raised his eyebrows in astonishment. "You've forgiven me?"

Grite stared at him for a long moment, then clicked his tongue. *"So, just tell them we're gonna save the world?"*

Arion couldn't help but laugh at the clear diversion. "That sounds good to me."

Cy had fallen in line with Arion, finally gaining control over himself again. He made a show of craning his head around to look at the group they had formed. *"We sure do make one hell of a team, don't we?"*

"Team Daddy Issues," Arion muttered before he could stop the thought from escaping his lips.

"Excuse me, but I don't have a dad," Cy quipped, lifting his nose into the air.

"And that sounds like an issue, now doesn't it?" Arion smirked as Cy's jaw dropped. His mouth flopped open and shut like a fish. On his other side, Kait burst into laughter, followed by the others.

The pillars standing on either side of them sent them all into silence as they approached the village. It was early evening, and the village was mostly empty. The few wanderers that were walking about the town eyed the newcomers suspiciously. It was clear that no one recognized them. It reminded Arion of how much they had all been through in such a short amount of time.

Cy sighed. *"Team Daddy Issues it is."* He stepped forth over the threshold, heading straight into the heart of the village where the mayor's house resided. Arion and the others quickly followed.

Arion kept his head straight and his eyes fixed on the

two-story manor that rose above all the rest, its chimney steadily spewing smoke. The upstairs window was painted with a rose, and a light flickered inside.

Murmurs rose around them as they neared the mayor's house, and more people had gathered in their doorways to watch. Once at the door, Arion knocked with false confidence. Out of the corner of his eye, he caught Kaitlyn hiding behind Cy, her face pale.

The door opened wide, and Mayor Benjamin stood with a question plain on his face. "Yes?" he asked slowly, his eyes raking over each of them. He was thinner than the last time Arion had seen him— though it had been years— and balder. The robe he wore hung loose on his shoulders, and the short man looked as though he were swimming in the fabric.

"Hi, Daddy." Kaitlyn peeked out from behind Cy. She looked just like normal now, her old normal, with two blonde braids hung over her shoulders.

The mayor burst from his home, pushing past Arion and Cy. He wrapped Kaitlyn in a hug that stole the air right from her lungs. "My sweet girl, you're alive!" he gasped. His breathing hitched in his throat as tears began to spill from his eyes.

He pulled away suddenly and cupped her face with both hands. He bent her head back and forth, examining every inch of her. He had no idea that even if she had been hurt, she wouldn't let him see it.

"Where have you been?" he begged, collapsing into another hug.

Arion found his courage to speak. "That's actually quite a long story."

Hesitantly, the mayor pulled back from Kaitlyn to see

who had spoken, though he didn't release her. His eyes narrowed as he surveyed the boy in front of him. "Arion?" he asked, his face paling as though he had seen a ghost. "We were told you were...that you had..."

The mayor's voice caught, unable to say the words.

Arion gave an apologetic grin. "Can we come in?"

* * *

Kaitlyn

Kaitlyn had never thought it could feel so awkward inside her own home. Her father had insisted she rest in one of their plush chairs, and ushered her to the one closest to the fireplace. It had only been embers when they arrived, but her father had stoked the flames until Kaitlyn was sweating. She held tightly to a steaming mug in her hand. She had only taken a few sips while Arion had begun his explanation.

The others were all standing around near the entrance, too timid to move further into the room. Kaitlyn was well aware of her father standing just beside her chair, a protective hand gripping the back. His immediate acceptance of her on his doorstep made Kaitlyn feel guilty for the way she had left. And for the secret of her powers that she was keeping from him.

"We need your help," Arion said. "We need the whole village's help. We seek refuge and a safe place to prepare. Crestyss is planning to start a war, and Theresa intends to meet him full force. The rest of Lontorra will be caught in the crossfire. I believe I can stop them before it gets that far, but we have nowhere else to go. There's no way to know where Crestyss or Theresa might have allies, but I do know neither of them can stand humans. This is the only safe place for us."

Arion was quiet for a moment. Kaitlyn tilted her head slowly to see her father. It wasn't often that Kait had seen Benjamin with such a serious expression. His normally round eyes were slits as he scrutinized the group.

Grite and Gil had stayed against the wall, Grite doing his best to stay in shadows. Kait doubted Benjamin would recognize him, but she couldn't deny that she didn't want to find out what would happen if the village found out what had really happened to Kraven.

Cy stood next to Arion. Kait was glad to see Cy backing him up, though Cy's face was so pale, she was worried he was slipping into his demon form. They needed to prove to her father that they were on his side, not scare him to death.

"If I recall correctly, you didn't think too fond of us either," Benjamin said slowly.

Kaitlyn winced and leaned forward to protest. Arion bowed his head, and the movement shocked her.

"I'm really sorry for everything I've done, and I'll accept whatever punishment I deserve later. For now, we are the best chance each other has. If Crestyss and Theresa are allowed to engage in their war, I don't believe Lontorra will survive. They'll destroy this land with their hate."

Benjamin leaned his weight against Kait's chair, nearly tipping it over. Kait pressed her feet to the ground to brace against the added weight.

"I suppose we had our own part to play in how things turned out. You weren't exactly welcomed here, even as a harmless child. I cannot guarantee that my people will be willing to help you, and I can't make them, either." Benjamin let out a heavy sigh and stepped away from Kaitlyn. He stepped up to Arion without hesitation, surprising Kaitlyn.

"I did my best to stifle the rumors about the storms, but there was no denying that magic was involved. It was such a phenomena for the village to be surrounded on all sides with such bad weather so often, while not a drop fell within our walls. It was easy for everyone to blame you, and the best I could do was to not confirm it."

Cy shot Arion a curious glance. "Thank you, but I didn't deserve that."

Benjamin waved his hand, then clamped it down on Arion's shoulder. "I have been alive a long time. Everyone has done things they are not proud of, but that does not make them bad people. Bad people do not wish to atone for their wrongdoings, nor do they try to protect others. Especially those that have caused them pain. You've grown, and you aren't the same person you used to be. I can see that, and I believe the village will as well."

Kaitlyn could see Arion's shoulders hitch, and he nodded silently.

"What do you need from us? I can speak to the village on your behalf, and try to get you what you need." Benjamin's question was soft.

It was warming to Kait to see Benjamin being so fatherly to someone else, especially after witnessing how Theresa treated Arion. She remembered how Arion's father had treated them when they were children, and realized Arion had never really experienced a parent like this before.

Arion cleared his throat, and answered, "We need a large space. There's something I need to build, and it won't fit within the village. And if there's a place to rest nearby the work site, I would prefer to stay close by to keep an eye on the project. The Wastelanders will be coming shortly with parts, but if there's any way you could gather excess cloth or old clothes. Any kind of fabric will do, but I need a lot of it, as much as you can get. Lastly, if there's anyone willing to volunteer, anyone skilled with a needle and thread, the extra hands would be a big help."

Benjamin nodded, deep in thought. "A place to sleep is easy, though it'll be a bit crowded with all of you. I'll see what I can do about the rest."

"Thank you," Arion said in relief. He finally lifted his head to meet Benjamin's gaze, and gave a nervous smile.

A knock sounded at the door, and Gil jumped at the sudden sound. Benjamin nodded to Gil with a chuckle as he went to open the door. A man close to Benjamin's age was standing just outside, a confused look on his face. Kaitlyn recognized him as one of her father's assistants.

"You called for me? You said it was urgent, but what's going on?" the man said.

"Walter, perfect timing. Take these young men and show them the old guard's cabin. They'll be staying with us for a little bit. After that, gather up the village for a meeting."

Walter nodded in the doorway, and waved his hand before walking away. Benjamin spun Arion by the shoulders and ushered them out. Gil and Grite ducked through the door first. Arion hurried to catch up with them. Cy lingered for a moment, glancing over his shoulder at Kaitlyn. She stood from her chair, the cup clinking against the wooden table to her side as she set it down.

"I'd like to talk with you, Kaitlyn. The boys will be fine by themselves for a little bit."

Kaitlyn swallowed a lump in her throat. "Of course, Dad." She tried to make her voice sound lighthearted, but she couldn't help but be worried about what he might have to say.

Cy nodded curtly and left the house, closing the door behind him.

Benjamin dropped himself into the nearest chair with a groan, the energy fading from his face. He rubbed his eyes tiredly, though the sun was far from setting.

"You can relax around me, Kait. It's fine."

Kaitlyn chuckled nervously. "I am relaxed, Dad."

Benjamin lowered his hand, his weary gaze looking her over. "That's not what I mean. You don't have to force yourself for my sake, you can let yourself be comfortable. I know what you can do, and I know this isn't who you are right now."

Kaitlyn's jaw dropped at the bluntness in her father's voice. Slowly, she did as she was told. Her body relaxed, and her hair fell away from her head until it was the short haircut she had already gotten used to. She could feel her expression harden ever so slightly, and her muscles grew to fit her clothes better.

Benjamin smiled softly and gestured for Kaitlyn to sit. "How did you know?" Kaitlyn asked.

"I've always known, even before you did. I'm sorry, Kaitlyn, but I have been lying to you your entire life. I'm not your father, at least not the one you share blood with. You were not born from my late wife."

"What do you mean?" Kaitlyn jumped up from her chair, her voice nearly a shriek. "You've always been my dad. I think I would know if I was someone else's child. If I was…"

Kaitlyn let her voice trail off, her eyes stinging with tears. Ever since she had gotten this power, these thoughts had been running constantly in her mind. She thought she'd never have to face them, because she had never intended to tell her father about her powers.

"Not human?" Benjamin offered. A tear ran down Kaitlyn's face, and she scrubbed it away. She winced as her cheek was cut, and she looked down to see scales covering the back of her hand. She shook them away violently, cursing herself for losing control.

Benjamin scoffed, and leaned forward to rest his elbows on his knees. "If I had told you sooner, you could have begun learning at a much younger age. You should have full control over it by now, but I... I was too much of a coward to tell you. I was afraid that you would leave me, or worse. I saw the way the village treated Arion even before his magic, who knows how they would have treated you if they knew you weren't human."

"How have you always known? What happened?" Kaitlyn gasped. She reached behind her until she felt the armrests of the chair, and fell back into the plush cushions.

"My late wife didn't have the best health, and when she got pregnant, she had to be on bedrest almost immediately. I spent every day terrified that I would lose her or our unborn child. When the baby came early, I panicked and was useless. The doctor did everything that he could, but my wife did not make it. The baby was so small and weak, a baby girl crying in my arms. The doctor couldn't guarantee she would make it through the night. Despite the doctor's orders, I snuck her away from the infirmary and took her home. All my wife had wanted was for our baby to sleep in the crib we had made together for her. All I could think about was honoring my wife's wishes.

"The doctor had been right. Within only a few hours, my baby girl had gone quiet and stopped breathing. I didn't have any tears left. I just sat in the darkness and silence, clutching my lost baby to my chest.

"Then I heard crying again, and thought it was my girl, but she had already gone cold. She had not come back, but the crying hadn't stopped. It took me a moment to realize that the crying was coming from outside. I laid my baby down in her crib, and went to look outside. On my doorstep was an infant bundled in a blanket and laid in a basket. Its face was bright blue, and I was afraid it was crying so hard it was losing air. On instinct, I picked the baby up and it immediately stopped crying, but their face remained blue. In fact, the hands that reached out from the blanket were just as blue. Every inch of their skin was blue, and they were bald. And as I stared in wonder, the color slowly drained until they were pale with freckles spread across their face, and blonde hair grew rapidly from their head.

"I tried to look around, but I couldn't find any sign of the parents. I'm not sure how they knew, or if they had just picked my house by chance. I lost one child, and was given another, a changeling child. That changeling was you. I watched and waited for you to change again, relieved when it never happened. I don't know why your power never manifested before. Maybe because you weren't in an environment with magic, or because you didn't need to before. It's honestly a relief to me now that you have your power. I thought I was crazy, or that I had hallucinated that night."

Benjamin sat back in his chair and chuckled under his breath. He looked like a great weight had been lifted from his shoulders. Sweat dripped down the side of his face, and he wiped it away with shaking hands.

"I'm so sorry I've kept this from you for so long, Kaitlyn. I couldn't stand the thought of losing you, too. But you've come home, and I can see how much you've grown in such a short time. You were always my strong-willed little girl, but now you look ready to take on the world. I'm so proud of you, and I'll do everything I can to help you and your friends."

Benjamin flashed Kaitlyn that big gleaming smile she had grown up with. Kait's chest tightened, and she jumped up from her chair. She launched herself across the room to fall across her father's lap. She felt his arms wrap around her, and she realized just how much she had missed his warmth.

"Thank you, Daddy. I love you." Kaitlyn said, her voice thick with tears.

"I love you, too, baby girl. And I'll always be here to support you, no matter what."

* * *

"You didn't tell him everything," Cy scolded, looming over Arion as he assessed the first delivery of parts from the wasteland. They had met the Wastelanders just outside the village. Arion insisted on needing a lot of space to properly inspect the pieces brought to him. Most were usable, but he needed cloth more than anything. Lots and lots of cloth.

"He doesn't need to know everything. Just enough to know we're the good guys in this fight." Arion shifted through the random junk for metal rods that were of similar widths.

Cy nudged pieces away from each other, digging out another long rod with a slight curve, though Arion thought it was supposed to be straight. *"You aren't telling us every-thing, either,"* Cy stated.

It wasn't a challenge, or accusation. Simply an observation. Somehow it hurt more than when Cy had yelled at him.. Arion almost wanted him to yell. If Cy was calm, there was no avoiding him.

All eyes had risen to look at Arion. They had all been given items to find among the rubble, but their tasks had been forgotten.

"No, I haven't," Arion admitted.

"What else is there?" Cy knelt down beside him, his tone surprisingly encouraging.

Arion wracked his brain, unsure where to begin. "I knew about the army. For a while now, I've known."

"Well, yeah, that much was clear when you literally unearthed them. There's a lot more going on inside that head of yours, I know it. We're a team, Arion, and we all need to be on the same page for whatever this plan of yours is to work," Cy pleaded.

Again, Arion wished he would just yell. This was only making Arion feel guilty, and his stomach roiled. He swallowed the guilt and let it all out.

"I found a book that describes everything that Theresa is doing... that Crestyss is doing. They're recreating an old legend, about the war where Mages fought for equality in Lontorra, not power. There was a metal army, where Mages, humans, *everybody* sacrificed themselves to put their souls into them so they could fight. But they couldn't return to their bodies afterward, they were just trapped. Their souls were nothing but fuel. It was like the people had never even existed once they made the choice to become one of them.

"Crestyss and Theresa both wanted me to power that

army for their own purposes. Crestyss to rule the world, and Theresa to destroy it. I found diaries of Theresa's, filled with rage and hatred. And journals of Crestyss and the different experiments he'd done over the years. Neither of them will stop until they're defeated, and now, that's up to us."

Arion looked around the group, begging for understanding. Gil's eyes were wide as he processed the information. Cy was looking far away, and Arion was worried he would lash out again. Kaitlyn's head was hung, her expression sullen.

"In the castle," Kait spoke slowly and softly at first, her voice threatening tears. "I found a strange room. The castle led me to it, actually. It looked like a medical room, with a lot of small beds stained dark and cabinets of bottles labeled with messy handwriting. One of the cabinets was locked and I...I broke into it. I thought there could be something useful, if it was still any good, at least. Inside were a bunch of books, patient logs. One of them was all about the same patient. He had a blood disease—"

"Seyano," Arion interrupted. He turned to Cy. "He's our uncle. He told me all about their childhood. He fell ill at a very young age, and their parents couldn't cure him. No one could, but Theresa managed to keep him alive by giving him blood transfusions and an animal form; an owl... Snow."

"That was him," Kaitlyn confirmed. "The book mentioned the other stuff, too. And that they had been chased out of every town, robbed of every ally when their parents died. She hated everyone, except for her brother. She truly hated the world."

"She still does," Arion continued. "And she'll have it burned to the ground if we don't stop her."

"What's this thing we're making, then? A secret weapon, I hope," Cy asked before the silence could fall too heavy in the air.

Arion hid a chuckle behind a cough. "Not exactly. It's another vehicle."

Cy groaned and threw himself back onto the ground. *"I don't care what it is, I'm not getting in it!"*

Laughter filled the air, chasing away the tension. "Don't worry, you don't have to. You'll have Vyekrin to fly you there."

"Fly?!" Cy's voice broke as he shot straight up. *"No way. I'm staying on the ground, thank you very much!"*

Everyone laughed again. Cy waved them off, trying to change the subject, *"Where is he, anyway? We could have used him back there."*

Kaitlyn reached into a bag that had been strung across her chest. Out came a sleeping lizard, laying limp in her hands. "I think the sound the metal dragon made knocked him out. He was already pretty tired from his disappearing trick. He still hasn't recovered."

"Disappearing?" Gil echoed. "That could be useful, right?" He asked the question aloud to the group, but his gaze was fixed on Arion.

Ignoring Gil's stare, Arion nodded. "Very. And we'll have our zeppelin."

"Our what *now?"*

"Zeppelin. I saw it in a book. It looks like a giant bag filled with air attached to a basket to carry people."

"And the book taught you how to make it, right?" Cy probed.

There was a long silence as Arion busied himself digging through the scrap in front of him. *"Arion,"* Cy growled.

Arion turned to look at him, forcing his eyes as wide as they could go to feign innocence. "Well, it didn't look that hard to make."

Cy pushed off of the ground and began to pace behind Arion. *"No way, I'll take the dragon any day over a* giant bag of air *flying through the sky!"*

Cy's theatrics sent them all into hysterics as he rambled on about how he would never touch another vehicle of any kind once this was all over. Or another dragon, for that matter.

"Seems pretty hard to keep working when it's this dark outside." Cy's voice drifted from behind Arion, startling him. He spoke flatly, a hint of concern creeping through as he finished his sentence.

The lampposts of the village didn't have the reach illuminate outside the walls where Arion had set up. They had all questioned just how big the zeppelin was going to be. Arion assured them that it wouldn't fit inside the village, and it would be easier to sort through the pieces where the Wastelanders delivered them.

Arion flinched and ducked his head below his shoulders. Pulling his knees to his chest, he raised his hand and created a small orb of light that hovered in the air beside him. "Better?" he asked quietly.

Footsteps were the only response Arion received. Arion busied himself as Cy knelt down beside him. His eyes raked over Arion and the donated clothes strewn across his lap.

"Want some company?" Cy offered.

Arion nodded once. "It doesn't feel right being inside the village. They're helping because they don't really have a choice. The only other sides to this fight want to kill them all. But they still look at me like..."

Arion didn't have to finish his sentence. Cy knew all too well what Arion meant, having lived it himself. It was better to just stay out of their way before they changed their minds.

"Starting with the balloon part?" Cy asked, seeming genuinely curious. Arion nodded and returned to stitching up the hole he was working on. The whole village had gathered every scrap of linen and cloth that could be spared. Tablecloths, bed sheets, clothing, even battered sails that old sailors had kept for mementos before Crestyss had banned ocean travel. Arion himself had even tried to raid his old house for anything useful, but there was nothing left from the fire and scavengers over the years. Nothing more than piles of blackened bricks and bitter memories.

Cy turned his head side to side, producing his own orb of lavender light beside him. It danced around his head as he turned, following his line of sight. He snatched something from the ground, and Arion felt tugging on the cloth he held.

He lifted his head to snap at Cy, but froze when he saw him holding his own makeshift needle and feeding the thick twine through the eye. Wordlessly, he lined a scrapped dress up the edge of cloth and began to sew them together. His stitches were big and uneven, his hands twisted as he struggled to hold the needle comfortably. Despite his awkward stitching, Arion could see his magic running through the thread, and fusing the two pieces together.

Arion dropped his head and continued his patching.

"Kaitlyn's mad at you," Arion whispered finally after a long silence.

Cy's hand jerked, pricking himself with the needle. He groaned under his breath as a bead of blood formed on his finger, and he popped it into his mouth. When he pulled it out, there was no sign of damage.

"You can tell?" Cy set the needle back to work, more cautiously this time.

"Of course," Arion answered. Another long pause set between them. From the corner of his eye, Arion could see that Cy's speed had increased as well as consistency.

Timing his words perfectly so he wouldn't make Cy hurt himself again, Arion pried, "Have you told her yet?"

Cy's face scrunched up. *"That's not why she's mad."*

"No, it's because of me. She doesn't like when we fight."

"Yeah, well, I'm not too crazy about it either, you know?"

Arion had finished the patch. There was far more work to be done, but he didn't want to fuss with the cloth and cause Cy to mess up. Instead, he twirled his needle between his fingers.

This needle was real and cold where the night air touched it. He pressed the point into his thumb, not enough to break skin. A chill ran down Arion's spine, and the needle slipped from his grasp and rolled along the fabric, settling in a crease made by legs beneath.

He was reminded of the needle he had wielded just days before, made of pure magic and used for a much nobler cause. An altruistic cause.

"I don't like it, either. I don't want to fight with you, or with *anyone*. I don't *want* to do this. I have to."

Cy's pace slowed, and Arion could see the thoughts

working through his head. While he was focused, Arion took the chance to watch Cy's hands move, smoothly and cleanly over the fabric. He had one leg tucked under the other. Arion could see his foot swaying side to side under the cloth. He bit at his lip, and Arion was amazed to see just how many muscles twitched in his face with every minute movement.

It really did work, Arion thought, proud of himself. Knowing that Cy had a true body now, a *real one* that could house and grow his own magic, had lifted a weight from Arion's shoulders. He let out a breath that seemed to grab Cy's attention.

"What about you?" Cy asked, an odd strain in his voice.

"What?" With a tilt of his head, Arion could see a few beads of sweat had formed on Cy's brow, and they slid slowly down his skin. They looked ready to freeze at the next wind that blew over them.

Cy's eyes darted over to Arion, pleading with him. *"You know,"* Cy started and jerked his head back toward the village. *"You've been getting along with Gil a lot better recently."*

Arion held his breath and stared at Cy, unsure how to react. Cy's mouth had become a thin line, and he was quietly awaiting any kind of response. Arion couldn't be sure what Cy meant by the question. The thought of Cy implying Arion and Gil were like Cy and Kait sent a rush of heat to his cheeks.

"I don't know what you mean. He won't stop following me around, so I just gave up trying to get him to leave," Arion explained in a rush.

Cy nodded slowly as his piece of twine ran out. He tucked the end round a stitch and tied a knot to hold it all in place.

"Well, you can't do this alone. And you definitely can't do it

without any sleep. The work will be here tomorrow." Cy stood abruptly, dropping the fabric to the ground. He turned to leave, but hesitated when Arion still stuck to the ground.

"I can't sleep," Arion whispered meekly. He almost hoped Cy hadn't heard him, but he couldn't be that lucky.

Cy groaned and put his hands on his hips as he looked down at Arion in disbelief. *"You think I can't tell just how exhausted you are? If you just lay down for a minute, I'm sure—"*

"I have nightmares," Arion cut him off, his tone harsher than he meant. A lump formed in his throat as he continued, but he refused to choke on his words. "I'm back in that cell, with Grite and Crestyss. Or in the dungeons facing down Kraven— Grite, again. I relive the torture and I'm scared. I don't want to see that again. I'd rather just die from the exhaustion, Cy."

Memories played out before him as he talked, though his eyes were still open wide. He shuddered, the pain of each memory still vibrant in his mind.

Then his arm was in a vise, tight enough that his hand was going numb. Cy shook him, and Arion turned to him, completely unguarded. Hot tears streaked down his cheeks. "I'm scared, Cy," he repeated, his voice breaking.

Arion could see his pain mirrored in Cy's eyes. In a flash, Cy had pulled Arion off his balance and into his arms. Cy held on so tight that Arion couldn't breathe, but Arion couldn't even think of asking him to loosen his grip. Reaching up slowly, Arion grabbed onto Cy's back desperately, and sunk into his embrace. The tears stopped as Arion buried his face into Cy's shoulder.

"Nothing like that is ever going to happen to you again, I swear," Cy promised, his own voice muffled against Arion.

Cy took a shaky breath and continued, *"I'm your brother. It's my job to protect you,"*

At his words, Arion began to cry again, steadily and silently. He nodded against Cy, his breath coming shallow.

"You're not alone, and you never will be again," Cy whispered.

For just that moment, Arion let himself believe it could be the truth, and guilt made his grip tighten on Cyllorian.

CHAPTER 11

Arion

A week passed quickly, with Arion busying himself with work on the zeppelin. Sleep had been coming easier, and it only fueled him into working well into the night more than it tempted him to get rest. A ball of green light bobbed beside his head as though riding invisible waves. It cast just enough light as Arion examined the seams of the carriage that was now assembled and attached to the giant balloon that had been sewn together in the first two days with the help of the village. The moon and stars were hidden behind clouds, and if not for his light, Arion would be lost in a sea of darkness.

It was the night they had been waiting for. The zeppelin had been finished just on time, though Arion's anxiety kept him going over every seam, every inch of the machine. He had never made something so big; a cabin fit to hold three people, at least, and the balloon that could have swallowed a third of the village had the wind chosen to blow it the wrong way.

Footsteps crunched the newly frozen grass.. The sound reminded him of the dropping temperatures and a chill slithered over his body. He hugged his coat closer with one hand, the other running over rivets and bolts holding the whole thing together.

"I thought we were done with this thing already." Gil's voice made Arion jump. He had been expecting Cyllorian, as he had been the one dragging him away from his work at different hours of the night. Gil knelt beside him with a loud yawn. Arion sat frozen.

The ball of light danced between them, casting strange shadows across Gil's face. He was looking forward at the machine with droopy eyes, though Arion doubted he was registering anything he was seeing.

"I thought Cy would be the one to get me," Arion mused aloud.

"Are you kidding? You're the one that had him doing all the heavy lifting today. He's already asleep. Everyone is. I woke up for a second and saw you weren't there, so I came to check. We finished it. Time for a break." Gil ended his rant with another yawn. His hand fell heavy on Arion's shoulder, and Gil tugged gently.

Arion thought for a moment, then said, "Yes, it's done. But are you really ready to fight?"

"We aren't going right this second," he said slowly, shaking his head. "Sleep first. You said we have another day or two, right?"

"Right," Arion echoed, but he still didn't move. He pursed his lips, aware of Gil's curious gaze on him.

Before he could stop himself, the questions escaped

him, "Why did you come with us all the way out here? Why did you try to save me? Why do you *care* so much?"

Gil's hand on his shoulder stiffened, and he finally turned away from Arion.

"You like me, don't you?" Arion asked quietly, trying to keep his voice even.

Gil's head shot up, his eyes wide. Arion started to curse himself. He'd thought too much of himself, even gotten his hopes up. But of course, he couldn't be right.

A deep purple flush came over Gil's face. He stuttered and stammered, tripping over his own tongue. "I didn't mean... I was trying— no, I *wasn't* trying to—"

He sputtered, making no sense to Arion. His head lowered slowly before he finally found his voice and mumbled, "I didn't think you could tell."

Arion couldn't help but laugh, and he stopped himself quickly, covering it with a cough. "You follow me around nonstop, you never stop talking, and you got jealous of a literal child whenever he was helping me."

"I was not jealous," Gil snapped. His hand dropped from Arion's shoulder, and he crossed his arms. He stared straight ahead at the zeppelin, pouting.

Arion glanced at Gil. His cheeks were still a deep purple, his lips pressed into a hard line. But there he sat, not leaving Arion's side.

It won't matter tomorrow, will it? Arion thought, his decision clear in his mind. In one swift movement, he grabbed Gil's collar, pulled him forward, and kissed him.

Gil froze instantly, a squeak sounding from deep in his throat. As Arion held him close, slowly, he melted. He grabbed onto Arion and pulled himself closer, kissing him back carefully.

Once they separated, they fell away from each other,

unable to hold their grip. It was only for a moment, but it left Arion breathless, realizing he hadn't taken a single gasp since he had moved.

Gil's face was completely flushed, even his ears tinted. Arion laughed at the stark color in his face, falling back into the frosted grass. It felt colder than ever against his heated skin, and he welcomed the help to cool off.

Gil stood over him, a hand outstretched to lift Arion up. The other hand was covering the lower half of his face. He jerked his head back to the village, "Are you coming?" he asked quietly.

In answer, Arion took his hand and let him pull him up. Gil's grip didn't loosen once Arion was upright, and he led them back toward the small cabin they had been granted. Allowing himself to simply enjoy the moment, Arion squeezed Gil's hand, smirking as Gil's stride faltered ever so slightly.

The cabin was lit inside by a soft glow. It had been a small guard cabin, meant only for one or two people at a time. It had only one room, and a small bathroom holding only a toilet and a sink. It was not meant for living, simply for the guards that would need a place to rest between shifts. Arion had insisted on staying near the edge of the village, and not in the mayor's house. Some of the villagers were less welcoming than others, and he preferred to be close to the zeppelin. Where Arion went, the others followed. Arion looked around at the sleeping bodies inhabiting it.

A small stove took up one corner, with only enough room for the single pot that hung on a hook nearby. Grite was sprawled out near the stove, his feet tucked underneath, glowing from the intense heat.

A bed was pressed against the opposite wall, and

Kaitlyn lay atop it. Her job had been to appease the village and recruit them for tasks that needed done. It was a tiring job, and she had been the first to sleep most nights.

Cy was leaning up against the bed next to her, resting his head on an empty spot on the mattress. One arm was tucked under his head as a pillow, the other holding Kait's hand that hung off the bed.

Arion usually slept propped against the wall right beside the door. The small room was always cramped with bodies, and Arion tended to pick odd parts of the days to sleep when the others were busy. He knew better than to hide away from the cabin. Cy had made it very clear he would destroy everything in his path to find Arion if he went missing.

Gil had made himself what looked like a nest in the remaining corner from the leftover cloth and blankets that had been donated. He pulled Arion over to it, spreading the blankets out to make room for Arion. Curling into one side of the pile, Gil pulled Arion into the other side, never releasing his hand. Arion sat next to him in the small space, and they laid back against the wall. Almost instantly, Gil went limp with sleep, his weight falling onto Arion's shoulder. He took a deep breath, wishing he could sleep as easily as Gil.

But he would not get sleep tonight.

Closing his eyes, Arion willed his magic out in strands around him, reaching for the others. It touched Gil first, then Cy, and Kait last. Once they all were within reach, Arion wrapped the magic around them, letting the spell seep into them. They all let out heavy breaths as their sleep deepened, and Arion knew the magic had taken full effect. He opened his eyes.

The spell helped them sleep, but that wasn't its

purpose. Arion relied on their exhaustion to keep them unconscious while he was gone. If their plan succeeded, Arion could be back before they awoke. And if he didn't return, the spell would make sure they felt no pain from his loss, because they would no longer remember him.

Grite was standing before him, the new brace on his leg holding his weight easily. *"Let's go,"* he said simply. Arion stood obediently, hesitating as Gil's grip held tight on his hand. He squeezed once, and shook his hand off.

He followed Grite out into the night.

* * *

"There's the Towers," Grite said, pointing out of the front window. The shadows of the Towers sprung up against the navy sky just above the horizon. *"We want a window near the middle. They aren't fortified or barred, and it'll be closer to his bedroom."*

Arion took a small step forward, though there was nowhere to go in the small cabin of the zeppelin. The metal groaned underfoot, and Arion prayed the hull would hold. If they fell through while the zeppelin was in the air, Arion wasn't sure if he could catch them before they hit the ground. He kept his left hand on the furnace hanging in the center of the room, the green fire he controlled filling the balloon with air and magic that kept them airborne. Steering was easy; he simply willed the magic whichever way he wanted, but he needed a steady flow of hot air and magic to keep the machine level.

Arion glanced over his shoulder out the back window. The first rays of sunlight were tinting the horizon scarlet, though they were an hour from sunrise. It was still rather dark out.

"Can you speed it up? We need to beat the light," Grite urged.

Arion took a deep breath, releasing it slowly. The air hissed out of him as the fire under his fingers flared to life. The zeppelin lurched forward, gaining speed. As they approached Centric, Arion's magic seeped out of the balloon. It stretched over the zeppelin like a web, bathing them in darkness. To any who looked up, they would see only the night sky.

Within minutes, they were passing over the outer wall, the residential houses, then the shops, all dark and quiet before dawn. Arion glanced down, but there wasn't a single soul to be found in the streets of Centric.

Arion spun the zeppelin so they would glide along the Tower. They hadn't accounted for the size of the balloon once inflated, and there was still at least ten feet between their cabin and the Tower wall.

The bricks gave way to a large window, a massive hole in the side of the building. Arion fortified the flame so it would hold the machine steady and approached the cabin door. He opened it slowly, cringing against the wind that rushed in to meet him. He made a rope of magic and threw it at the top of the window. It stuck into the brickwork, and Arion tugged to be sure it wouldn't fall. He attached it to the frame of the zeppelin, and it merged with the magic covering the zeppelin.

As sure as he could be, Arion grabbed the rope and slid down it into the Tower. He landed on his feet easily, and stepped cautiously into the stairwell they had fallen into. He heard Grite land less agilely behind him, but he quickly got to his feet. Glancing out the window, Arion was relieved that he could only see darkness, the spell on the zeppelin keeping it hidden while the rope held it in place.

Grite started downward on the stairs. *"His room's this way,"* he whispered.

"No," Arion said simply. His gaze was fixed at the shadows waiting atop the stairs. Something was pulling him, beckoning him to the top of the Tower. "We go up."

They ascended quickly, though Arion did his best to preserve his energy. The further they went, the stronger the pull was inside his chest. Just before the stairs gave way to a large room, Arion placed the feeling.

Magic.

It was magic guiding him, his or Crestyss', he couldn't be sure. And that thought terrified him.

Silently, Arion stepped into the room. Directly across from him was a large stained-glass window made of jagged hues of green and gold. Near the top was a ring of gold, sitting perfectly to halo the figure standing against the window.

"I'm afraid you're a little early for the festivities. The party starts tomorrow— once I save this world from Theresa's wrath." Crestyss spoke with a cold, clipped tone. He stared out the window, his hands clasped behind his back.

"There's not going to be a party, Crestyss. Not after war and bloodshed. This ends tonight." Arion stepped forward, left hand raising to strike.

"Aren't you going to ask why I'm here? Why I'm not sound asleep, dreaming of my perfect world? Or how I knew you were coming?" Crestyss taunted.

Arion hesitated. The plan had been to kill Crestyss in his sleep. He wasn't sure if it was best to keep him talking, or to strike first.

Grite spoke before Arion could stop him, a low growl in

his throat. *"I thought you always woke up this early. You need time to get your hair and makeup perfect for the day."*

Crestyss shot a quick glare over his shoulder, but his face smoothed in an instant. He lifted a hand slowly and flicked his wrist. Lying in his palm was a crystal ball, the surface cloudy. A ripple ran through the ball and settled on an image of Crestyss standing, holding the crystal ball.

"You never thought to dig the bullet out of your skull, did you Grite?" Crestyss sneered at them smugly.

Grite threw a hand over one eye in shock, and the image on the ball went half dark. Crestyss had been watching them. Grite had gone deathly pale, though his eyes were alight in rage. He had been used by Crestyss again, completely unaware.

"It doesn't matter," Arion spat. "This ends tonight."

The stones shook underfoot, and Arion fought to catch himself. He looked to Crestyss, wondering what he had done. But Crestyss' head was turned, gazing out the side of the window with fury in his eyes.

"It seems you are correct," he hissed. He whirled away from the window just as another tremor shook. Even through the stone and glass, Arion could hear the crashing of buildings, and a high-pitched whining that made him feel like his ears would start bleeding any minute. Behind Crestyss, through the window, a red haze rose up. But dawn was still far away.

As the horizon bled red, the sky quickly darkened, filling with smoke. The edges of Centric were ablaze. Screaming joined the sounds of destruction, and Crestyss sneered.

"I don't have time for children," he snarled. His hand shot out toward them, lightning fast. Arion had only a second to duck before a dagger, dripping with thick green goop, lodged itself in the wall behind him.

From the dagger burst strands of lightning that spread through the stonework, reaching for Arion's feet. He jumped away just as the entire Tower shook, sending him onto his hands and knees. The whole thing lurched toward the window with a great crunching sound of stones crumbling. Turning back to Crestyss, Arion saw the giant claws protruding from the walls around the window.

The wall gave way and the room was filled with hot smoke as Vyekrin tucked his head in and roared in Crestyss' face. The man jumped away from the ground that gave way beneath him at Vyekrin's weight. Between him and the dragon, Cyllorian and Kaitlyn jumped down from Vyekrin's neck.

Cyllorian was fully in his demon form, with pale white skin. A black streak ran from his chin and disappeared into his collar. Four black eyes pierced Crestyss where he stood as Cy brandished his talons. His muscles were pulled tight, ready to strike.

Kaitlyn stood tall beside him, taller than she should. Scales covered her entire body. The bottom of her shirt lay torn from the wings that sprouted from her back. A tail that looked like it was tipped with metal swung behind her, stirring the smoke that swelled around them.

"You didn't really think you could leave us behind, did you?" Cy hissed, his eyes never leaving Crestyss.

Pressing his back against the closest wall, Crestyss stared down Arion's reinforcements. Though Vyekrin covered the sight outside, the hole in the wall only made the sounds of war louder. They rang in Arion's ears, and guilt gripped at his throat.

"You shouldn't be here!" he yelled, stepping back. He

avoided the mess of magic cracks around him as he grabbed the dagger and ripped it from the wall with his right hand, keeping his left free to defend. "You were supposed to stay back! You were supposed to stay—"

Cy cut him off, peeling his gaze away from Crestyss just long enough to leer at Arion. *"I told you I was done with the martyr shit, Arion. You're not doing this alone!"*

"We're all helping, Arion! Gil is on the ground, trying to find Theresa so she can stop the fighting!" Kaitlyn called. Her voice came out more like a growl than her usual rhythmic tones.

Arion's stomach dropped even further at her words, but he forced the concern from his mind. He had to tell himself that the ground would be safer than here. He would finish this quickly, and—

Cy crouched, preparing to pounce, but Crestyss' slick smile froze him in place. "How sweet," he hissed, and venom literally dripped from his tongue. It landed on the stones and ate away the floor like acid.

Arion growled, jumping forward to stab at Crestyss. He danced away from attack after attack, laughing under his breath. Arion closed the distance until the dagger snagged on the cloak flowing around Crestyss. Tripping over his cape, Arion took the opportunity to grab Crestyss with his left hand. Instantly, Crestyss convulsed from the electricity coursing through his body. While he spasmed, Arion drove the dagger into his side, under his ribs until the hilt stopped at his flesh. Crestyss' legs gave out from under him, and he collapsed to the floor.

And began to laugh. The hysterical sound drowned out the chorus of metal clanging and the city falling outside. The others gathered closely, waiting for his breath to cease.

He spread his hands on the ground, as though he were going to stand.

Waves of magic poured from his hands. They all jumped back, but Arion felt nothing from the magic as it passed under him. They all stood silently, waiting for the room to burst into flames, or the walls to fall around them. But nothing came from the magic Crestyss set loose

Vyekrin roared outside, a guttural sound filled with pain. Kaitlyn's scream echoed Vyekrin's, and she stumbled forward. Arion looked from Kaitlyn to Vyekrin. Another dragon, this one made of metal and nearly twice as big with six legs, had latched onto Vyekrin. A barbed tail wrapped around, tearing through Vyekrin's scales and flesh in large chunks. Vyekrin struggled under the added weight, the Tower being torn away by the two of them.

While Arion was distracted, Crestyss shot up and snatched Kaitlyn by the hair. He wrenched the dagger from his own body and buried it into Kaitlyn's stomach. The blood that filled her mouth stifled her screams. Vyekrin bellowed once more as Crestyss shoved Kaitlyn away. She stumbled toward the growing hole in the Tower. Cy caught her just before she reached the edge, clutching her tightly in his arms. The scales started to fall from her body in large patches, but her breathing was even. Arion had a moment to be grateful that Crestyss had left the blade in her so that she wouldn't bleed out.

His vision went red. A visceral yell tore through Arion's throat as he launched himself forward at Crestyss, grabbing his head between his hands. His own talons, now extended in rage, cut into his scalp. With the might of his magic, Arion lifted Crestyss to his knees. He felt the sickening crunch of bones breaking under his palms. Crestyss' face was crushed, blood poured from his orifices.

Crestyss laughter finally ceased, and Arion tossed his body aside so it hung half out of the ruined Tower, limp and lifeless.

"Damn," Grite breathed behind him. Arion shook the blood from his hands, breathing deep to control himself. With the haze of anger gone from his mind, he stepped toward Cy and Kaitlyn.

The metal dragon began to groan, the magic sputtering from it. Its head landed heavily on Vyekrin, causing him to lose his grip. He tried to cling to the tower, but only managed to tear the rest of the roof free. His arm came down hard beside Cy and Kait, and the floor around them gave way.

Arion ran for them, willing all of his strength to push him faster, but it was too late. Cy and Kait went down with the dragons and the stones. Arion reached the edge of what was left and stared down. The rocks tumbled slowly to the ground. The metal dragon landed first, with Vyekrin right on top. A clawed hand from the metal dragon stuck out from Vyekrin's chest, leaving him a bloody mess.

Among the rocks and debris that plummeted to the ground was Cy, holding tightly to Kaitlyn as they fell. Dust rose as the rubble piled on the ground, and when it cleared, there was no sign of Cyllorian or Kaitlyn. Only bloody stones barely covering Vyekrin's corpse.

Arion turned and bolted down the stairs. Faster he propelled himself down the winding stairs. He shoved his way past confused shoulders, mustering magic into every inch of his being to electrocute any who touched him. The ground floor didn't come quickly enough and he rounded the building.

The rubble stood at least ten feet high. Dust still

swarmed around the edges of the debris. Arion shot forward, his claws ready to dig at the pile until they bled.

A hand snatched his wrist and yanked him back. "The tyranny of Crestyss has been ended!" Theresa's voice announced from Arion's side. He turned to her slowly. It took everything in him to wrench his gaze from the destruction before him.

As his gaze shifted, he saw Crestyss' crumbled and broken body among the rubble, his bottom half crushed. His stomach roiled. If he'd had anything in him, it would have come up.

Theresa pulled him away from the rubble and into a throng of people cheering and shouting. They surrounded him, and Theresa's grip was harsher than he ever thought possible for her. An ecstatic smile beamed on her face as she addressed the crowd.

Arion twisted, trying to pry his arm free. He felt Theresa's nails prick his wrist. In an instant, he lost control of his body. His limbs felt heavy. The world around him started to spin and blur. Inside his chest, his heartbeat slowed, and he could feel his blood thicken in his veins. He tried desperately to find his own magic, but his mind was a muddied mess. It was all he could do to keep himself breathing.

Theresa had poisoned him, and he had no choice but to be dragged along by her. She was taking him away from everything he cared about, and he could do nothing.

"A new era begins today!" she yelled into the crowd. A chorus of elation arose from the mob of people. Arion didn't recognize a single face, though he noticed not a single Void could be seen anywhere. None that were still standing, at least. His vision swam as he looked desperately for Gil.

Kait said he was down here. Where is he? He needs to be here. He needs to get Cy and Kait.

Panicked thoughts filled Arion's head, while his mind was still his own. He could feel the poison seeping deeper into his being. There was no telling how much longer he could stay conscious. Gil was nowhere in sight, and Arion was at Theresa's mercy.

He turned away from the crowd, wishing he could return to the rubble, that he could search. But as he turned, his vision righted itself. In that second of clarity he could see shimmering blue scales covered in blood, and a pale hand crushed completely.

<h1 style="text-align:center">CHAPTER 12</h1>

Cyllorian

Darkness. Cyllorian was enveloped in an empty sea of thick darkness. He tried to suck in a breath, and felt the shadows fill him, writhing within. He released them immediately.

A few bubbles formed near the edge of his vision, bobbing up and down as they floated from left to right slowly. Cy tried to turn as they spun around him, but he could not move. Though he was mysteriously stuck in place, the bubbles never left his vision. He was sure they were spinning all around him.

Intrigued, Cy reached for the bubbles, but could not find his hand. He struggled against the torrents of blackness, but couldn't feel or see an inch of his body. He instantly thought of the crystal ball he had spent years trapped in. It was a vague memory now, but the familiarity of *then* and *now* was uncanny. Panic threatened to suffocate him.

Think, think! What was I doing? What happened? His thoughts floated in the space around him, echoing off of impossible surfaces. He racked his brain, which felt even more empty than whatever void he had found himself in.

Suddenly, the bubbles popped silently. As they faded, an image appeared before him.

Arion stood admiring the great metal flying balloon beast he had created, now completed. Cy wanted to share in his pride, but his fear of the sky made him feel sick.

Arion did it, he built the damned thing. Did we use it, did we fight? Did we win or lose? Am I dead?

Cyllorian's frantic voice filled the space around him. With the endless echoes of his fear came more and more bubbles, crowding around him. They swirled, faster and faster, as his thoughts caught in a whirlpool. They spun around him at a speed he couldn't follow, until the sounds of his voice were long gone. Just as easily, they slowed to a pace that Cy could have counted each one, had he wanted.

But all he wanted were answers.

The largest of the bubbles bounced to his right and popped. Instead of the silence, a muffled voice boomed beside him, a single word that he couldn't make out. Before the echo of that word could fade, the rest of the bubbles started popping, one after the other, and the voice came through loud and clear.

"I summon you, demon, upon the mortal plane so that your power shall be mine to wield!" The voice was booming all around him. Pride and cowardice both were clear within his words.

The last of the bubbles vanished, revealing what looked like a crack in front of him, golden light leaking through it.

Desperation and some strong force deep in his soul

pushed him to act, to move. He could feel the faintest shape about him, not that of a body, but of his essence, floating freely like a cloud of smoke. He stretched and contorted himself forward. He could feel the light shining on him, repelling the darkness away from his body. Upon touching the light, his talon manifested, and the break split larger until a hole had formed.

He plunged his hand forward through the hole. His hand came into existence, followed by his wrist and arm. Slamming his hand down onto the floor, the cold of the stones sent a chill through him.

Some force from the other side grabbed hold of him and pulled him through. Air slammed into his lungs as they formed, and he gasped desperately for air. He fell forward onto the stone floor, the light in the room blinding him. Goosebumps spread across his skin, and he quickly formed clothing to cover him.

His vision slowly became clear. Rings of charcoal had been drawn on the floor around him, filled with runes and symbols that Cyllorian didn't recognize. There looked to be words mixed in, written in a curly script, but Cy couldn't read them.

"It worked," an elated voice breathed.

Cy raised his head to find the sound, and was met by a balding man dressed in oddly pressed clothes, a buttoned jacket over what looked like silk, an odd scarf tied close to his neck. "Rise, demon, so that you may obey!" he barked.

Cy twisted his face at the man, but stood slowly. There was crunching under his foot. He lifted it to find a silver ring, its gem loosed from its holding and broken on the stones. Cy wondered if he had been the one to break the ring when he fell. A twinge of guilt crept in his mind, but he ignored it. There were more pressing matters.

The man cackled under his breath as approached the rings. Cy walked to meet him but was held back as he reached the innermost ring. Realization that he was trapped hit him, and he snarled at the man.

"That's no way to address your master," the man hissed, an air of forced competence coming into his voice. "You are here to do as I say, and my orders are to punish those that dare to cross me. Starting with her."

Cy followed the man's pointed finger and froze.

Knelt on the ground in front of large double doors was a small girl, no more than ten. Tears cleaned the grime from her cheeks as they flowed, revealing a dusting of freckles across her cheeks. Crystal blue eyes met Cy's, terror clear in the girl. Gnarled blonde braids hung from her head. Her wrists were tied in front of her, and two men stood on either side of her, one holding the end of the rope.

Kaitlyn, Cy thought, and his breathing hitched at the thought. But this girl was far too young, despite her being the spitting image of a young Kaitlyn.

"*A child?*" Cyllorian spat. "*You're too weak and cowardly to handle a child, so you summon me to bloody my hands in your stead?*"

The man sneered. "Don't let her appearance fool you. That is not a child, it's a monster. And you will dispose of it."

Cy turned back to the man and cocked his head in defiance. "*I don't think so.*"

The man's face turned red, and he stomped his foot, much like a child himself throwing a tantrum. "I have summoned you from your dimension, and you are mine to control!"

Cy looked the man up and down. He hadn't noticed at first how the clothing squeezed his body, or the pudgy fingers that were now pointed at him. Cy chortled and taunted, *"You can't even control your appetite, and yet you dare try to command a demon?"*

Sputtering uselessly with his words, the man's face began to turn purple. Before he could find his voice through his rage, the girl's laughter rang out in the small room. "You're such an idiot," she snapped.

Her voice held more conviction than Cy had expected — more maturity. She pulled herself up on her knees, standing taller than Cy thought possible for her age. Her head was held high as she spoke, "You really should have planned out your summoning circle a little better. And not put me right in front of where the master's name goes."

She swung her legs out from under her and leaned back, watching the man carefully. Cy craned his neck to see what she had revealed, but the scrawling word was upside down to him, and impossible to read.

"You little whelp! How dare you cross me again!" the man burst. He started for the girl, but she simply turned back to Cy.

"Get me out of here," she ordered. A force welled within Cy's stomach, and he launched forward from the entrapment before he knew what he was doing. He slashed at the men beside the girl until they backed away, then he quickly slashed the ropes binding her. She stood quickly, and her small size surprised Cy. She was at least two feet shorter than him, but she looked ready to take on the world. Wordlessly, Cy scooped her up into her arms and bolted for the double doors.

He kicked them open, and jumped down the small flight of steps leading to a small courtyard. The gate that kept them in was too high for him to jump while carrying the girl, so he spun and ran around the side of the large estate. Near the back corner, he found a pile of firewood. He climbed the wood and vaulted over the wall with ease, landing in a narrow alleyway. On instinct, he felt himself shift to his human form. The last thing he wanted was to draw attention.

To his right, he saw a road filled with people walking by, and something strange passed by in a rush. It looked like something Arion might have made. It piqued Cy's interest, and he started to shift his weight that direction.

"Go left," the girl commanded, and the choice was no longer his. He immediately turned left and ran for the end of the alley. She gave orders as he ran, guiding them through a maze of back streets and alleyways. The sounds of life faded behind the abandoned buildings they passed. Finally, the walls opened up into a small courtyard, the intricate stonework overrun by weeds.

"They won't follow us this far. You can put me down now," the girl said.

There was a lack of pressure in his gut, and Cy realized this wasn't a command, though he obliged anyway. The girl slowly slid from Cy's arms, catching herself lightly on the uneven ground. The girl walked over to a broken window of what might have been a shop at one point. Cy took the chance to gauge his surroundings.

The buildings looked like nothing he had seen, all standing at least two stories high and looking expertly made. The brickwork appeared to be perfectly laid, or it had been when the buildings were made. Small awnings stood out above every door, most of them ripped by the elements. While the craftsmanship was extraordinary, the buildings themselves were plain. Cy's stomach twisted as he thought of the homes he had seen in Centric, each one carefully crafted to reflect those who dwelled there. He remembered Jemmina's heart shaped windows, wishing for any sense of familiarity.

"Why did he want to kill you, anyway?" Cy asked, willing his sorrow to leave him.

"I stole from him," the girl said, very matter of fact. "A lot." She was boasting now, laughter in her voice. "It took him so long to catch me. You should have seen his face when he finally figured out it was always me. Hilarious."

Cy turned back to the girl. She was now perched on the windowsill, kicking her feet against the wall. Each time her heel hit the stone, dust cascaded to the ground. *"What do you mean?"*

The girl cocked her head to the side, a wicked grin split across her face. "He was right, you know? I *am* a monster, but I'm the best kind."

Before Cy could ask what she meant, she changed. The filthy braids fell out, leaving her with short black hair that stuck out from her head like spikes. Her blue eyes dimmed to a gray blue. Her heels were nearly touching the ground now that she was taller. And the clothes that Cy hadn't even noticed were far too big, fit her grown form perfectly.

"I can't even count how many bodies I've used to steal from him. He just thought he had really bad luck, but it was all me," she bragged, and now her voice matched with the body she was in. She jumped down from the sill suddenly, and stretched out her limbs. Cy could hear her joints popping despite the distance between them. She made for the furthest opening, nearly invisible in the shadows.

When Cy didn't immediately follow, she stopped and turned back to him. "You coming? We've got a great place for freaks." She smiled, mischief and warmth intertwining.

Cy looked around again. *"I don't know..."* he said, unsure

of how to finish. *Where I am. What happened? How long it's been.* Too many questions filled his head for him to even begin.

While Cy lost himself in his worries, the girl had approached him. "You can't go anywhere else. This world hates magic, and anyone who has it. I think there's someone that can help. You saved me, now let me help you. Unless you really want to go back to wherever you came from."

Cy thought of the darkness he had woken up in, and shuddered. *"Some help would be nice,"* he said simply. The girl smiled softly, and led the way into the darkness.

"My name is Zayla, but you can call me Zee. Everyone else does," she said over her shoulder as they walked.

"Cyllorian," Cy said, not wanting to be rude. *"Cy is fine, too."*

"That's strange."

"What?"

The girl eyed him while she turned a corner. "That's not the name he used to summon you."

More questions filled Cy's mind, but he pushed the harder ones aside from later. *"Zayla's an odd name. What made your parents choose it?"* Cy asked, trying to make conversation. Finding out about this girl seemed far easier than trying to solve everything else.

"They didn't. I did."

"You did? Why?"

Zee shrugged. "Because I couldn't remember my real name. I can't remember anything beyond a couple years ago. These outcasts took me in, and I help them however I can."

Something in her voice made it clear that the conversation ended with that, and Cy didn't dare press further. The uncertainty in his gut only grew stronger.

Cy could hear muffled voices now. They crossed under most of an archway into a garden where people had gathered. They were dirty, with worn clothing that didn't quite fit. They were outcasts, but they were all chatting happily.

From a nearby house on the border of the garden, a small boy darted out of an open door, arms waving in the air. He looked to be about two years old, by the way he toddled when he ran, and the babble that was coming from his mouth. He ran straight for Zee, giggling at her feet.

The boy noticed Cy and stepped up to him with no hesitation. Surprising Cy, the boy held his arms up, grabbing at the air above him. Cautiously, Cy bent to pick the boy up.

The boy giggled again as he was lifted into the air. He reached to wrap his arms around Cy's neck, and went rigid against his chest. Cy watched the boy, scared he had done something wrong. He was fully aware that everyone else in the square was watching him, but he had no idea what to do.

Wails filled the air as the boy squirmed in Cy's arms, desperately trying to get free. Cy panicked, and bent down to set the crying boy down on the ground. He ran off back toward the house.

"Mommy!" he yelled as he went. A figure stepped into the doorway and lovingly scooped the boys into her arms to rock him, but the boy never settled. "Hurts, Mommy! Big rocks hurt!" he cried over and over.

A headache split Cy's skull. Cy doubled over, pressing his palms to his eyelids as he fought against the pain and the wave of memories that flooded his mind.

Waking to find Arion and Grite gone, along with the

zeppelin. The rush to catch up to them on Vyekrin. Centric under attack by Theresa's army, complete with Voids scattered about her crowd. Gil urging them to let him search for Theresa and stop her. Vyekrin tearing open the Tower. Him and Kaitlyn jumping in to help. Cresytss stabbing Kaitlyn. And the tower crumbling beneath him.

He and Kait plummeting to the ground... the debris of the Tower falling around them.

"It's about time you showed up," a soft voice called from the house. Cy struggled to catch his breath, the pain subsiding. He raised his head to see the figure holding the boy had stepped out from the house. Her long black hair was in a thick braid going down her back. A tattered purple dress hung loose on her frame. Bright purple eyes rested on Cyllorian, and he was surprised by the warmth in them.

"Jemmina?" he breathed through the pain.

A smirk crept onto her face. "It is good to see you, Cyllorian. Though I did wonder how long I would have to wait."

The pain had finally subsided while Jemmina spoke. Cy stood slowly, sputtering for words. He had so many questions to ask, he couldn't decide which would be first. Zee was looking between the two of them.

"You know him?" she asked incredulously. "He came out of thin air."

Jemmina pursed her lips together, obviously thinking of how best to answer. While she contemplated, a strange humming noise droned in Cy's ears. Everyone around him had shifted their attention to the skies, and it was clear they heard it, too.

Zee grabbed Cy by the arm and pulled him into the nearest house. Cy was thankful that it had no inhabitants to startle. *"What are you doing?"* he asked.

The answer came in the form of strong winds forming just outside the door, and the humming noise drowned out his own thoughts. Cy craned his neck to see out the doorway, squinting his eyes against the dust blowing into the air.

A zeppelin flew overhead, not unlike the one Arion had made, though this one didn't look like it was made of scraps. The metal glistened in the light, blinding Cy. It looked as though something fell off of it, plummeting toward the ground, but Cy didn't think it could have been that poorly made.

Zee grabbed him and yanked him back into the house. "Get back in here!" she yelled. Cy fell into the open room just in time for the air to fill with thick, black smoke. It swirled in the open spaces just outside, lingering near the doorframe threateningly. It piled against the doorway, as though an invisible wall held it at bay.

Just as quickly as the smoke had formed, it vanished. Cy stared in awe as the smoke seeped into the cracks in the ground.

By the time the air was clean again, the zeppelin was long out of view, and Cy could hear nothing. It was like it had never happened. Cy looked back at Zee for confirmation, and found her scowling at the sky.

"*What was that?*" Cy cautioned a question, despite Zee's expression.

"An attack," she said bitterly, stepping toward the door. She stared up into the sky in the direction the zeppelin had disappeared. "That Mage bastard across the sea has been sending them for as long as I can remember. They used to hit the big cities, but now they're just warnings for us to leave him alone."

Bastard across the sea? She can't be talking about... Cy

thought to himself. He sprung to his feet and slid out the door around Zee, turning sharply toward the house Jemmina had come from.

Jemmina leaned against the wall outside, and Cy had to stop fast to avoid hitting her. The boy was no longer with her. "Go on," she said softly.

Cy took a deep breath. *"What happened?"*

Jemmina sighed. "You have to start with the hard one, don't you? Arion set out for an ambush with Grite. Theresa attacked at the same time. Crestyss was ready. Arion managed to kill him, but it cost him. You fell from the tower,"

"I was— Kaitlyn! We were crushed," Cy finished.

Jemmina shook her head. "You *should* have been. And you would have, if Holten hadn't seen you fall. He managed to fill the space around you two with ice, sparing you from most of the damage."

"Then how did I get here? Where am I? What—"

Jemmina held a hand up to stop Cy's rant. He shut his mouth, and took a slow breath through his nose.

"When I arrived, Theresa had snatched Arion and offered him to the crowd of people as the victor. The other demon was trying to dig you out from the rubble. Holten helped, and we got you both out."

Jemmina paused, and there was a deep sorrow in her silence. With another shaky breath, she continued, "Theresa was determined to keep you dead. I pleaded with her to spare you, to allow me to bring you with me when I left Lontorra. She agreed, but she stripped you to your essence, and bound you to that ring." Jemmina rubbed her hands together, playing with her pinky. It was only then Cy noticed how barren she was, devoid of any jewelry or accessories. "It had been my mother's. That's how I knew it would be strong enough to hold you."

The little boy peeked his head out from the door, then ran to Jemmina's legs. He tugged at her dress until she lifted him, and he settled perfectly in the crook of her neck.

The sight of the boy reminded Cy, and he asked, *"How long have I been trapped?"*

Staring at the sky, Jemmina looked lost in thought. "It's been almost two years."

Jemmina smiled then, humor in her eyes. "I nearly forgot. Congratulations are in order. Happy birthday, Cyllorian. You turn twenty today."

CHAPTER 13

Cyllorian

"What do you mean there's no magic here?" Cy asked in shock.

Jemmina kept a steady stride ahead of him. "Just that. We are far from Lontorra, across the ocean. This land is called Molanse, and it has traded magic for technology. Now, come along. We have allies to see."

"Allies?"

Jemmina looked over her shoulder at him, confusion in her eyes. "Yes, allies. You don't think you're going to cross the sea on your own."

Zee bounded forward to catch up with Cy. "Across the sea?" she echoed excitedly. "We're going across the sea?"

"We?" Cy barked, sounding harsher than he meant. *"Why do you want to come?"*

Zee thought for a moment, staring straight ahead. "Well, you're going to put a stop to those attacks, aren't you? I want to help. Besides, I've always dreamed of an adventure." Her eyes glimmered.

A lump formed in Cy's throat, but he swallowed his curiosity. If he had been brought to this new land, could this girl be Kaitlyn? She had her powers, her personality.

But she didn't look like Kaitlyn, despite the shifting powers she held. This body is what she seemed to feel comfortable in. What were the odds that Cy would meet someone with the exact same powers immediately upon waking up?

Someone they passed had grabbed hold of Zee and kept her back for a moment. Cy moved closer to Jemmina so he could talk quieter.

"Jemmina, you said you and Holten pulled us both out. Where's Kaitlyn?" Cy pressed, unable to resist the question any longer.

Jemmina shot him a nervous glance, then answered tensely, "She was injured, but not gravely. I did what I could for her, and brought her with us to Molanse."

"Is Zee—"

Cy was cut off by Jemmina's stern gaze. "There has been no way to bring her memories back, nor to convince her of anything but this narrative she made for herself. After what she went through, we thought it best to let her be."

Jemmina's words were a warning. Cy couldn't deny that Kait's life would have been harder had she known she was missing a part of her life. Cy's heart thudded in his chest. Did it matter that she survived if she wasn't the person he had known before?

Before Cy could push for more information, Zee ran to catch up with them. She shot Cy a curious glance. He could feel Jemmina staring him down, and he was forced to agree to leave the matter alone. Until Cy could find a way to bring her memories back, the person beside him was Zee, not Kaitlyn, and he had to focus on finding Arion first.

"That zeppelin before, was it..." Cy asked carefully instead. He watched Zee out of the corner of her eye, waiting for her reaction. Her eyes darted to him for a second, her jaw hardening.

"The reports state that Arion took control of Lontorra right after Crestyss' fall. The attacks came soon after. I suspect Theresa forced him into a leader's role, but that she was actually in charge. I doubt Arion actually had much power." Jemmina's answer was cryptic.

Zee spoke before Cy could ask for details. "What did we ever do to him, anyway?" Her question was left unanswered as they slowed.

Despite Jemmina's obvious doubt that Arion was behind the attacks, Zee seemed to have already made up her mind. *I need to get to Arion, but I can't let these people know that I'm on his side, let alone that I'm his brother. They'd never help me if they thought I was with who they think is their enemy.*

"We're here," Jemmina said, stepping to the side of an iron archway that opened into a communal garden filled with fruits, vegetables and even an apple tree filled with ripe apples. Many people were crouched among the rows, tending to the crops. Cy scanned over the faces, unsure what, or who, he was looking for. He turned to Jemmina, her attention fixed across the garden where a large tool shed sat open. There, Cy found a familiar face.

Cy marched across the garden, careful to step around the crops and people. He ignored the glances he gained from those he passed, focused on the person ahead of him. He was sitting on a large box, propping a rake in one hand

and holding a dirty rag in the other. He raised the rag to his face. Dirt came away with the rag, revealing gray skin dotted with light freckles. His long silver hair had been cropped on the sides, the rest pulled back and tied behind his head.

A shadow fell over the person as Cy stepped up to him. He lifted his head, and was met by Cy's closed fist connecting directly with his cheek.

Jayr fell to the ground, and the chatter around them ceased. Jayr pressed his dirty rag to his cheek. The rake had fallen from his grip, and he raised his free hand to wave off the concern of the others.

"I'm fine," he said simply. Then he looked up at Cy. "So, you're finally here."

Using the rake to help himself to his feet, Jayr rose to face Cy. He looked past Cy to Jemmina still perched at the entrance. "Time to go?" he called out to her. Cy turned to catch Jemmina nod.

"Don't tell me you're the ally?" Cy quipped.

Jayr sighed. "I've been using someone at the docks to smuggle letters across to Lontorra. I've been keeping tabs on how things are going, thanks to a member of the rebel force there."

"Rebel force?" Cy cut him off.

"Arion hasn't exactly been making friends while you've been gone. You saw the attack just a little while ago. And they've gotten worse in the past year. It seems Theresa *had* been keeping him under control, but she went missing. Arion has too, for that matter. It seems, without him to give the orders to stop, the attacks will just keep coming. The people of Lontorra aren't happy and want to take back control. We're going to need them to find him."

"I bet I can find him just fine on my own," Cy snarled.

"But how will you get over there? I say the word, and my smuggler can get us on the next ship. Which just so happens to leave tonight!"

Cy glared at him. *"Tonight. How convenient."*

"It is when I've been keeping track of every ship that's come and left the ports in the last two years," Jayr snapped back.

A long moment of silence passed between them. Cy wasn't sure if he could be trusted after everything. *"How did you get here, Jayr? Why aren't you beside Theresa like the lap dog that you are?"*

Jayr looked away from him, and dropped the rag on the box. "I have my reasons. If you want to get to Lontorra, Jemmina will take you to the docks at nightfall. If I'm leaving, I'm doing as much work as I can before I go."

With that, Jayr left Cy to find whoever needed help in the garden. He started barking orders as he made his way up and down the rows, enticing the workers to move faster.

He'll have nowhere to run on the ship, Cy thought, resolving himself to continue his interrogation later.

Night fell quickly while Cy busied himself with work around the garden. He even made a run to pick up supplies with a few others. He took the chance to admire the machinery they had around town. Large vehicles that could hold entire families and admitted black smog as they went. Flameless lights shown in windows as the sun began to dip beyond the horizon. And the people marched along the road, bustling from shop to shop, blissfully unaware that they walked among a demon.

Not that any of them even believed in demons, if what Jemmina had said about this land's lack of magic led him to believe. He was in utter awe of this new land, but a sickness had settled to roll around in his stomach throughout the day.

The docks that laid out before him looked the most similar to Lontorra of what he had seen. Plain wooden docks stretched out into the sea, loaded with sailboats. A few stood taller than the others with smokestacks that reached for the stars overhead. It was strange, but Cy was sure that there were less stars here, or perhaps they were just covered by clouds.

They hid among a large stack of boxes, most empty and waiting for their cargo. Zee was perched at the edge of their hiding spot. She watched the workers eagerly, eyeing every boat that was handled or loaded. She was muttering to herself about which boat she thought could take her farther or faster.

Jemmina had given her a set of new clothes for the journey. A pair of slacks hung loose around her legs, a white shirt with billowy sleeves that clasped at the wrist with shiny metal buttons, and a vest that tightened and contoured to fit her perfectly. Beneath the vest, Cy could see a thin leather strap running across her chest. She clung to it nervously as she rambled on about the coming adventure.

Jayr sat patiently against a box, twirling something in his fingers. He fumbled it into his lap. He snatched it up quickly, but Cy caught a glimpse of it. It looked like a dragon tooth on a string.

"What happened that day, Jayr?" Cy whispered. Jayr looked away from him, shoving the tooth into his pocket. *"Look, we've had our differences and arguments. But now I*

need to know if I can trust you. You were the most loyal person to Theresa, yet you're here. Helping me to get back to Arion, no less. I need to know."

Jayr pulled his fist back out and opened it. The tooth rocked in the palm of his hand, the string falling. He had made it into a necklace. It looked stained with blood.

"Arion was right about the army. I had been following Theresa for so long, but I had no idea it even existed. I definitely didn't expect her to use it." Jayr took a shaky breath, caressing the tooth with his thumb. "Kaliyah was the first to volunteer to be put into a suit. She was so desperate to fight. It was just supposed to be a different body, like the one you had. You made it look easy, switching bodies like that. But not these...*things*. She wasn't Kaliyah anymore. There was nothing left but a soldier, obedient to Theresa to a fault. And that's saying something coming from me.

"I don't know how Polae survived. Not that it mattered. She killed herself trying to protect Kaliyah— the thing that Kaliyah had become. The machine didn't even miss a step when Polae died. It just marched forward. I lost sight of it in the fire, but I know that there wasn't a single one that made it through the fight."

Jayr stared off toward the sea, but his mind seemed to be lost elsewhere. His eyes were glossy, his breathing hitched. A tear rolled silently down his cheek.

"I wasn't ready for war. I trained endlessly, day after day. It never mattered. It was complete chaos. I didn't know who was friend or foe after only a couple minutes. Magic filled the air, and I couldn't keep up. I stumbled around and found myself surrounded by Mages. Wayonn found me and crushed them. One of them managed to set off an explosion just before he died under Wayonn's weight. His entire side was missing. I just stared at him, lying on the ground. I didn't know what else to do. I just grabbed this, and I ran. I don't remember much else. Jemmina found me days later after I snuck on the boat she took to come here."

Cy sat stunned. An empty pit of sorrow had opened in his chest, listening to Jayr's recounting of that day. They had arrived just after the fighting had started. It felt like it all had lasted mere minutes, but so much death and destruction had come from it.

A whistle shrieked in the air around them. In one swift move, Jayr stood and dropped the tooth into his pocket. "Time to go," he said, his voice rough with pain. A man rounded the corner and hustled them onto the boat. They tucked away between a row of filled boxes and the wall of the ship. The salty water that splashed onto Cy was freezing. He shivered as he looked toward the horizon. He could just barely make out the tip of Mount Draken stabbing into the night sky.

* * *

The boat was docked at the coastal base of the mountain, cut off from the rest of Lontorra, just after daybreak. The three of them jumped over the side of the boat as instructed, and waded through the water away from the workers.

Cy was surprised to see Droll and Draken working together to unload the boats, and the humans from Molanse seemed utterly at ease around them. This close to the sea and the mountain, they retained their scaled skin and webbed features.

A raised platform held a few older members giving direction to the workers, dividing the supplies by group and who would receive them. Among them was Kolry, the Droll that had led them around Lorile on their visit.

"Stay here. I'm going to talk to someone." Cy looked at the other two. Zee was admiring the new creatures around her, her skin already glistening with shiny new scales.

Jayr nodded while he scanned over the crowd himself. "Hurry. I'm meeting someone myself."

Cy nodded and ran toward the platform, hoping he wouldn't draw too much attention to himself. Everyone was far too busy to care about what looked to be some delinquent human boy shirking his duties. He ducked under the edge of the platform, grateful that Kolry was standing at the end of the row of people.

"Kolry!" Cy hissed to get his attention. The Droll jumped and looked around for the source of his name. His gaze finally found Cy, and his eyes widened. He stepped to the edge and knelt before Cy. He studied Cy for a long moment, his scrutinizing gaze stopping Cy from speaking.

"Cyllorian?" Kolry finally breathed. "How? You were not among those we knew to have survived."

Cy groaned, but fought to control his temper. Of course, Theresa had declared him dead, even unofficially. *"It was a close call, but I'm still kicking. I'm surprised you recognize me."*

"I'd never forget the eyes of the first demon I have ever met," Kolry said proudly.

Cy chuckled, relief washing over him. *"Can always count on you, huh, Mr. Boss,"* Cy teased.

Kolry puffed before him, but his disdain quickly dissolved into laughter. "I must say, I did grow quite fond of that name."

Cy laughed with him. It was strange how simply having Lontorra beneath his feet again had made his shoulders feel so much lighter. But now was not the time for jokes. He had to save Arion.

Again.

"Hey!" a voice yelled out from behind Kolry. A Droll jumped from the platform and marched up to a human who had dropped a box while trying to set it down. It had fallen less than a foot to the ground, but the Droll was furious. "What do you think you're doing? You come here to help, and yet you look down us, don't you? Just get your ass back to your boat and leave. We don't need or want help from useless humans like you!"

The human, a slim human teenager, cowered before the Droll. He inched away from the Droll, his hands raised. Retreat was clear in his face. The confrontation had gained everyone's attention, but no one stepped forward to help the poor boy.

Cy's hand came down hard on the Droll's shoulder. *"If the food can survive the rough seas to get here, it can survive a little tumble, don't you think?"* Cy growled.

He was well aware of Kolry calling after him, but he didn't care. These people were helping. They didn't deserve to be treated like this.

He yanked on the Droll's shoulder, forcing him to turn around. Cy's hand fell limp as the enraged face stared him down. Behind the sheer rage, Cy recognized his eyes. A thick scar started on the right side of his forehead, stretching back along the top of his head.

"Who are you? Get back to work!" he spat. He shoved Cy, and he stumbled a few steps back from the shock.

Kolry was at their side, grabbing the other Droll and holding him back. "Stop it, Gil. That's enough," Kolry begged.

"Gil?" Cy questioned, unwilling to believe it. *"What*

happened? Where's Arion?"

Gil barked a sarcastic chuckle. "That coward went into hiding. He knew what was good for him."

Gil ripped away from Kolry, yelling orders for everyone to get back to work. He bent over the box that had been dropped. He inspected the contents, his face now twisted in worry.

Cy was pulled away by Kolry, his eyes never leaving Gil as he dug through the rations. *"What happened to him? I didn't even recognize him since he's so...so..."*

"Angry," Kolry finished. "And hurt. I don't know what occurred during the battle, but he was found with a head wound and brought back. He slept for three days, and when he awoke, his memories were gone. Nearly a year's worth. He doesn't remember a thing leading up to the war, nor of the time you were here last. The last thing he remembered was his sister's passing. He was never able to get over that pain, not like he had when he traveled with you. He's been bitter ever since."

Uncertainty washed over Cyllorian. He trudged over toward Gil, who was nearly buried in the food rations as he inspected them. Cy tapped him on the shoulder, and Gil spun on his heels with a sigh.

"You don't remember me?" Cy asked, pointing to his face.

Gil scoffed and stood upright. He met Cy's eyes unflinchingly, but also, without any recognition in him. He shook his head, scrunching his face. "Not at all. Can't say I'm all too disappointed about it. Sorry," Gil quipped. His words sounded dead on his tongue as he spoke.

Even though Cy had originally met him while he was still grieving his sister, he had never been like this. Cy could only remember the mischievous side of Gil, or the serious side that had stood beside him in a fight.

"What about Arion?" Cy didn't have time to process the thought before he spoke it aloud.

Gil's face changed instantly. His eyes narrowed as a scowl ingrained itself on his face. "What about him?" Gil hissed through gritted teeth.

"Don't you remember him? You can't have lost all of your memories, right?"

Footsteps sounded behind Cy. A quick glance over his shoulder showed Jayr and Zee had come to find him. He hadn't meant to be gone for so long, or to cause such a scene. Despite their being stowaways, no one seemed to pay them any mind as they stood beside Kolry.

Gil laughed— a forced sound. "The only thing I know about him is that he's a coward. He *used* to supervise the shipments, but I swear, he only did it because he was a masochist. He would just stand there silently. Didn't even care when I yelled at him. At least, I thought he didn't, but he hasn't come in almost a year. Not since he killed Theresa and left the rest of us to rot."

"Theresa is dead?" Jayr asked, stepping forward. "What do you mean she's dead?"

Gil looked at Jayr with even more disgust than he showed Cy. Cy was shocked that it was even possible. "Arion threw her from the Tower," Gil snapped.

Cy stood stunned. Gil huffed his breath out, and turned back to directing the workers.

Jayr nudged Cy, freeing him from the stream of broken thoughts in his mind. "I need to go find my informant. Do you know where Arion is?" he asked hurriedly.

"He'll be hiding," Cy said simply.

Jayr nodded in understanding. He shot a worried glance at Gil. "Make him go with you. Lontorra isn't the same as we left it; you'll need a knowledgeable guide."

"How am I supposed to do that when he's like this?" Cy threw his hand out toward Gil, his raised tone drawing his attention. Gil glared at Cy. He barked out orders, his eyes never leaving the newcomers.

Kolry stepped forward and paused beside Cyllorian. "I suspect you are here to set things right. No one has been brave enough to stand up in Theresa and Arion's absence. No one has dared to take responsibility for Lontorra. I will handle Gil. Take what rations you'll need and prepare yourselves."

"Thanks, Mr. Boss." Kolry smiled at the nickname, and strode over to speak in hushed voices with Gil. Cy was not unaware of the deadly glances he was getting from Gil, but he chose to ignore them.

I hope an adventure will be as good for him as it was the first time. Cy's thoughts flooded his mind, and he wondered if he was truly in over his head this time.

Jayr was at his side before he noticed a hand on Cy's shoulder. "Don't let them near Arion. The rebel forces are beyond my knowledge," Jayr whispered. Jayr's eyes darted between Gil and Zee.

Cy swallowed hard and nodded once. It was a strange feeling to trust Jayr over the others, but Jayr's motivation was the only one he knew. Without another word, Jayr turned and ran for the mountain.

Cy guided Zee to an unattended cargo box. Another worker brought over large bags, and Cy mindlessly stuffed them with food and water. Zee followed suit, but her attention was divided as she awed over every inch that she could see of Lontorra. She spent a long while with her head craned back. Cy followed her gaze to see the silhouettes of dragons in the sky.

"Dragons," Cy said simply, returning to his packing.

"Real dragons?" she mused. "I want to ride one."

"You'd love it," Cy muttered, his voice barely audible even to his own voice.

"What was that?" Zee asked. Her eyes were now fixed to Cy, and they glowed with a wonder that was so utterly familiar that it stabbed at Cy's heart. Cy cursed at himself.

She's not Kaitlyn. Even if she was before, she isn't now.

"Just that my bag's done. You should hurry up," Cy covered quickly. He swung at the strap of the bag. It wasn't even half full yet, and Cy was already fastening his shut. He stood and threw the bag over his shoulders.

Gil approached, his arms crossed. Kolry was standing a little behind him. "Where are we going?" he barked. There was an attempt at strained civility, but it fell flat.

Zee joined them, the bag hanging heavily off one shoulder. Cy noticed Gill had a smaller bag at his hip, its strap strung across his chest.

Cy closed his eyes. He let his magic thrum throughout his body. Rubbing his left arm, Cy remembered how Arion had carved letters into his arm. They were connected. Mixed in with his magic, Cy felt a thin strand of something else. It surged through him like lightning.

He opened his eyes to see a thin band of green light wrapped around his wrist. He ignored the stares he was getting from the others. He rubbed a thumb over the band and felt his senses explode. The sound of rustling pages filled his ears. His eyes clouded over with darkness. The smell of mildew and coldness surrounding him. Underfoot, he could feel cold rough stones. His skin felt like paper.

The vision passed as he dropped his hand. He recognized the library from the castle. He knew where Arion was.

"Home."

CHAPTER 14

Cyllorian

Gil led Cy and Zee through newly built tunnels beneath Mount Draken. They had been made to aid in the transport of the emergency supplies coming from overseas. They had a nearly straight path from the docks to the outskirts of Centric. Cy was thankful not to have to waste time either climbing the mountain or going around it.

Unlike the last time Cy needed to trek through Centric, they took a main entrance into the outer ring. Gil pushed through the crowds of Mages, rushing ahead of Cy and Zee. Zee was keeping an especially slow pace, as she gawked at everything around her. Cy was worried her head would start spinning atop her shoulders.

To Cy's surprise, the Tower had never been rebuilt. Only a jagged husk of the one he fell from jutted up over the roofs of the houses they passed. The others stood intact. Even from this distance, they looked abandoned.

"There's a stable on the other side. Let's go," Gil barked behind him, sounding just as he had at the docks.

Cy grabbed Zee's wrist and pulled her forward to catch up with Gil. *"We're supposed to be a team here, you know."*

Gil glared at Cy without breaking stride. "I still don't have a single reason to trust you."

A growl escaped Cy's lips. *"What if I told you I could get your memories back?"*

At that, Gil stopped. "You really think you could have better luck than everyone else that's tried? I've been to at least a dozen doctors, a dozen Mages, even a few people that have come in on the ships. No one has been able to do a damn thing about it. All I know is there's this magic wall inside my head, blocking the memories."

"Magic wall?" Cy echoed. He had to keep a firm grasp on Zee to keep her from wandering from them. Now that Cy had finally gotten Gil to talk to him, he didn't want to let this opportunity slip away.

Gil scoffed at his clear ignorance. "Yeah. A big magic wall made out of green lightning. What do you think you can do that no one else could?"

A triumphant grin spread across Cy's face. *"You may have been seen by a dozen Mages, but not the right ones. I can get your memory back, but you have to help me first. I can fix your memories, and everything else, too. You trusted me before. You can do it again."*

Cy extended his hand in allegiance. Gil scrutinized it, his expression softening just the slightest. "Kolry trusts you. That's good enough. For now."

Without another word, Gil strode away into the crowds of people, heading east. Cy fought to keep up with him, pulling a distracted Zee behind him. The rest of the time spent in Centric was done so in silence, until Gil had to pay for the horses and carriage they would take the rest of the way. While they waited for the animals to be saddled, they rested for lunch.

Cy tried to make conversation again, but Gil didn't so much as meet his eye. Meanwhile, Zee rambled on as fast as her tongue could move as she reviewed everything she had seen so far. Sitting closer to Gil than Cy dared, she ignored her lunch in favor of examining the glistening scales that covered his skin. They had started to fade from the hours away from Lorile, his skin paling underneath, but enough were present that they caught Zee's attention like a child. Cy was shocked at Gil's indifference as Zee grabbed an arm and twisted it this way and that while trying to count the remaining scales.

Within a half hour the carriage was ready, and they set off onto the road again heading east. Gil took the reins, guiding the horses clumsily, but confidently. Just outside Centric, it looked as though the road truly had split the world in two. One side of the barren dirt was a lush green field of overgrown weeds and wildflowers, the woods holding the castle a thin line on the horizon. Opposite the vast sea of green was a blackened mud that dried and cracked in the sun beating down. The dirt itself looked like ashes, filling the air with dust and smoke upon even the gentlest breeze.

"Kindling Woods," Gil finally said. His voice held a detached sorrow when he spoke.

Cy registered his words a moment, saying them over and over again in his head. *"What?"* he asked, unable to comprehend the words on his own. He turned to Gil, but he was staring over the ravaged land himself.

"The day of the attack, the Kindling Woods were set on fire. People say it was on purpose, but I don't understand why. There was nothing there. It was probably an accident, I heard there were a lot of dragons around. Some of Centric burned down, too. The fire probably started there, then spread to the trees."

"No one helped put out the flames?" Cy asked, reigning in the conversation.

"The fire spread faster than it should have. There was no time. Nothing survived. Well, almost nothing."

Cy cocked his head in question. Gil raised his hand to point out the answer. They had traveled along nearly half of the original length of the Kindling Woods. Not far from the road stood a dark, gnarled shape resembling a small dead tree.

Cy vaulted from the carriage and sprinted for the tree. Behind him, he heard Gil stop the horses, and he and Zee were behind him.

The tree trunk stopped just below his shoulders, with two large branches raised toward the sky. Thin branches twisted out from the limbs in a mess.

Cy moved to rest his hand atop the tree. A small light tumbled from the bramble on the trunk. It fell a short way before shooting back up to hover just in front of Cy's face.

Noma's wings fluttered, her wings sputtering as she fought to keep her altitude. Cy swallowed the lump that had formed in his throat as his fears were confirmed. *"Hey there, bug,"* he said softly.

Noma's mouth fell open, and she seemed to forget how to fly entirely. She dropped, but Cy caught her easily, lifting her back level with him.

"It is you," she breathed. Her voice was hoarse, causing a coughing fit from the effort to speak.

"I'm back to try to fix things," he said simply. Noma nodded where she sat in his hand. Cy thought he felt tiny

tears fall on his palms, but he couldn't be sure. *"What happened?"* he pressed softly.

Noma's shoulders hunched forward. Her arms wrapped around her, one hand tugging at a twitching wing. "We were on our way to Centric, following Theresa. We didn't know what else to do; she called us all to fight so suddenly. Just before we reached the walls, my lady just fell over. I couldn't hear anything over her screams. She grabbed her chest and her skin...it turned to dust under her fingers. She could feel the Woods, her home, burning. It was then we saw the light from the flames. It danced across the tops of the trees. The other Kindling must have spread it as they tried to flee. My lady managed to get to her feet, and she ran for the trees.

"It was too late. Every single leaf was already ablaze. She rushed in, but she couldn't avoid the fire. She was the last to catch, and the last to burn. I don't know why, but her body remained right here, where she burned. She now stands as a reminder of all we lost that day."

"Arion probably did it, when he attacked Centric," Gil hissed.

Cy bit his cheek to keep his temper in check. Once he had control again, he retorted, *"Arion wouldn't do this. It must have been one of Crestyss' people. He knew the Kindling would pose too great a threat. Right, Noma?"*

Noma looked between the two boys, defeat on her face. "I don't know who started the fire. Just that it started near Centric."

Cy doubled down. *"Crestyss was ready for an attack that night. He was waiting for Arion, and he had defenses in place for Theresa. He planned everything. This had to be him."*

Noma nodded absently. She turned her head to glance back at the tree, drawing a ragged breath. She felt cold in Cy's hands, and light. He couldn't help but worry for her.

"You can come with us," he offered gently. Noma lowered her head for a moment, her eyes wide. Then, she made her decision.

Puffing her chest, Noma stood on shaky legs. "My place will always be with my lady." Her words rang with bravery, and a deep sorrow. Cy nodded and held her out toward Adoette. She climbed atop the twigs that entangled what had been Adoette's head. Noma lay down where she could. Cy tried not to flinch as he watched Noma's light dim slightly. He told himself the sunlight had just gotten harsher.

"Do what you can to set things right. We will be here." Noma's words were both encouraging and grim. Cy chose to hold on to the positive meaning. Noma's eyes closed, and Cy marched back to the carriage. Gil and Zee followed close behind.

Gil climbed to the driver's seat, a solemn dread now washed over him. Zee had tear streaks on her face, though her eyes had already cleared. She stared at the final grave of all the Kindling as Gil urged the horses forward at a faster pace than before.

Just before Adoette was out of sight, and their destination began to loom in front of them, Cy watched as the tree glowed brightly. Flowers sprung to life for mere seconds, before they drifted away on the wind.

* * *

"There's nothing here," Gil griped. They stared forward into the mess of trees that surrounded the castle. Though the trees were obviously thinner than last Cy had seen, they still protected the castle.

"He's here." Cy stepped over the threshold of the woods. As soon as his foot touched the ground, the woods came to life. Wind rushed through the branches, sounding like music. The grass lapped at his foot, shimmering with dew that should have dried long ago. Distant rustling could be heard, drawing closer. Cy froze, and readied himself for an attack.

From a thick shadow emerged a large wolf, crouched low to the ground with teeth bared. He raised his head, starting to growl, but quickly stopped. His nose furiously sniffed the air, his eyes wild as he investigated the intruders.

"Easy, Tuft," Cy said. He extended his hand slowly in greeting.

Tuft barked and bounded for Cy. The large wolf tackled Cy to the ground, drowning him in slobber as Tuft licked his face. Cy laughed as he tried to fend the beast off. *"I said, easy, Tuft! Get off already."*

Tuft backed off with a whine. "What are you..? How are you..? When? Why? How are you here?"

Tuft yipped, bouncing back and forth in front of Cyllorian. He struggled to get the questions out through his excited panting.

"I survived, but was banished overseas. I'll give you one guess as to who ordered that."

Tuft froze and growled low in his throat.

"Exactly. Now I need to get inside, and find Arion." Cy pushed himself to his feet, wiping the drool from his face. While Cy was distracted cleaning himself, his company had joined him carefully.

Zee inched her way toward Tuft, nearly crawling on the

ground with one hand held out. She presented her palm to Tuft, and he sniffed it dutifully. Within seconds, Tuft curled himself into Zee's lap, nuzzling her hands with his nose.

Gil watched from a safe distance away. "No sense of urgency, I see. Not much of a guard dog, either."

Tuft whipped his head to glare at Gil. "You're the first people to set foot in here since Arion returned. I'd say we have a pretty good record," he barked.

"Has anyone else tried?" Gil taunted. He smirked when Tuft growled in response, but was cut short. Tuft jumped up and closed the distance between them in seconds, examining Gil closely.

"You smell the same," he mused aloud. "So what happened?"

"Long story, Tuft. But he's right. We need to get moving," Cy answered, gathering all of their attention. Zee groaned in disappointment, but rose to her feet.

Tuft guided them swiftly and silently through the woods. It took less time than Cy remembered before they reached the gates to the castle.

One gate had been completely ripped from its hinges, and was lying about ten feet away in the castle's courtyard. The plaque that once held the bolt insignia had a hole melted through the center of it. Cy grimaced at the damage as they passed through the gate and over the uneven stone path to the large doors.

The castle was eerily quiet and dim, lifeless from the years gone by. It looked utterly abandoned, but there was something in Cy that told him he was in exactly the right place. His left arm tingled as though he had been shocked, and he was reminded of the connection he and Arion shared.

The doors were heavy, even with all four of them pushing against them. Cy pulled away, frustrated, and the rest copied. The whole castle had been overrun with vines, and rust covered the doors hinges. Placing a hand to the door, Cy closed his eyes and thought of entering.

The wood fell away from his hand. A smaller door was now carved just in front of him, swinging open on hinges made of smoke. He stepped through cautiously, and beckoned the others in behind him.

The entry room was dark. The windows had all been covered, blocking out most of the sunlight. Thin rays of light seeped through cracks in the walls and unmarked corners of the windows. It was cold enough inside that Cy could see his breath stirring within the trails of light.

Raising his hand above his head, Cy conjured a large cloud of wispy smoke. He swirled it around and around. Strands broke off in every direction. The smoke slithered to the windows, wiping the grime and soot from them. The room filled with light slowly.

"I need you three to wait here for me," Cy said. *"It's going to be a lot for him, and it could get dangerous. Tuft, watch them."*

Tuft raised his chin dutifully, then spun on his heels to watch Zee and Gil.

Zee was meandering along the walls, taking in the grand pictures portrayed by the painted glass. Gil was having a staring contest with Tuft, his body stiff.

"I'll be back," Cy said, and took off down the hall.

The innards of the castle were much like he remembered. The layout hadn't changed since the day they had fled, and a few hallways had collapsed near the outside walls. Debris littered the floor.

He found his way to the library easily. It was faint, but

a flickering light shone from under the doors. They opened easily when Cy pushed, and he inched his way into the room.

A few shelves were on the floor, their contents spilled or piled in the corners. One of the tables was broken in half, its chairs nowhere to be found. Books were stacked in a ring in the center of the room, some of them open to seemingly random pages.

Arion sat in the center of the ring, his back to Cyllorian.

"Leave me alone!" Arion called. He tossed a book from his side. It landed with a thud and slid until it hit a fallen shelf.

"I think I'll pass," Cy quipped back. The words came out thick through his tightened throat.

Arion whirled around to face Cy. His skin was deathly pale, his cheeks hollow in his face. Dark shadows swallowed his eyes. His brow was furrowed in anger. "I said, *leave!*" he shouted.

Arion didn't lose his memory, too, did he? Cy thought in a panic.

There was clear recognition when Arion had looked at him, but also a fierce rage. Cy's chest tightened. He hadn't expected a perfect reunion, but he hadn't thought Arion would throw a tantrum, either.

He flung another book, this one larger than the first, straight at Cyllorian. It fell short, landing a short ways in front of Cyllorian. "I don't want to see this, so just go away!"

Cy felt a crackle in the air that made his hair stand on end. He began to close the distance between them slowly. *"I know it's been a while, but just let me explain—"*

"No!" Arion yelled. He wrapped his arms over his head, like he was trying to protect himself. Lightning lashed out around him, singing anything it came in contact with. "I don't want to see! Go away. Go away. Go away!"

Arion started wildly flinging books around him in every direction, though most were aimed toward Cyllorian. He dodged them as best as he could, but inevitably was struck right in his chest. He grunted at the impact, though it had been a small book that hadn't done any damage. It landed at his feet, and he kicked it away.

Arion was frozen on the floor. His face had paled even further. His eyes were burning with rage. He got to his feet shakily, his eyes never leaving Cy where he stood.

"How *dare* you," he hissed. "Why in hell would you think this is okay?"

"What are you talking about? Look, I know it's a lot to take in, but I really did think you would be happy to—"

"Happy? You seriously think I would want to see you like this? Even for you, this is one disgusting joke, Grite. I would have rather you been a hallucination, instead." Arion was shaking violently, magic oozing from his fingertips. Cy could see faint green lines glowing just under the skin of Arion's hands.

Cy gawked in amazement. *"You think I'm Grite? Is that what this tantrum is about? Has he done this to you before? I promise, Arion, I'm not Grite!"*

"Maybe you thought it would be a good idea today. Either cheer me up, or drive me fully insane. I don't care why you did it, but it needs to stop!" Arion charged forward. He stumbled on the books scattered over the floor, giving Cy enough time to react.

Cy held up one hand to fend off Arion, while the other tugged at his shirt. *"I swear, Arion, I can explain. Just calm down."*

"No. I'm done with you, you damned demon! Just leave me alone already."

With one hand, Cy lifted his shirt, and dug his other thumb into the hem of his pants. He pulled the fabric aside, revealing the scar nestled in his hip bone. *"Grite doesn't know about this scar, does he? No one does, Arion. Only you and me. It's me, Arion. I really am Cyllorian."*

Arion was barely a foot away, standing so still that even his shaking had stopped. His wide eyes were fixed to that scar. The magic pouring from him slowed and ceased. His bottom lip began to quiver.

"How..." Arion started, and his voice caught in his throat. He swallowed audibly before continuing. "How do you remember me?"

"What are you talking about, why do you think I would forget you?"

"The spell, it didn't work right. Gil doesn't remember anything, he doesn't remember *me!* It wasn't supposed to happen like this. That's not what the spell was supposed to do," Arion pleaded.

"What spell, Arion? What are you talking about?" Cy took a step forward, reaching slowly. Arion flinched away from him initially, then froze.

"I wasn't going to come back from the Tower, Cy. I was going to go down with Crestyss if I had to. But I couldn't leave and hurt everyone. The only thing I could think of was a forgetting spell. It was only supposed to work if I died, but something went wrong. Gil was attacked on the ground. A whole group of people ambushed him, they beat him so much. The wound on his head was too deep, it activated the spell, and I can't undo it. I can't fix him, I can't fix anything. I don't know what to do, Cy."

Arion stumbled forward and Cy caught him by the

shoulders, holding him up straight. *"I'm here. We'll work together and set everything straight, I promise. One thing at a time. I'm not going anywhere."*

"Cy," he breathed.

"I'm back, kid."

Arion collapsed into Cy's arms, sobbing.

CHAPTER 15

Cyllorian

"*W*hat the hell is all the yelling for?" Grite complained as he burst into the library. He froze when he saw Cy holding Arion up, his tears now dry. *"Isn't this a surprise."*

Arion took a step away from Cy and toward Grite. He was shaking again, though he seemed more stable than he had before. "Did you know?" Arion asked quietly.

Grite leaned away from him, resting his hands behind his head. His eyes shot up to the ceiling. There was a metallic tapping sound, and Cy noticed the mechanical boot that covered his entire wounded leg. It looked like a splint made of silver beams, and it bent smoothly at the knee due to gears.

Grite's silence brought a new wave of anger into Arion. "Answer me! Did you know about Cy?"

"Well, I certainly didn't know he would show up today," Grite muttered.

Arion lunged forward, but his legs gave out beneath him. Cy stooped to catch him before he hit the ground. He was so much lighter than Cy expected. Arion had grown so weak while Cy had been gone. He felt a mix of guilt and anger that they had been separated.

"Why didn't you tell me?" Arion hissed.

"Look it's not like Theresa told me what she was doing with their bodies! I dug them mostly out of the rubble, but Theresa got there faster than I expected. I ran, okay? I never knew what she did with them." Grite's answer came in one big rush. He backed away further while he talked.

Arion's head drooped. He grew heavier in Cy's arms, but he held him up easily. "Cy's been alive this whole time. You knew there was *something*, and you never told me. He was alive, and you let me..."

Cy tried to keep Arion steady as his shaking grew worse. *"I know I've been gone a while, Arion, but I can help now. What happened while I was gone?"* Cy asked gently.

"Why did it take you *two years* to come find me?" Arion shook his head. His voice was trembling again, his breath coming short.

"I was trapped somewhere else. Like before you freed me from the music box. I just got out yesterday Arion, trust me. I got here as fast as I could," Cy explained. The guilt in him was growing from the pain in Arion's voice.

"Yesterday?" The word was strained. Arion felt like he was buzzing in Cy's grasp, and he knew he had to calm Arion down. Small green sparks were flying from his fists clenched in his lap.

"I had to sneak on a boat and everything. But I'm here now. It's okay," Cy coaxed.

Arion doubled over suddenly, pressing his forehead to the ground. Cy tried to lift him back up, but it was too late.

Arion pressed his palms to the stone floor, and a shock-wave of magic shot out from him in all directions.

Cy tensed from the immediate pain, and he heard Grite crash to the ground.

Just as suddenly, Arion collapsed to the ground. Cy rolled him over as gently as he could. They were both breathing heavily from the pain. Arion's hand was bleeding from the lightning bolt on his palm, the blood mixing with the remains of his magic, making it glow as it slowly dripped to the floor.

Grite was spewing profanities from the ground. His brace had locked in place, partially bent, and he clawed at it until the magic faded completely and it loosened up.

"We really need to find a better way for you to manage when you build up magic, kid," Cy said through gasping breaths.

Arion was quiet for a moment, and Cy thought he might have passed out from the exhaustion. "I'm not a kid anymore," Arion said in one drawn out breath.

Cy chuckled. Relief washed over him, and he felt himself finally relax since he had woken up in the summoning circle. *"You'll always be a kid to me,"* Cy teased. He'd hoped Arion would laugh with him, but there was silence.

"I killed Theresa," Arion whispered beside him. He stared up at the ceiling expressionless. "Last year. On the anniversary of... She wanted to *celebrate*," Arion spat the word out like it was poison. "She wouldn't leave me alone. Just kept saying that it didn't matter, and it was a good day. I lost control and...she fell out of the tower window. The magic destroyed her before she hit the ground."

Cy clambered into a sitting position. *"Arion—"*

"I ran away here while everyone panicked. Grite didn't have anywhere else to go, so he came, too."

Grite had long since gone quiet, busying himself with testing the mechanisms of his brace.

Rushed footsteps cut off Cy before he could think of a proper response. Gil and Zee ran into the room to find them all on the ground.

"What happened?" Zee questioned. Her skin had gone pale, with thin green lines running underneath. They pulsed like veins. Her hair was a tangled mess, sticking up in odd places. "There was this loud sound, and then we got shocked. Gil just started running, so I followed him and…"

She caught herself on the wall before she fell. She took deep breaths and shook her hands until the magic veins faded.

Gil was glaring silently at Arion. "What did you do?" he asked Arion directly. Arion crawled to his feet silently, refusing to look at Gil.

"Sorry," Arion muttered, wrapping his arms around himself. A thin smear of blood was left on his arm.

Gil stepped forward, but Cy jumped to his feet to stop him. *"Easy. Give him a chance."*

"A *chance*?" Gil shouted. "A chance to what? Kill us? Take our memories so he can just run away again?"

Arion flinched and turned further away from Gil. Cy put himself fully between Gil and Arion and tried to force Gil to focus on him instead. *"Calm down, and we'll figure things out,"* he said slowly, making the threat clear in his tone.

"Figure what out? You just heard him admit to killing Theresa! Are you just going to do whatever he wants? He's ruined everything!"

"It's not his fault!" Cy yelled. His outburst finally got Gil

to look at him. He sneered and took a step back from Cy, pointing past him at Arion.

"Really? It's not his fault? Ever since he took over in Centric, Lontorra has fallen to ruin. Peace between the races was lost when everyone had to fend for themselves. Overseas trade was banned, so we had to smuggle supplies just to stay alive. We all lived happily under Crestyss, but Arion killed him. Then when Thersa wanted to make things better, he killed her, too. He ruined everyone's lives, then ran off when the people were sick of him. He's the one who took my memories!" Gil yelled, growing louder with each accusation.

Arion finally spoke up for himself, "So what if I took your memories? You don't want them, anyway!"

Gil lunged forward, but Cy caught him. "What do you know about me? You don't know what I want, you bastard! Give them back!"

"I tried! Believe me, I tried, but you're blocking them just as much as my magic is. This was never supposed to happen, and I can't fix it!" Tears welled up in Arion's eyes again, and he scrubbed them away.

Gil peeled himself away from Cy and paced back toward the door. He punched it, and it swung against the wall with the force. His knuckles were scraped bad enough to draw blood when he pulled it away.

"What do you mean? Why would I block my own memories?"

Arion clenched his own fists, obviously fighting with himself. He forced himself to calm down before he spoke again, slowly and deliberately, "What if you weren't on the side you think you were? You defend Theresa now, but if you and I weren't working together, I wouldn't have had access to you in order to use magic on you. Theresa used me and lied to you. You've decided I'm the bad guy, and you don't want to remember anything different."

They were all quiet for a moment. Gil stared down at the wound on his hand, flexing his fingers. "I want the truth," he admitted.

Arion sighed. "The truth is, you received a head injury in the battle, and it messed up the magic. I can't undo it. I told you; I tried."

"Then try again," Gil barked, whirling around. He moved closer to Arion slowly, and Cy stood ready to intercept.

Arion tilted his head back. "I can't," he whispered, and his speech was slurred. He swayed on his feet for a second before his legs gave out underneath him.

Cy managed to catch him again just before his head hit the ground. He was completely passed out, heavy and limp in Cy's arms. He picked him up easily, and set him down on the only table clear of books across the room.

He went back to the group, and stopped mere inches away from Gil. *"Behave,"* he hissed sharply. Cy grabbed Grite and pulled him just outside the room. Once out of earshot, he released Grite, and the other demon leaned defiantly against the wall.

"What?" Grite snapped.

"Two years is a long time. I'm sure I've missed some stuff," Cy pressed.

Grite groaned and dropped his arms to his side. *"You heard the kid. He got pissed and killed the old lady. What more do you want?"*

Cy simply narrowed his eyes and tapped his talons against the stones of the wall.

Grite rolled his eyes, but continued without the attitude. *"Theresa used him as a figurehead the whole first year, since Arion was technically the one to take Crestyss out of power. She made all of the decisions, and he got all of the blame and the praise. It was mostly blame, though. Theresa repaired most of Centric, but her good deeds pretty much stopped there. At least, what was good for everyone. Oh, and she started communications with the next land over across the ocean, but that didn't last long. Once she was dead and Arion disappeared, it all collapsed. No one else wanted to take control, at least not at first. I send the wolves out sometimes to get information. There were rumors that Arion was just biding his time before he came back worse than before. Not that Arion's even gotten close to the front door since we got here, but the masses need someone to blame. We've just been hiding out here ever since, and no one's come looking until today. I'd say we're doing pretty good for ourselves, just staying out of trouble."* Grite examined his own talons once he finished speaking.

"What about the zeppelins? In the other land, there was an attack; a smoke bomb dropped from a zeppelin."

Grite shook his head, his lips a thin line. *"Not Arion. The only thing he's made is this."*

Grite lifted his leg to show off his brace. It looked similar to the workings of Cy's old metal body, though most of the metal was wrapped in thin leather. It looked like the leather had writing or imprints on them, and Cy realized they were book covers stitched together.

Grite's head shot up, and he raised a finger. *"Almost forgot. There's a very angry, secret group of people in Lontorra that wants Arion dead. That seems important."*

"It is," a voice echoed through the halls. Cy jumped to attention, but dropped his guard in disappointment as Jayr stepped into the light pouring from the library.

"So glad you could make it," Cy cheered sarcastically.

Jayr had donned a set of light armor over his chest and

legs, leather bracers around his wrists. His thick boots stomped through the corridors. He looked around in the small space outside the library. "Where are they?" he inquired. His tone was harsh, tense.

"Arion passed out. The others are still in there." Cy jerked his thumb to the open door behind them. It was only now he thought it strange how quiet they were being.

Jayr's face twisted as he bolted for the door. "You idiot!" Jayr growled. "Gil's part of that rebel group now!"

* * *

Zayla

Zee crossed the room to the books strewn across the floor. The years of use were clear in the broken spines and bent pages. She grimaced at the damage, and scooped a pile into her arms. Balancing them carefully, she made her way around the mess and stacked the books neatly on a standing table. It wobbled under the added weight.

Once her arms were free, her gaze wandered to the sleeping boy on the table nearest the door. His hands twitched at his sides. Moans and whimpers escaped his lips, but he didn't wake. Gil had been pacing in front of the door, but quickly changed his mind and sat on the floor near the table Zee was stacking the books.

Zee's hands wrapped around the strap across her chest. It tightened on her, pressing the metal into her back and sending a chill down her spine. With a sigh, she loosened the buckle, and the whole thing fell from her heavily. She caught it easily, and swung it up on the table beside the books. The thin dagger thudded against the wood of the table.

"He's...not what I expected," she mused aloud, and went back to the mess of books on the floor. She closed the open ones gently, and stacked them atop each other. She used an especially large one as the base of her pile since it could hold two normal sized books side by side atop it. The only sound in the room was the fluttering of pages and the thud of leather on leather as she piled the books as high as she could carry.

On her second trip to the table, Gil spoke. "You're from across the ocean, aren't you?"

Zee hesitated, book in hand. "Yes," she answered, her guard up immediately. It was the first time they had really talked since they had teamed up together, and something in his tone threw her off. She had heard him angry, and this wasn't it. This was a terrifying calm.

"I heard about the attacks. You know *he's* the one who made those flying machines in the first place, right? No one had ever seen anything like it before."

"There's all sorts of technology in Molanse. Maybe you should visit sometime, educate yourself." She cast a worried glance at Gil. He was staring at the boy, still sound asleep. He had rolled onto his side, and one hand had fallen off the table. He was mumbling in his sleep, but Zee couldn't make out the words. The large, open library distorted most sounds.

Finished with her second stack upon the table, Zee returned to the mess. She set to sorting the books into separate piles ready for transporting. "You don't have to watch him like that. He's asleep, and besides, he certainly doesn't seem like a threat to me."

She felt Gil's glare hot on her back. "So you and I didn't feel the same wave of magic knock us to the ground back there?" Gil shot back.

"I didn't say he wasn't powerful, just that he's not a threat. When we came in, he was a wreck. Without his magic, he doesn't even look like he could lift a book, let alone a weapon. I know it sounds crazy, but I don't think he's to blame. I know you think he's the one that took your memories. It's frustrating, trust me— I know. I can't remember anything before a few years ago, myself. But you don't see me taking it out on everyone around me."

Gil huffed, and she heard him get to his feet. "I can fix it, though. Get rid of the source." His whispers roamed the library, reaching Zee's ears.

She spun to ask him what he meant, and saw Gil glowering over Arion, defenseless in his slumber.

There was a blur of gray and gleaming silver as someone bolted into the room, headed straight for Gil. They tackled him away from Arion and backed him against another table. She couldn't see the newcomer's face, and panic filled her. Zee was running after him before she knew it, unsure what she was even planning to do. She didn't particularly trust Gil, or even like him, but she couldn't trust a stranger, either. Something caught the light, and changed her mind immediately. The small familiar blue gem of her dagger flashed in the light, now in Gil's hands.

Zee slammed into the wall next to the two men, and wrestled her knife away from Gil. Once the knife was back in her possession, she turned it toward the intruder. A snarl started low in her throat, but she cut it off instantly, lowering the dagger as she did. Holding Gil against the wall was Jayr.

The two men were yelling at each other. Zee's mind was spinning with thought, and most of their argument was lost on her. All she caught were the repeated words of *Droll* and *Draken* used as insults.

Cy and the other demon were behind them instantly, Cy placing himself as a shield before Arion. His voice boomed over everything else, *"What the hell is going on?"*

Jayr released Gil mostly, but one arm remained across his chest to keep him on the wall. He spoke bluntly, "Gil was going to kill him."

Gil rushed to defend himself, pulling Jayr's arm, "It's not even my knife! You said you know me, Cy. Are you really going to trust this Draken over me? Get him off already!"

Cy looked between the two of them, and then to the dagger in Zee's hands. She tucked it behind her back, her cheeks burning red.

"It's yours?" Cy asked, jumping straight to the conclusion she so wished he wouldn't have. She pulled her hands out sheepishly.

"I wasn't going to use it," she lied. "It was just for self defense. It's a new land to me, you know."

Cy flinched at her words, and disappointment filled his eyes. The expression tore a hole in her stomach that she couldn't understand. *I've barely known him for a day. Why do I care what he thinks of me?*

"It was on the table," she tried again, nearly begging Cy to believe her. "He grabbed it while I wasn't looking. I was just picking up the books, I swear."

Cy nodded, though his expression didn't soften.

Suddenly, Gil growled and ripped himself free of the other man. "Why are you defending him? After everything he's done, you treat him like some dumb child. He's destroying everything!"

"Actually, he's not. Someone else is," Jayr said. Gil shoved him away, but the Draken simply bit his lip and stepped away.

"What do you mean, Jayr?" Cy asked.

Jayr sighed heavily. "Theresa's alive."

Cy gasped, but Gil was the one to speak. "What do you know? If she was still alive, I would know about it."

Jayr glared at Gil, and leaned against the wall. "Just because you're part of the rebel group doesn't mean you get all the information. Even after being gone for two years, I have a higher rank than you."

"How is that?" Gil spat.

"Because I used to be Theresa's biggest supporter, her right hand man. And they think I'm still on her side."

"You expect us to just trust whoever you've been talking to? Why couldn't they come and tell us themselves?"

Jayr sneered. "If I had brought anyone back with me, they would have tried to kill Arion. Much like you just did."

Gil narrowed his eyes, but Jayr didn't give him a chance to speak. "A few people are claiming to be getting letters from Theresa, commands. I saw them myself, and the handwriting looks to be hers. She's trying to start a war overseas with Molanse. She wants them to wipe out Lontorra all together. She's telling her followers Lontorra is beyond saving, and the only thing to do is destroy it and start over. Everyone is so desperate that they don't have a choice but go along with her. Her supporters were guaranteed to be evacuated, but that's probably a lie."

There was a strained pause from Jayr as he broke off to stare at the wall.

"What else?" Cy asked. He shoved Jayr's shoulder lightly, but the Draken didn't move.

"The Drakens are the ones that made the zeppelins, and the ones sending them over. We're a race of fighters, and most of them are restless. She's been using our blacksmiths for their craftsmanship, and getting the Mages to make the smoke bombs. They all think they can get out before an attack, or fight their way out if they need to. I don't trust Theresa to let my people go so easily. I managed to convince them to stall the next zeppelin, but not for long. I told them I came to warn them that Molanse was getting close to declaring war, but we need to be unpredictable to give them the final push. We can't let Theresa wreak havoc any longer, we have to stop her."

"So, what? She's still pulling the strings from wherever she's hiding?" Cy asked.

Jayr nodded, and Cy groaned. *"Please tell me you know where that is."*

"No one does," Jayr said as he shook his head. "Or at least, no one's saying. There's not much information that I can't get, so my guess is just no one actually knows."

"I know," Arion said, struggling into a sitting position. Zee tucked the dagger behind her again, hoping he didn't know how close to death he had just been.

"Arion, what did you say?" Cy asked, incredulous.

Arion looked around at the people around him. "If you're right and Theresa isn't dead, then I think I know where she would have gone."

CHAPTER 16

Zayla

Arion dug through Zee's neat stacks of books she had made on the table, returning them to utter chaos. She clenched her fists to hold herself back from attacking him, tight enough that her nails bit into her palms. Having not found what he was looking for, he left the destruction and moved to the nearest shelf, where he picked up books seemingly at random, studied them, and threw them over his shoulder when he was done with them.

Zee turned her back on the chaos, and busied herself with the books on the table. She stacked them hurriedly, not having the focus to sort them back the way they had been. She grumbled under her breath, "He has this massive library, and doesn't even care or respect all these books. How could he?"

"Found it," Arion called. She took a deep breath, and turned slowly, keeping her gaze fixed above the cluttered floor. Arion was approaching the group, a small black leather-bound book raised above his head. As he got closer, Zee could see a tiny white point sticking out from the pages somewhere in the middle of the book.

Arion let it fall open in his hands, and thumbed through the pages quickly. As he passed the saved page, a fluffy white feather drifted to the floor. "This book wasn't always here," Arion began to explain as he searched the book's contents. The words were scrawled across the page in a neat looping script. The words were thin and packed close together, even overlapping in some places, and more words were lost in the edges and bindings of the book. It looked like some sort of journal.

"I don't even know when it appeared. It was just here one day. Snow has been by a few times, checking in. He must have left it, but he never told me."

Cy moved to Arion's side, easily reading the book over Arion's shoulder. Despite Arion's earlier behavior, he was handling the pages with great care. Zee forced herself to relax as she watched Arion lift the book to show something to Cy.

"Here," Arion said, pointing. Cy read the page silently, his mouth moving as he went.

"*This is...*" Cy started, the color draining from his face.

Arion nodded enthusiastically. "It's Crestyss'. These are the experiments he did with blood and magic. What he did to the Vamyr kids."

Cy backed away, his lip twisted in disgust. *"How does this help us find Theresa?"*

Arion opened his mouth, then bent back over the book. He flipped a few more pages, and stopped. On one side was a sketch of what looked like the ocean, the other page filled with more of the same script. Arion read aloud, *"The world starts and stops here, where glass covers the ground instead of sand. When the sun dips to touch the horizon, the sea and sky glow as violet as her eyes. And when the stars gleam, there is a touch of humanity across the water. To be able to watch the sun move across the world— bathing the Wastelands, sitting as a halo on Talgrin, and vanishing behind the mountains before reemerging on the water— is such a gift that I could never have asked for."*

Arion finished the recital, and looked up at the others expectantly. Zee looked around as well, and found confused faces. Far behind her, the other demon erupted in laughter. *"Crestyss wrote that? You have got to be kidding me!"*

"Grite!" Arion barked. He glared across the room, but the corner of his mouth was twitching. The other demon turned away, covering his mouth. He continued to snicker to himself, but kept the noise contained.

When no one else spoke up, Arion answered himself. "The southernmost edge of Lontorra. There's a beach there — my owls saw it. Crestyss' lab has to be down there."

"The south beach is uninhabitable. Nothing's there," Gil argued. His arms had been folded across his chest since they had taken the dagger from him, and Zee had belted it back around her hip. There was no need to hide it now that they all knew it existed, and the weight of it felt better than when it had been pressed between her shoulder blades.

Jayr spoke up then, "The group has looked everywhere they could think of. But like you, none of them even considered the southern beaches. They are treacherous, impossible to reach, and unlivable. Which would make them a perfect hiding spot, for Crestyss and his experiments, or for Theresa."

Gil snorted. "You said it yourself they're impossible to reach. How would a weak and injured Theresa get there?"

"The tunnels," Cy offered.

Arion dropped his head. "Maybe. They were still intact when we got here, but..."

"But now they're not, huh," Cy finished. Arion nodded in shame, though there was no anger or shame in Cy's tone.

Cy ruffled Arion's hair playfully. *"Don't worry about it, kid. We'll figure it out."*

Arion ducked out from under Cy's hand, and sat on the floor. He was suddenly short of breath, clutching the book to his chest. He closed his eyes, slowly gaining control over his breathing.

Cy stepped aside with Jayr and Grite. *"Watch him for me?"* Cy asked Zee. She nodded, and the three of them moved to the other side of the room. Jayr pulled a map out from inside his armor and spread it across the table.

Zee crouched in front of Arion. He was breathing more normally, but his face was paler than it had been before. He looked like he was fighting against sleep.

"Are you okay?" Zee asked softly.

Arion's eyes fluttered open. They wandered for a moment, and finally focused on her. He swallowed audibly, and nodded once. "I will be."

"What's wrong?" she asked, but Arion lowered his head in response. He was playing with his hands. And Zee saw they were smeared with dried blood. She snatched one of his hands. "You're hurt!"

Whimpering from her grip, Arion tried to pull his hand away, but didn't have the strength. Zee's fingers wrapped around his wrist far too easily, overlapping from how thin he was. She shrugged her pack from her shoulder and retrieved a cloth and her water bottle. She laid the cloth across her knee and carefully poured a little water on it. Balling the wet cloth in her hand, she dabbed gently at the blood until it washed away. She released him once she was finished, and held her hand out for the other. Arion hesitated, but relented his other hand over to her.

"Did you cut yourself?" Zee asked. Arion shook her head.

"Did you cough it up? Are you sick?"

Arion shook his head again.

Zee scrunched her face up as she thought. Where else could the blood have come from?

"My magic," Arion finally said as the last traces of blood disappeared from his skin. "Sometimes it's too much for me."

Zee gazed down at the lightning bolt on his hand, and ran her thumb over it. It was an impression in his hand, soft and smooth like a scar.

Forcing a reassuring smile, Zee looked from his scar to his face. "It can't be all bad, can it? I'm sure your magic can do great things, too."

Arion didn't raise his head, but something filled his eyes. They watered a little bit, but he blinked and the tears were gone. "Do you want to see a trick?" he asked.

"Sure." Zee's smile was no longer forced, the idea of something new sparking her genuine interest.

A faint glow emanated from Arion's scar. All around them, the room filled with bright balls of light. They looked like tiny stars, dancing in the air mere inches from her face. The room filled with the heat they gave off, but it felt soothing. Not like the impressing heat of a fire, but more of that of an embrace. As she watched them dance, one star wove between them and landed on the tip of her nose. Her eyes crossed as she followed its path, and she giggled at the sight of it perched on her nose.

The magic in it surged through her, and she felt her

body change. Air tickled the back of her neck as her hair shortened. The glow of the star burned brighter, and she knew that to mean her eyes had lightened.

"Kaitlyn," Arion gasped, a quiver in his voice.

The star on her nose detached and flew away. Distracted by its course, Zee ignored Arion's outburst and followed the star as it went. The whole library was filled with such stars. Cy, Jayr and Grite were swatting them out of the way of the map. Jayr looked mildly annoyed, while Cy watched a few stars with a smile.

Movement from the corner of her eye drew Zee's attention. Gil was swinging for the stars, trying to catch them. He managed to trap one, the fire bright in his cupped hands. He stared at it a long time, clearly lost in thought. Before Zee could ask him what he was thinking, he closed his hand on the star, and the light was gone. He turned to stare at a barren wall, his guard back up.

Cy broke away from the others and approached Gil. They spoke in hushed tones, and Zee wished she could hear them.

Whatever was said, Gil didn't like it. Cy grabbed Gil by the arm and pulled him over to where Zee and Arion were sitting. It was only then that Zee noticed most of the stars had died out. Behind her, Arion's eye's were drooping. He didn't seem to have much energy for himself, reinforcing her idea that he wasn't dangerous.

"*We're going to trade,*" Cy said. He nudged Gil forward, and ropes of purple smoke formed around his wrists. "*Can you come with me?*"

Zee stood, and Cy shoved Gil until he sat down awkwardly next to Arion. This startled Arion to attention, and he pulled his knees to his chest. He eyed Gil oddly, his cheeks flushing. *Of course he's not going to want to sit next to someone so hostile toward him.*

"Are you sure this is a good idea?" Zee asked as Cy led her over to the table.

"We're going to need Arion at full strength, so he needs to sleep. We're not going to leave them alone, so it'll be fine," Cy answered, but he didn't sound very sure himself.

"Do you really think they're going to be willing to help?" Jayr's hushed voice came into earshot as they reached the table.

"Willing, forced, I don't see why the specifics matter. They are going to make what we need," Grite said.

Zee looked between the two demons, wondering how they could really be of the same species. While Cy preferred to look human, the other one, Grite, was a sickly green color and had a tail protruding from his pants. A weird mechanism was wrapped around his leg, but Zee was honestly afraid to ask about it. His voice was hoarse and nasally. Zee got the impression that Grite enjoyed other people's suffering.

"Who's making what?" Zee asked, her curiosity getting the better of her.

"The outcasts in the wasteland. If they can make us some kind of vehicle, we should be able to get to the beach quickly and easily. It's the only thing we can think of."

"A vehicle," Zee echoed. "I thought you only had magic here, not technology."

"We're a bit behind Molanse, but there are a few of us here that believe in technological advancement," Cy quipped.

"The outcasts expanded their territory. The Wastelands wrap around the woods now. We should be able to communicate with them easily," Grite added. This time, his voice sounded

more normal, and it only added to Zee's confusion surrounding the creature.

On cue, in walked the wolf that had escorted them to the castle. He had remained at the entry room when Gil and Zee ran to find the source of the shockwave, saying that his job was to guard the castle. He jumped up on the edge of the table and looked over the map, now with a few lines drawn on it with possible routes.

After a moment of scrutinizing the lines, he placed his paw right in between two of them. "The woods have thinned even more in the back. You don't have to go around, but the path won't be easy. It should still be quicker, though," Tuft informed them.

Tuft was standing so close to Zee, and it took all her strength not to pet him. She had easily gotten over the fact that he could speak. Of all she'd seen that day, a talking animal of any kind was almost expected of this strange land.

"We need the scavengers' help. Can you go to the Wastelands ahead of us and ask for their aide? We need to know before we waste time getting there," Cy asked.

Tuft nodded obediently. He dropped from the table and held himself proudly with his new errand.

Before he left, Tuft went to Arion. He was starting to doze, despite how uncomfortable he had seemed with Gil. Gil was turned away from him, but he stayed where Cy had put him. Tuft nuzzled against Arion's hand, and Arion smiled sleepily at the touch. Zee saw his mouth move, but couldn't hear anything from him. Gil was watching the two of them over his shoulder, his expression softer than Zee would have expected. Arion's head lolled to the side, and his chest rose and fell steadily with sleep. He lay perfectly still otherwise— nothing like the restlessness that had gripped him before.

Tuft squared his shoulders, then bounded from the room silently.

"Seems we have some time to prepare," Jayr said. He set his pencil against the map, tracing the path that Tuft had laid out for them.

"Tuft is fast," Grite warned. *"I'd say he'll be back in an hour, two tops."*

Cy left the table to kneel before Arion and Gil. He lifted the book Arion had showed them. *"Then let's get started."*

While Cy began to scan the book's contents, Zee's attention was stuck to Gil, still watching Arion over his shoulder. She wondered if he thought he was doing it sneakily, but if Zee had noticed, there was no way the others hadn't. But still, no one said a thing.

As though he sensed Zee's gaze, Gil turned away abruptly. Though he was mostly hidden behind his back, Zee could see Gil lift his hand and open it. A green light was cast over his shoulder, the last of the stars Arion had made.

* * *

CY HAD to force Arion to let him carry him on his back once they exited the castle. Arion had nearly tripped over the smoothest halls inside the castle, and his pace was slower than the others. He hung on tightly around Cy's neck, facing away from the rest of the group.

Where it had taken Tuft just over an hour there and back, it took the group almost two just to reach the edge of the woods, where trash had begun to spill from the Wastelands' borders. Arion wasn't the only one weakened; Grite needed frequent stops, though his pace had matched the others for the most part. Cy had used his magic to reinforce the brace on his leg after the third rest, and they were able to make it to their destination without another hindrance.

Arion made Cy put him on the ground at the first sight of debris, not wanting to reveal his weakened state. Cy protested, but Jayr agreed that they shouldn't let anyone else know how easy Arion would be to kill.

Tuft was waiting at the border, along with an older bearded man. He wore ragged and torn clothes, even worse than anything Zee had ever had to wear. They were stained with black oil and red rust spots. Zee couldn't even be sure of the clothing's original color through the grime and dirt that covered him. His skin matched his clothing, dirty and tanned and splotched with oil. A crooked smile broke through his gnarled beard that tangled with his long, gray hair. A patchwork belt was slung across his chest, pockets spilling screws and small scraps.

"Good to see ya, boys!" the man yelled out. "What are we making? Everyone's itching for another one of your big ideas."

The man swung his arm over Arion's shoulders, and he groaned with the weight. He slunk out of the embrace and faced the group that had quickly formed.

Arion cleared his throat, and his voice came out surprisingly strong. "We need something like the bikes we made before, but sturdier. Bigger, better, more wheels, the works. All of us need to fit, and we're going over rough terrain. Who's up for a challenge?"

The crowd cheered and scattered among the piles of garbage. They returned one by one, getting the approval or dismissal from Arion on what could and couldn't be used.

Arion had fallen into a leader role easily, and it surprised Zee.

Inching toward Cy, Zee whispered, "Is it a good idea to use this...junk?"

Cy chuckled. *"The original zeppelin came from this junk. Not the ones you saw, but the first one Arion made that inspired the others. It got him to Centric, so it worked. Don't worry, they know what they're doing."*

Arion was being swarmed by people asking him about parts, or for advice, or to jump on the machine himself. Cy stepped forward, yelling over the crowd that he would assist them, and Arion was in charge of planning.

"Stay with these two," Jayr instructed as he joined the crowd, helping a scavenger that was struggling to lift a large piece. Zee tried to stop him, but he was gone before she could get a word out in her defense.

Grite had sat down in the shadows of a tree as soon as they had stopped. Cy's magic had faded from his leg. The brace was at his side. His pants had been rolled up, and Zee turned away quickly at the sight. It looked like there was a hole ripped straight through his leg, but there was no way anyone could survive something like that, not even a demon. She glanced over carefully, and morbidly wondered about the cloth tied around his head.

Gil leaned against the tree beside her. His hands were still bound by magic in front him. Jayr had been in charge of carrying his and Cyllorian's bags for the trip, and they were now resting at her feet. "Can I have some water?" Gil asked sheepishly.

There was something strange in his tone, and he held himself as if he were wounded. He looked defeated and exhausted. Zee retrieved Gil's water from his pack and handed it to him. "Finally given up?" she joked while he drank.

Gil finished and corked his bottle, returning it to Zee. "You still don't think he's dangerous? Just look at the way he rallied a whole colony of people behind him," Gil pushed.

"Just because you're a successful leader doesn't mean you're a bad person. I'm sure you're still pissed about the memory thing, I get it. But he said he's tried, and it can't be removed. Aren't you getting tired of being mad all the time?" Zee spat.

She felt a twinge in the back of her throat, and swallowed it down. She hated thinking about her own lost memories. *At least you had a childhood, and know who your parents are. I have nothing, and you don't see me trying to kill people because of it!* She wanted to scream her thoughts at Gil, but unleashing her own anger wouldn't help either of them.

Gil was staring down at the magic that bound him. The purple smoke swirled endlessly around his wrists, surging in bright colors at every move he made. He didn't answer.

Instead, he pushed away from the tree and started toward Cyllorian. Zee followed close behind him, her hand hovering over the dagger at her hip. She was grateful that Arion wasn't near Cy, but...where was he?

She scanned the crowd quickly, and found Arion kneeling in front of a large carriage, magic sparking from his fingertips. The scavengers had reached Cy, and he was watching over Arion with obvious pride and relief.

Gil stepped to block Cy's view, and raised his bound hands in his face. Cy glared at him, but Gil said, "I want to help."

Cy's eyes went wide. Then he called out, *"Hey, Arion?"*

Arion turned immediately. *"You need another hand?"* Cy asked, gesturing to Gil.

Arion looked between the two of them. His cheeks lit up bright red, and he nodded while turning back to the machine.

Cy sighed, but released the magic. Gil shook his hands out, and went to kneel beside Arion. The crowd of scavengers parted to let him in, and Arion instructed Gil to hold the next piece that needed to be attached.

"Progress," Cy muttered, amusement in his voice.

Chapter 17

Arion

It was a surprise to everyone when Zee was the first to volunteer to drive the massive, six-wheeled beast Arion and the scavengers had managed to build in only two days. She admitted to stealing vehicles overseas for what she called "joyriding." Cy was all too willing to relinquish control, and Arion hadn't the strength to take on the task.

The car, as Zee had called it, bumped over the uneven earth. The large tires didn't care about rocks or branches or roots that got in their way, it simply bounded over everything. Which had been the plan, but none of them had been prepared for the trip.

Arion busied himself studying the group that had willingly joined him. Behind him, Grite and Gil were fighting over the limited seat space. This time, no one had argued about Grite joining them, though Arion was sure Cy still had reasons to despise him. After everything that had happened, Arion couldn't bring himself to send Grite away.

Any minute now, Arion was sure he would wake up. This had to be a twisted dream his own mind had created to torture him, just like all his other nightmares. He had to admit that his usual nightmares hadn't been bothering him as much as they had in the past. This would be a new breed of suffering all of his own making, and he couldn't say that he didn't deserve it.

If he wasn't dreaming, perhaps he had finally lost all control of himself and this was his afterlife. Perhaps Cy was still dead, and was bound to wander aimlessly with Arion, and it was all his fault. If he'd only been quicker, been smarter, or stronger. Maybe if he'd been more ruthless and had destroyed the tower himself with Crestyss in it, none of them would have had to die. If it wasn't for Arion, they all could have lived happily—

An astoundingly big bump in the path jerked Arion from his depressive memory. A branch reached into the car and slashed Arion's arm. His breath came in a hiss at the pain that shot through him. Blood dripped steadily as he waited for the wound to close. *There's no pain inside dreams. And blood means that my heart is beating. This is real.*

I'm not dead, yet, he told himself as he set his mind back to the task at hand; killing Theresa.

Again.

This time he had help, and he knew better than to push them away.

Jayr had one hand outside of the car, gripping the roof like his life depended on it. His other hand was struggling to hold the map across his lap against the wind's best attempts to snatch it from him. They had fit the front of the car with a pane of glass at Zee's advice, but the sides were left open to save on time. Only a thick frame and belts slung across their bodies kept them in the vehicle.

Jayr's motives were questionable. Last Arion suspected, Jayr should have been angry at him for embarrassing him in front of Theresa. They had never spoken a word otherwise. Though he was suspicious, Arion couldn't deny that having someone that had previously been so close to Theresa was useful.

Zee was the only one making any noise, a solid stream of curses pouring from her mouth with everything the car hit. Every so often, Jayr would shout out a direction, loudly so he could be heard over the wind. Zee would jerk the car to follow, and everyone would cling to the body of the car as they were thrown around.

Arion glanced beside him at Cyllorian. He looked to be doing better than he had been on the bikes, but this couldn't go nearly as fast. Still faster than walking, but slower than the bikes. His talons were dug into the seat between them.

Arion flinched as Gil shouted at Grite behind him, when a sudden turn had knocked the demon into him. "Will you stop touching me!" he snapped, shoving Grite away. Grite laughed and began to tease Gil. They had been trapped in such small proximity for hours already, their speed hindered while in the woods, and there was no telling just how much longer the journey would be.

Arion took the opportunity with everyone distracted to speak to Cy. "Are you scared?"

Cy looked at him quizzically. *"Theresa didn't have any magic left two years ago, I doubt she has much going for her. She's hiding because she can't fight back."*

"That's not what I meant. I was talking about me."

"I gotta say, you aren't looking too good. But after this we'll

get you eating better, and figure out your nightmares. You'll be back to normal in no time."

Arion gritted his teeth. He couldn't tell if Cy was really this oblivious, or if he was avoiding Arion's real question on purpose. "Are you scared *of me*, not for me!"

Cy sighed, staring straight ahead at the trees Zee was barely dodging. *"Arion,"* he started in exasperation.

"I know you were afraid of me, everyone was. Everyone except…"

Arion cut himself off. It wasn't the conversation he wanted to have, and he focused himself. "I was out of control. I know you were all terrified of what I would do."

Cy thought for a long moment, long enough that Arion nearly gave up on getting a straight answer out of him. *"I was never scared of you, at least, not in the way you think. I was afraid of what you would do to yourself, the complete disregard for your own safety. It's gotten us in so many messes, I can't even count. But I think the fact that you can acknowledge that means you're doing better. Yes, I knew you were wild and unpredictable. You didn't always make the best call. But I'll be honest with you, after everything and with how well I know you, a big part of me didn't even expect to find you still alive when I got here."*

"I couldn't do it," Arion admitted. "I wanted to, but I couldn't."

"Why didn't you?" Cy asked. It didn't sound like he actually wanted an answer— or to be talking about it at all.

"I knew you would be mad if I did."

Cy huffed loudly. *"Damn right, I would have. I'm still plenty pissed that you tried to go after Crestyss by yourself."*

"Grite was with me," Arion offered, knowing just how ridiculous it sounded even to him.

"*Yeah, 'cause he's the best role model you could ever ask for.*"

Arion laughed, a weight off his shoulders. Cy surprised him when he spoke again.

"*It seems like something finally clicked in your head. I wouldn't say you're completely better, but you're different from before. We'll handle Theresa, together, then we'll do whatever it takes to help you get better. We can do whatever you want, we won't have anything to worry about anymore. Hell, we can leave Lontorra altogether if you want to. Just get away from everything.*"

Arion thought for a long moment. It was a future he had never granted himself even a glimpse at. Complete freedom, no worries, and Cy beside him.

A pit of guilt opened in his stomach at the thought of leaving. "I think Lontorra needs some help, too," Arion suggested.

"*Then we'll do that together, too. This place really has gone to shit, hasn't it? Not that it was the best to begin with, but there's always room for improvement.*"

A smile settled on Arion's face, but he was shook from his reverie as the car veered sharply. One side lifted high into the air, and Arion feared the thing would tip over completely. It slammed back down onto the ground, and Zee yelled a curse that broke through everything.

The woods were behind them, and they had just crossed a border of boulders buried in the sand around the empty beach. The horizon glinted on all sides, the world open in a way that they could see everything.

And everything meant absolutely nothing, because there was nothing at all to be found as far as the eye could see.

The car slowed drastically, the tires sinking into the

soft sand. Zee was leaning forward, slamming her fist against the steering will. "Move, dammit!" she yelled at the car. Her rage was getting the better of her, and her hair was flaring bright red, flowing in the wind like flames.

Arion thought back to the glimpse he had gotten of her when his magic touched her, the seamless change, until she looked like Kaitlyn exactly as he had remembered. He turned to ask Cy what he knew about her, but Grite lunged forward between them, pointing straight ahead.

"The colors!" he shouted excitedly. They all stared at the horizon. The sun was nearly touching the water, and the scenery was bathed in violet light. Arion could no longer tell where the sky ended and the ocean began, only a vibrant purple that threatened to swallow them.

Jayr jumped from the car, and the others followed his lead. Zee kicked at the front tire once she was out, cursing the machine again. Almost in a trance, Arion stepped forward, blindly walking to what looked like the end of the world.

Something clinked under foot, breaking his stride. He looked down, and found shimmering stones of every color. He lifted a blue one the size of his palm and held it up to the light. The world contorted behind the stone, as though he were looking through one of the painted windows of the castle.

"Glass covers the ground instead of sand. This is it," Arion breathed.

"And it's exactly what we thought we'd find. Nothing," Gil quipped bitterly. He picked up a purple rock and threw it as hard as he could. It clattered among the glass beach, musical sounds echoing around them.

The group scattered over the beach, walking the length of it slowly. Zee had gone the closest to the edge, and was staring across the water. The violet hue over the world was fading, and the horizon held peaks and ridges in the far distance.

"There's so much more out there, isn't there?" Zee asked loudly.

The others glanced at her, but she didn't seem to be looking for an answer from any of them. They wandered the grounds in near silence. Waves splashed messily over the stones, the wind whistled around them, and the glass clinked noisily where they walked. They had entered a whole new world of music at the edge of Lontorra.

It was a world that obviously no other had seen before.

Slowly, Arion approached Gil, who had paused for a moment to launch glass rocks into the sea. He stood just inside the reach of the coming tide, the cold water lapping over his bare feet. The sun and water reflected the scales that had returned where the water touched him.

"I'm sorry," Arion breathed. He made sure he was out of range if Gil retaliated. His words made Gil pause, and he dropped the rock he had been about to throw. He turned toward Arion, his expression blank.

Arion missed the Gil that had chased him around the castle before, the Gil who would talk his ear off without even caring whether he was listening or not. He cursed himself for being so selfish, for ever thinking that lost memories could be a good thing.

He had thought it would be easier for all of them to move on after his intentions of going down with Crestyss. But it had done nothing but blow up in his face. Arion had been the one to lose everything, but he wasn't the only one to suffer.

"You really can't get my memories back, can you?" Gil

finally asked, surprising Arion. He didn't sound angry, he sounded defeated and desperate.

Arion struggled with his own voice, "I—I tried before. I promise, I couldn't—"

"Try again," Gil cut him off. He stepped toward Arion.

Instinctively, Arion backed away. He hated to, but he couldn't help thinking of the sight of Gil holding a dagger over him. He had tried to forget it, ignore it, to pretend he didn't know it happened. But the image was burned in his mind. He hadn't realized there could be something worse than losing Cy and Kait...and Gil, but to see one of them try to kill him was even worse than his nightmares.

"You said it didn't work before because I didn't want my memories back. What if I changed my mind? What if I want them now?" Gil pressed.

The possibilities flooded Arion's mind, along with his own memories. He felt his cheeks burn, and he forced himself to calm down. He couldn't guarantee it would work. And if it did, there was no telling if Gil would go back to how he had been before. He could still just as likely hate Arion, maybe even more than he did without his memories.

"Well? Can you try again?" Gil asked. Gil was standing directly in front of Arion now. He was so close that Arion froze. Gil had spent the last two years as far from Arion as he could be. The last time they had been so close was when Arion kissed him.

Arion nodded sheepishly. Gil let out a sigh of relief and closed his eyes.

Arion's hand shook as he reached forward and pressed his palm to Gil's forehead. Closing his own eyes, the bolt on his hand began to burn. Gil squirmed under his touch, but didn't pull away. Arion focused on the magic, and dove into Gil's mind. It wasn't hard to find the block that had formed. Arion knew right where it was from the last time he had tried, though physical contact made it even easier to reach. He could see it as though it were in his own mind, glowing and pulsing. The magic surged as it flowed, spilling sparks from it. Somehow it seemed weaker than he remembered, the light dimmer. Through the sparks, Arion thought he could see a crack forming in the center.

Unsure what else to do, he attacked the wall with his magic, aiming for the cracks within it.

His magic rebounded instantly, sending a shock back through Arion's arm. He felt his chest tighten and his heart skipped a beat. Collapsing to the ground, he struggled to find his breath. He fought back his tears, both from the pain and the disappointment.

"I can't," Arion croaked, and coughed. "I can't break it."

Gil didn't speak. Disappointment was plastered to his face as he turned and walked further into the coming waves. He walked along the shore, away from Arion.

Once the pain had subsided, Arion stood and trudged back to the border between the glass and the sand. He found his own path to search in the stretching shadows of the trees beyond.

An hour passed and the sun had nearly gone by the time they had paced up and down the beach, returning to where they had left the vehicle. Taking a break to snack on their provisions, they gathered to rest themselves. Grite climbed into the vehicle, stretching his damaged leg across an entire bench. He was the only one that seemed to be eating normally. The others ate absentmindedly, picking at their rations.

Gil ate from a mix of nuts and berries with one hand, and launched glass stones across the beach with the other.

Zee had her eyes fixed on the now-glowing land across the sea. Jayr was studying his map as he sat a noticeable distance away from the others. He muttered to himself around a mouthful of food, and had to sweep crumbs from the map.

Cy was watching them all in turn, and when his eyes came to rest on Arion, he turned away from the concern they held.

Arion had the journal spread over one leg, using his other knee to hold it open while he scanned the pages. There must have been something he missed, some clue that would help him find Crestyss' lab.

"We better start digging," Gil said with a groan. Arion's head shot up at the idea, and immediately buried his hands in the stones. He managed to get deep enough that the glass wrapped around his wrists. His fingers found cold, wet, rough stones beneath, and he searched blindly.

"What are you doing?" Gil snapped. He was towering above Arion, glaring down at him. Everyone else had stood and were surrounding the vehicle. They were scraping sand away from the tires, rocking the vehicle out of the ruts they made.

Arion's face burned. "Digging?" he offered.

Gil scoffed. "We've wasted all day on this, and now you're just playing? The night here will get brutally cold, and we need to leave before that happens. Get off your ass and help us get out of here. Use your magic to get this thing to move."

"What about Theresa? We have to find her!" Arion jumped to his feet, scraping his hands on the rocks as he yanked them free. He shook the water from them, feeling the salt seep into the shallow cuts before they could heal.

"She's not here!" Gil yelled, startling Arion. He flinched

away, and Gil seemed to force himself to soften his tone. "We've looked, and there's nothing here. We don't even know when your book was written. Crestyss could have destroyed the lab years ago to hide any evidence, if it even existed in the first place. We tried, and we have to move on. If Theresa really is alive, she's somewhere else."

"There's nowhere left to look. Her followers have scoured every other inch of Lontorra," Jayr interjected.

"Then she's not on Lontorra," Gil shot back, exasperated.

Cy stepped between Gil and Jayr before either of them could speak again. *"If she's not in Lontorra, we'll never find her."*

"She's here," Arion whispered. "I can feel it. Two years ago, in the Tower, I could feel where Crestyss was. Now, I can feel Theresa."

Gil huffed and walked back to the vehicle. He dropped into the front seat, crossing his arms. "Then you can look by yourself. Can't you do anything with your magic?"

Cy started to berate Gil for the clear insult, but Arion hadn't taken it so harshly. He'd been so focused on *looking...*

Standing to face north, inland to Lontorra, Arion ran backwards until the remains of Talgrin peeked out from over the tree. He could practically see an imprint in the sky where the sun would have ringed the top of the Tower, just as Crestyss had written it. Behind him, humanity rested on the horizon, clear as ever. This was the spot.

Arion buried his left hand in the stones until he felt the cold water on his fingertips. He used the water to send a current of magic out from him, covering the whole of the beach. Light surged upward, a rainbow of colors shown through each and every piece of glass.

The light faded slowly just as the sun fell beneath the horizon. Arion looked up to see the navy black sky speckled with brilliant stars. The wind had died and the tide calmed. Not even a breath could be heard as Arion waited.

Not more than a foot in front of him, the ground lifted where a metal door opened in the earth.

CHAPTER 18

Arion

The halls of the underground laboratory were a maze in themselves. Arion held the journal open in front of him, guiding the group through tunnels and avoiding traps. With his magic, the pages of the book were aglow. Beside him, Cy held his hand and cast a soft purple light through the halls.

"Not too bright," Arion cautioned as they entered the first room to be found. "We can't let Theresa know we're here."

Cy clicked his tongue, but obliged. The light receded into his palm, and shadows threatened to overtake the room.

The room was filled with shelves lining the walls. The mix of empty and filled jars reflected the light grotesquely across the walls. Arion didn't have to look to know the jars' contents— the book told him more than he ever wanted to know.

Zee had wandered over to a shelf, and just as quickly retreated, her hand covering her mouth. "How much blood did he need?" she whispered. Her face was pale in the light. Arion wasn't sure if the green in her cheeks was a reflection from a jar of mold, or from disgust.

In the center of the room sat an ornate desk, covered in dust. It faced toward them, the chair that sat behind it obscuring the doorway on the opposite wall.

Jayr's armor clinked as he tried the drawers on the desk, but they held shut. Small, rusted keyholes shone as Arion stepped closer, the light from the book crawling over the surface of the desk. Ignoring the dust, Arion scooped a stack of papers from the desk and shuffled through them. They were overflowing with more of Crestyss' scrolling script. The ink had bled from time and damage, most of the words unreadable. Arion left them a mess in the dirt, and summoned the others to the next doorway.

The next hall was unusually wide, allowing them through in two lines. Cy and Jayr walked alongside Arion in the front, Jayr helping to decipher a scrawled map that took up half a page. Zee, Grite and Gil took up the rear. Zee had changed herself to give her talons and a spiked tail that swung heavily behind her. She was careful not to let it hit the wall, but it came close. Grite was struggling to keep up, bracing himself against the opposite wall so he wouldn't break stride.

Arion was hyper aware of Gil directly behind him, and the loaded crossbow pointed just over his right shoulder. It was nice to have Gil on his side again. He swallowed the lump in his throat as he wondered how long it would last once this was all over.

"*What's that?*" Cy hissed, making the group stop. He had paused in front of a thick door with a large glass window. A metal bar was spread across the door. Cy wiped at the grimy window, squinting through it. With a groan he hefted the bar up and out of the way.

The door squeaked on rusted hinges, opening into a small room. A long table sat to one side, the metal still gleaming despite its age. On the other side was a small desk, an array of tools spread out over the top.

Cy stepped into the room, and lost his footing. He stumbled forward, but caught himself easily once he realized what had thrown him off. The floor was angled toward the center, where holes opened up in the steel tiles for a drain.

Arion shivered at the sight, his memories of the torture coming back to him. He spared a glance back at Grite, but the demon was focused on the table, a dark look in his eyes.

He caught Arion staring at him, and said, *"It took a lot of work to make a human body accept a demon's essence."*

A brief glimpse of a memory flashed in Arion's mind—one of Grite's before this body had changed owners. There was a blinding light, and white hot pain, then darkness. In the darkness, Arion's ears rang with the sounds of distant screams.

Across the room at the table, Cy held up one tool after another. There was a long, thin knife, a strange hook with an eye like a needle on the end, syringes, flat pliers, and many more tools beyond Arion's imagination for their uses.

Cy picked up an especially cruel looking one; a large spoon with a thick handle. There was a thin bar that hugged the inside of the scoop. Cy pressed a lever on the side, and the metal slid along the inside, and back into place. Cy grimaced, then slowly held the thing in front of his eye. It was the perfect size for removing eyes.

Cy chucked the scoop against the table, then grimaced at the loud sound that echoed in the room around him. Arion whirled, but found the door had closed silently behind him. He sighed in relief that the sound had been contained along with them.

"Let's go," Arion offered, shoving his weight against the door. Gil was the closest one to Arion, and he added his weight to the door. They shoved it open with great effort, the metal groaning in protest. They exited quickly, and Arion turned to thank Gil, but he had already fallen back into a defensive position, waiting obediently.

They passed several similar rooms, with slightly different tools inside. One room had a table built with railings and restraints. The walls were lined with sealed vats, thick tubes spreading from them like tentacles as they reached for the table.

The surgery rooms ended, and the containment rooms began. They were sealed with the same thick metal doors, their windows larger than before. Small slits had been cut in the doors, barely thick enough to fit a hand through. Inside were soiled beds, holes in the floor, and empty bowls in the corner. Some rooms even had multiple beds, or small cages nestled within them. The floors weren't as clean as the surgical rooms had been, stained dark with any number of things.

The hallway ended abruptly, with the side opening into a large room with a domed ceiling, the highest they had seen since they had gone underground. Arion wondered just how far they had come— what part of Lontorra were they under?

This room had the worst damage of them all. The

walls, the floor, even the ceiling were pitch black. At first, Arion thought it had just been made from dark stones, but the trails of dried fluid clung to the walls. He touched it, and it came away thick like sludge on his finger, revealing the copper brickwork beneath the mess. Arion swallowed the bile that rose in his throat, wiping the sludge low on his pants.

"Don't touch anything," he whispered as he took a cautious step into the room. He urged his light just a tiny bit brighter, willing it to reach the four walls and nothing more.

Scraps of furniture were spread around the room, burned and torn to such pieces that he couldn't tell what they had been originally. One table seemed to have barely survived against one wall. Most of it was charred black, and the flasks it held were spilled over it, but it stood nonetheless.

Against the other wall, thick chains had been set into the stone. Three of them lay curled on the floor, rungs broken in half.

Surrounding the chains, the wall held deep etchings of flowers in both the grime and the stone beneath.

A thick black whip lashed out from the shadows of the corner. It swung wildly side by side. The tip of it slashed into Zee's head. Her eyes rolled back into her skull, and she fell to the ground with a spasm.

As the whip came round again, it thudded into Gil with the heaviest part, launching him across the room. He crashed into the table, and it crumbled beneath him. He was covered with wood splinters and glass shards as a half full vial broke over his head. He lay still in the wreckage, groaning.

The whip pulled back, and Cy lunged for Zee. The whip

swept across the floor, coating itself in gunk, and caught Cy's ankle. He twisted to catch himself, but his hands slipped on the grime covering the floor. His face slammed down, and his own red blood poured from his nose to mix with the black goop now blinding him. He wiped his face with a low growl, shifting into his demon form.

Arion felt his magic surge with anger, and he filled the room with electricity that cut through the grime, disintegrating it where they collided. Across the room, the attacker recoiled at the light, but quickly recovered. Their head lifted with jerking movements, until the familiar smile greeted them.

Twila had one chain bound to her right wrist. Her left wrist was bare, save for a long black gash in her flesh, from which the whip protruded. Her tattered dress was splotched black and red like an animal hide. Black tears poured silently from her eyes. A tongue lashed out from between the twisted, cracked smile, to lap them up.

The whip sprung to life again, slashing across the room faster than before. Twila was dragged into the wall, her side colliding with the base of the chain that held her. Her smile spread wider as she screamed, an eerie yell that sounded more animal than human. Her blackened eyes rolled back, her body going limp, but the whip's movement immediately brought her back to consciousness.

Arion pulled a small tube from his wrist, and flicked it outward. A spear sprung forth from the handle, catching the whip as it curled toward him. "Jayr, keep this thing busy! Cy get me a handcuff!" Arion yelled.

He bolted forward without waiting for a reply, ducking and weaving around the pulsing tentacle made of magic and blood.

The whip stilled just before it slammed down on Arion.

He heard Jayr grunting behind him. Out of the corner of his eye, he could see Cy inching along the wall toward the pile of ruined chains.

Twila screamed again, and the tentacle split into four smaller ones, moving even faster than the original had. Blood splattered when it broke apart, and the drops burned where they touched Arion's skin. He shook them off, refusing to slow down.

He stabbed one into the ground and it writhed disgustingly. Twila cried out in pain again, but it was clear she was losing her strength. The four tentacles were throwing her around the far end of the room, moving as though they had minds of their own. Her head lolled to the side, and she locked eyes with Arion. There was desperation clear in her eyes, mixed with guilt.

Arion jerked his spear free from the stone, slicing the tentacle off in one swift movement. It spasmed and retreated, but Arion was relieved to see that it didn't grow back. He smiled as he spun the spear upwards, nearly cutting through another one. It fell to the floor, sweeping back and forth weakly.

The other two were busy trying to pry the sword from Jayr. Arion spared him a glance. Blood was running into his eye from a cut on his head, but he was winning his fight. Both of the tentacles were significantly shorter than they had been, and small chunks littered the floor at Jayr's feet.

Arion dove forward, ducking under the whips so he wouldn't draw their attention. "*Cyllorian!*"

Cy had been slowly making his way along the left wall. Gashes were in the grime on the floor from Cy dragging the chains around. He was inspecting the third chain, slashing at the end with his talons. He was covered in black gunk from his search, but he didn't even seem to notice when it splattered on his face as he sawed through the chain.

Cy held up the cuff in triumph. Just as Arion slid under the base of the weakened tentacle, Cy tossed the cuff to him. Arion threw his spear to the ground and caught the cuff, nearly slipping on the fresh blood that slicked the floor.

Twila's head was rolled back, and the arm that held the whips was bent at an unnatural angle. She was muttering something quietly, but it sounded more like an animal whimpering than it did human speech.

Arion snatched his spear and it swept it along the floor. It splashed through the puddles of blood and caught on Twila's ankle. There was a sickening *snap* in the air when it connected, and her legs gave out from under her. Jayr yelped in surprise as the tentacles were ripped away, pulled down to the ground as Twila fell.

Arion pounced on top of her and slammed the cuff down around her bare wrist. The tentacles lashed out desperately, cutting into Arion's face and arms. He grit his teeth, and sent a surge of magic into the cuff. It glowed red hot under his touch, and he felt his skin searing where they touched. The metal twisted and bent until it squeezed Twila's wrist, melding together seamlessly as though it had never been broken.

Twila spasmed under him. Magic shot throughout the tentacles, ripping them apart from the inside out. The tentacles jerked feebly until his magic had turned them completely into dust. Black blood pooled in the gash on Twila's arm, coagulating into a thick bubbled mess on the skin.

Twila collapsed, and in the sudden calm, Arion could

finally make sense of what she had been saying, "I'm sorry, Hunter. Hunter. I'm so sorry."

She repeated the words over and over. Arion wasn't sure if she even knew any other words, after all she must have gone through.

Arion wiped the tears from her cheeks, relieved to see they had actually stopped flowing. "Is Theresa here?" Arion asked slowly.

Twila's eyes whirled in her head, and she tried to focus on Arion. The whites were bloodshot with blackened veins. Lifting the arm that wasn't broken, she pointed behind her. Where Arion thought the wall was especially thick with grime was actually a doorway, which Twila had been guarding.

Arion nodded and laid her down gently on the ground. She groaned through the smile that was still stuck to her face, drawing in ragged breaths. He turned to survey his team.

Cy had gone instantly to Zee, who was only now starting to stir. She looked around the room in terror, her whole body shaking.

Her gaze finally fell on Cy who was desperately asking about her injuries. She grabbed his arm tight, her talons cutting through fabric and flesh alike. "Cyllorian?!"

Cy shushed her, placing his hand against the wound on her forward. There was a wisp of purple smoke that drifted under them, and the cut was completely gone when he pulled away. He helped her back to her feet. She was still obviously dazed, and she clung to Cy to stay upright.

Across the room, Jayr was helping Gil to his feet. Arion didn't know when he had come to, but he looked mostly unscathed, despite having been buried in debris. His head and shoulders were damp with a thin green liquid, and his clothes were torn where they had caught on splintered wood. He shook off Jayr once he was on his feet. He kept his head low, and Arion worried the glass of the bottle had cut or stuck into him.

He looked just as shaken as Zee as he scanned the remains of the room slowly. His gaze fell on Arion, and he turned away quickly. Arion stood to check his injuries, but Jayr was already upon him.

"She's deeper in?" he asked. Arion nodded. Twila groaned again at his feet. One hand gripped the hem of his coat, her eyes closed.

Cy and Zee approached, both watching Twila carefully. Cy with suspicion, and Zee with concern.

"*What is she doing here? What was all that?*" Cy asked, stepping forward.

"Twila Vamyr. Theresa never let her out of her sight, but where's her brother?" Jayr looked around the room, but there were no signs there was anyone else nearby. Twila whimpered again on the ground, curling in on herself.

"*What did Theresa do to her?*"

Arion patted the pocket of his coat that held Cresytss's journal. "Theresa continued Crestyss' experiments, and created a strong and uncontrollable magic. It didn't look like Twila was in control of the magic, she was being swung around like a puppet. She must have done something to Twila to make her attack, turning her into a trap."

"We can't leave her here," Zee said. She sounded so much like Kaitlyn that it felt like a knife stabbing into Arion's heart.

I should be thankful to get Cy back, I couldn't possibly have hoped for both of them, he thought to himself bitterly. He reminded himself that he held the brunt of the blame, and accepted that this life was what he deserved.

"I've got her," Jayr offered, surprising all of them. Before anyone else could speak. He knelt in front of Twila and picked her up easily. He spun her around onto his back, leaning forward so she wouldn't fall if her grip faltered.

"Deeper we go," Jayr said ominously once Twila was settled on his back.

The hall forward was narrow, and darker than any others. Abandoning all hope of an ambush after the previous fight, Arion pressed his hand to the wall. Cracks broke through the stone and light poured from them. It stretched a few feet in front of them, moving with them as they walked in silence.

Cy set his own palm against the wall, smoke winding through the cracks Arion made. *"I don't feel anything. Arion?"*

Arion shook his head. They walked on in silence for what felt like hours, Arion's and Cy's magic working together to be their guide. They twisted and curved, passing rooms filled with beds... enough to fit all of Lontorra it seemed.

A long mess hall stretched to their left, and a large domed room with weapons lining the walls on their right. Theresa hadn't been the only one prepared for a war.

The magic pulsed just on the edge of their vision, and Arion froze. The group nearly crashed into him at the sudden stop. He raised his hand, seeing Cy about to speak. A ringing sound had filled the halls, so slight that it had gone unnoticed between their footsteps and Twila's mumbling.

Even lighter still, hidden by the ringing, was the sound of something skittering in the dark.

"We haven't seen any rats," Gil whispered, his voice

barely louder than a whisper. At his words, all sound ceased, even from the now-unconscious Twila.

Arion drew in a deep breath, and shoved outwardly with his magic. The cracks grew at incredible speed, racing down the walls and flooding the space with light. Just outside of where the light had originally reached, the tunnel ended in a polished wooden door, blocked by a shadow.

Theresa stood with wide eyes, blinking the shock away. Thick robes hung heavy on her body, bent under their weight. The shadows played tricks over her face, casting the shapes ominously. Her eyes were ringed in black, and her cheeks and jaw protruded sharply. She looked more like a skeleton than a person, a perfect visage of death.

Her gaze darted over each of them quickly, ending with Arion. Her cracked lips split in a sneer. Arion stepped forward, unsure if what he was seeing was real, or another hallucination.

"Theresa," Cy growled, confirming that the others were seeing what Arion did. Theresa flinched, and Arion knew they had to move fast. He charged at her, his magic fading slowly from the walls.

Just before the light died, Theresa dove through the wooden door. Arion reached it mere seconds later, and burst into the room.

It was a small, round area, lit up instantly as Cy emerged behind Arion. It was furnished exactly like the bedrooms in the castle. Though there was nowhere to hide, Theresa was gone.

"Where is she?" Cy yelled, spinning in circles in the center of the room. He stomped over to the bed and threw it onto its side.

Arion stared at the wall across from the door, his magic

spreading from his feet. It slithered through the stones like lightning. Across from the wooden door, his magic gathered, outlining the shape of a door.

A triumphant smile set upon his face, and he ran toward the wall without hesitation. He could hear Cy yelling at him to stop, could see Gil trying to grab him, though he was already out of reach. The stones neared his face, and...

Pitch blackness swallowed him. Then the wind was whipping at his hair, threatening to tear his coat from his back. His heart sunk into the ground as he looked out over the darkened city of Centric.

The ruined walls of the Tower Talgrin rose around him, just like his nightmares.

CHAPTER 19

Arion

Theresa stood, looking out over the darkened city of Centric, its people still hustling about in the early evening. Lights dotted the ground, and chatter rose up to greet them. She held herself against the ruined wall, gazing down at the city below. "What do you hope to accomplish by coming back here, Arion? Do you truly think these people would ever forgive you after you killed Crestyss and dragged Lontorra into ruin?"

Theresa's taunts drifted on the wind to Arion. He shook the painful memories of this room from his head, focused on the task at hand.

"There's no more running, Theresa. No more hiding and no more lying. It's time to admit the truth of what you've done. To me, and to everyone else," Arion called out. He brandished the spear in his right hand, magic sparking in his left.

He heard the shuffle of footsteps as the others followed

him through the portal, and filled out the room behind him.

Theresa laughed, and turned on him with a snarl. "You moronic little abomination. You really think I'm still running?" she hissed.

From her cloak, she pulled a large black bottle, the liquid sloshed as she swung it around. It wasn't the glass that was black, but the potion inside, staining the bottle a disgusting color.

"You think it matters what *I've* done in this pitiful world? What matters is what I didn't do— that I didn't slaughter you in your crib, or spill Crestyss' guts while he slept. What matters is that I didn't storm the towns with a bloodthirsty army, that I didn't mow down the humans like cattle when I wanted to! All of those missed chances have led to this moment, and I plan on making up for lost time."

Arion lunged forward, but Theresa was faster than he had anticipated. She lifted the bottle over her head, leaned back, and poured it into her mouth. It splattered on her face and soaked the front of her robes. The liquid sizzled where it touched her, burning through, but she didn't stop until the bottle was completely empty.

Dragging her arm across her chin to wipe away the mess, she dropped the bottle over the edge of the tower. The sound of the thick glass shattering carried to them even over the buzz of people, and Theresa laughed again.

Her laughter was cut short as she doubled over, gripping her stomach in pain. Her robes tore where she pulled at them. Blackness oozed from her lips while she gagged. Arion stood frozen, praying that she wouldn't have the strength to survive whatever she had ingested.

Theresa raised her head shakily to look at them. Her

eyes had turned pitch black, darker even than a demon's. Her lips split in a sickening smile. More black liquid poured from her mouth. She wiped it away with sharp movements. Arion flinched as he saw the liquid rippling on her skin.

"The only thing I'll confess to is your murders when I'm through with you all," Theresa growled through the blood filling her mouth.

A strange tearing sound cut through the air, and Theresa's body burst open with a dozen black whips lunging forward. They struck through the air, scattering the group as most jumped out of the way.

Arion faced two of them head on. At the last moment, he sidestepped one and stabbed the other into the ground. It exploded, releasing hundreds of needles. They dug into Arion, burning where they touched. He quickly shook them off, but not before the other tentacle wrapped around him, squeezing his legs. Losing his balance, Arion fell to the ground. He twisted in midair, raising his spear to strike. The needles in his arm dug in deeper. A spasm went through his arm, forcing him to drop his spear. The tentacle tightened its grip, curling under his body to cover it entirely.

A scythe came down and severed the tentacle where it held Arion. The grip loosened just enough for Arion to breathe, and he pressed his left hand to the oily surface. Lightning shot through it, tearing it to pieces. Arion flung the chunks off of him, and found a hand outstretched to help him to his feet. He took it gratefully, about to thank Cyllorian for saving him.

Cy growled from the far side of the tower. Arion stood stunned, watching Cy in full demon form slicing through the onslaught of smaller tentacles that had targeted him.

Pressed to his back was a familiar body covered in shimmering blue scales. She slashed at the writhing whips with her own talons, her tail swishing about their feet to keep any stray tendrils from grabbing their ankles.

Arion had to blink to be sure he wasn't seeing things. It felt like his heart was about to stop, his memories of that night playing out in front of him. As she whirled and snarled, there was no denying it any longer; Zee had been Kaitlyn all along, and it looked like she remembered who she truly was. But there was no time to rejoice if Arion wanted this fight to turn out differently than the last one they had shared in this tower.

Kaitlyn reared back and roared as she struck a tendril that was descending from the ceiling toward their heads. Black ooze dripped from her hands, and Arion was unsure how much of it was from the tentacles, and how much was her own poison. The tendrils recoiled at even the slightest cut from her, and he guessed most of it was poison.

Arion was pulled out of his memories and back into the fight at hand as Gil yanked him to his feet. He thrust Arion's spear back into his grip, eyeing over Arion for any injuries. Arion shook him off, not needing another distraction. Gil spun and brought the scythe around in a large arch over his head, catching two more whips as they lurched for them.

At the back wall, Jayr and Grite were working together, albeit awkwardly, to guard Twila, who was hunched over on the ground between two piles of debris. Grite stood closest to her, fending off the few stray tendrils that slipped past Jayr and his sword.

The floor of the tower was littered with severed hunks of flesh, some of them still writhing. Theresa had clawed her way to her feet, clinging to the broken wall to hold herself up. Her cackling could only barely be heard over the slashing of weapons, and the splatter of blood on every possible surface. Despite how many of her tentacles had been cut down, more and more tendrils flew from her body from the many wounds that had opened along her exposed skin. Her robe hung on her in mere scraps, held in place simply by the mass of tentacles escaping her body.

Arion stared in horror as the whips lashed out at the wall around her, knocking and throwing large stones to the ground below. Screams erupted from the crowds that had gathered at the commotion. Theresa smiled wider as the screams joined the chorus of their fight. Arion prayed that no one had been caught in the rubble, but he doubted there would be no civilian casualties.

"All of you will burn in hell with me, and I can't wait to watch you suffer!" she screamed hysterically. Her face was entirely covered in black from the blood that poured from her eyes and her wounds. She contorted her body unnaturally around the tentacles so she could watch the people fleeing below, chortling maniacally.

Arion lunged forward and grabbed one of the largest tentacles. Spikes sprung from it, stabbing through Arion's hand. He smiled grimly. He couldn't get away even if he wanted to. He took a deep breath and expelled as much magic as he could without passing out. The tendril writhed and spasmed, trying to shake him off, but his hand was thoroughly stuck by the spikes.

Theresa screamed and fell forward. The tentacle in Arion's hand melted into goo that fell on the floor, along with every other one that had been fighting. Theresa held herself up on shaky arms, breathing hard through the pain and blood loss.

"Nothing will be left after this night is over," Theresa hissed. "Nothing at all."

The blood beneath their feet came to life, slithering along the ground like snakes. It wrapped around them, covering them. While they fought off the new pests, more tentacles emerged from Theresa's skin. Four large ones that swung her weak body around like a puppet. They reached up for the sky, looming over them like a black ceiling. They swayed slowly back and forth, dragging Theresa along the ground with them.

Arion stomped the ground, sending a current of magic through the floor. Lightning shot up from the cracks, slicing through the snakes that wriggled on the ground and setting the pieces ablaze. He cringed at the inhuman shrieks that filled the air as they burned.

In one quick move Arion switched his spear to his left hand, filled it with magic, and lunged forward, aiming perfectly for Theresa's heart.

Two of the four tendrils fell upon him, faster than should have been possible. They curled around him, threatening to tear him in half. The other two reached around him, fending off the others so they couldn't help. One whip wrenched his spear from his hands. A scream echoed from his throat as a few of his fingers broke from the effort to hold on. The tendril squeezed him again, cutting off his air so his scream fell short.

He was pulled forward until he was face to face with Theresa. She cocked her head to the side with one sharp movement, and Arion cringed at the sickening *pop* that her neck made. There was nothing human left in her— her eyes had been eaten away by the acidic blood, and the empty sockets stared at Arion.

Theresa's mouth opened slowly, and she spoke with a

voice that was so far from her own it sent chills down Arion's spine. "Did you really think you could play the hero after all this time? After all the pain you've caused? Look around you. Your friends that are fighting right now? You've hurt them all, scarred them all. You've ruined every single one of them. Not me, *you.* What makes you any better than me? After all, you are my child."

Arion fell limp. Prying his eyes away from Theresa's face, he turned to see his friends fighting for their lives for him yet again. Gil was hacking at one of the tentacles holding Arion, slicing small pieces from its flesh, but it never relented. Despite Arion taking his memories, he still fought.

Behind Gil was Jayr and Grite shielding Twila. They had never even been friends with Arion, and yet, he owed them his life. Jayr had actively despised him, even before everything had collapsed, but he saw Theresa as just as much his enemy as Arion's.

And Cy. They had spent years tormenting each other, but if Arion had never been born, he could have lived a happy life, free from pain and death. Yet he stood against Theresa, when once he had wanted nothing more than a mother, just as Arion had. He was fighting her for Arion's sake, all alone.

Alone? Arion thought. *Why is he alone?* The thoughts flooded Arion, chasing away his insecurities.

Kaitlyn dropped from the air just behind Theresa, large wings spreading out behind her. The tendrils froze for just a moment as Theresa slowly twisted her head toward the sound.

Kaitlyn didn't give her a chance. She leapt onto Theresa's back, sinking her sharpened teeth into her shoulder. Black blood spurted from the wound, mixed with something that shone blue in the moonlight. Theresa opened her mouth to cry out, but black and blue bubbled up into her mouth and spilled over.

Arion fell to the ground as the tendrils retreated. They wrapped around Theresa's back, much slower than before. Veins of blue pulsed in them, bulging and ready to burst. Kaitlyn released Theresa with a shove, sending the woman onto her knees.

Wings beating heavily, Kaitlyn took to the sky, narrowly avoiding the tendrils as they curled around Theresa for protection. She landed just in front of Arion, pulling him to his feet. Her blue eyes shone with warmth.

"Since when have I *ever* let someone bully you?" she asked. Kait's hand was warm where she still gripped his, and Arion had to hold his breath against the tears that welled in the back of his throat.

Something cold fit into his other hand. Cy was at his side, returning Arion's spear. Gil stepped up beside him, close enough that their shoulders were touching. Kaitlyn released Arion's hand and stood beside Cy, bumping into him so Cy in turn bumped Arion. Together, they formed a wall ready to take down Theresa.

She was a huddled mess of blood and tendrils. Small ones wiggled meekly from the puncture wounds on her shoulder. They slowly untangled themselves, revealing Theresa. One arm looked to be nothing but tendrils twined around each other like rope. She held herself at an odd angle. Arion gagged when he realized one of her legs had completely melted into goo.

Theresa roared, and all of her tendrils sprung into action. At the last second, it split again, slashing out at all of them. They swung back and forth wildly, like a wounded animal fending off death. A black spike was aimed straight for Arion's face, and he raised his spear to block it.

A quick flash of silver, and the tendril fell to the ground. Gil's scythe had carved it perfectly before it could reach Arion.

"Get her!" Gil said as he stepped forward against the onslaught. A second scythe glinted in the moonlight, and both curved blades danced through the air, accurately hacking the never ending tentacles to pieces.

Kaitlyn had taken to the sky, protecting them from an overhead attack. She wrestled with the thickest whip, ripping chunks of flesh from it. Blood rained down on them, but they paid it no mind.

Cyllorian was darting back and forth, fending off the strays that tried to curl around and ensnare them. Jayr joined him, now that the tendrils were focused on the group and no longer going near Twila. He swung his sword in wide arcs, cutting through multiple at a time. He didn't miss a beat as the tendrils were replaced just as quickly as they fell.

Raising his spear, Arion charged forward. He weaved around Gil, gliding along the tendrils he was fighting. He ducked under another that shot out at him, and watched it fall back immediately, torn to ribbons.

Theresa was screaming, her eyes closed and head tilted to the sky. Through the gurgling blood in her mouth, Arion thought he could hear words in her screeching. There was no sense to her madness, the darkness had nearly taken over. Arion jumped forward, over another tentacle that swept along the ground to trip him. He stabbed forward with his spear, straight for Theresa's heart.

The screaming stopped abruptly, followed by the sounds of battle. For a moment the whole world was frozen, Theresa staring blankly at the stars above. The whips trembled in the air, unmoving otherwise. With a jerk, Theresa's head dropped to look at Arion.

Arion took in his breath, and sent a current of magic straight through his spear and into Theresa's heart. She spasmed violently, and more of her body sunk to the ground as it melted. A sound like raindrops came over Arion's ears, quickly turning into a downpour as the whips melted themselves, pooling on the ground around them.

Before Theresa fell, Arion stepped forward. He gripped his spear just below the blade, pressed his foot to Theresa's shoulder, and ripped the spear from her chest. She stopped moving, and slowly fell backward over the edge. There was silence as she plummeted. Arion watched her tumble over herself, dissolving midair until there was nothing left of her.

On the ground lay a pile of tattered cloth in a puddle of thick, black goop, still sparking with green magic.

A crowd had formed at the base of the tower at the commotion, those brave enough to face the risk of it falling on them. They turned their heads up to Arion. Behind him, Arion could feel his team gather around him.

Shouts and questions rose up from the crowd, over-whelming Arion. His spear clattered to the ground. Arion would have followed if Gil hadn't grabbed hold of him. He pressed his body against Arion's, giving him something to lean against. He was staring at the crowd like a dog ready to attack, his cheeks flushed.

Adrenaline, Arion told himself. He looked around him in wonder that they had all survived. Everyone was covered in blood, both red and black, and sweat. Small cuts littered their exposed skin and clothes.

Beside him, Cy stood proudly in his demon form. He

clutched Kaitlyn's hand firmly, the veins popping out from under his pale skin. Arion guessed his talons would have pierced Kait's skin if she wasn't still covered in dragon scales. Her wings were spread out brilliantly behind him, and her tail swished back and forth steadily.

Jayr and Grite carried Twila forward, now conscious. She limped along with them, her arms strung across their shoulders. They had to hunch down so that her feet would touch the ground, but they supported her well. Her face was finally free of her cursed smile, and tears were clearing a path down her cheek through the grime that covered her.

The crowd below grew louder, and it sounded like a fight was about to break out. Gazing down, Arion could see two groups of people gathered on either side of Theresa's remains. One person seemed to have come forward as a leader of each side, and they were yelling at each other.

"If we had gotten here sooner, none of this would have happened! Theresa would still be alive! We have to avenge her and kill Arion— it's the only way to help ourselves!" one side shouted. Arion recognized the shine of armor made from dragon scales. A Draken.

"If she's been alive this whole time, why have we been suffering? And you knew she was alive, but did nothing to help the rest of us! I haven't even seen him for a year. How do we know Theresa hasn't been running everything from the shadow? She certainly had the means to, with you people around!" the other side argued. He waved his hands vigorously, and red magic sparked from his hands in his agitation. He dropped them to his sides, clenching his fists, but it didn't calm him down.

Arion shifted his weight, surprised that Gil held him tightly... almost defiantly. Not wanting to argue, he leaned into Gil and pressed him to turn around.

"*Where are you going?*" Cy yelled.

Arion paused for a moment. "We have to tell them what happened."

"*There's an angry mob down there, half of which want to kill you. And you want to just waltz down there? The bitch is dead, let's just go and let them figure it out themselves. At least give them all time to cool down.*"

"I told you, Cy, I'm done running. Lontorra needs our help. No one else is going to step up to fix this mess, so we have to. You said we'd do this together, didn't you?"

Arion reached his hand out to Cy with a smirk. Cy groaned, but stepped forward to clasp his hand on Arion's shoulder. Kaitlyn followed a step behind, entwining her fingers with Cy's.

"*Fine, but if I have to kill any civilians that get too rowdy, it's on you.*"

With a chuckle, Arion turned to the door leading to the winding stairs out of the Tower. Pulling his family along with him, Arion said, "We've got a lot of explaining to do."

EPILOGUE

1 Month Later

Gil strode across the docks, giving direction where need be. The yard was filled with ships bringing stock from overseas.

One of the first things Arion had done was send an owl across the sea to apologize and explain what had been happening. It took a lot of back and forth, but they had finally convinced them, and trade was booming between the two lands.

Along with cargo, the ships were even carrying visitors. So many were curious about the neighboring country, and a few ships had been designated just for passengers. Gil watched as the next ship docked, and a flood of people with wide eyes and gaping mouths stepped from the boat. He waved at them, and watched as a few began whispering among themselves. A Mage quickly stepped forward to rally the group of tourists, leading them to a few carriages being pulled by horses. They eyed them strangely, but obliged.

Gil liked seeing the docks so lively. He remembered how he used to sneak out to visit them when he was younger, and how desolate they had been. Now it was as though they had never been abandoned in the first place.

He hadn't spent as much time on the docks in the month since Theresa's death, instead being forced to spend most of his time keeping the peace in the courts at Lorile. He was forced to play messenger between Lorile and Centric, though he didn't complain about getting an excuse to visit. They had all been busy, and there was no sign of any of them getting rest any time soon.

Kaitlyn had found herself easily at a clinic in Centric, helping those that had been injured during the fight. A lot of the tower had been thrown around and damaged by Theresa. Gil visited when he could, and found Kait was a natural healer. She had learned a lot from Theresa's medicinal research— one of the few good things Theresa had left to offer Lontorra— and she used that knowledge with her own powers to make a few medicines and balms with her own body.

Twila had been locked in a room above the clinic at her own request, and Kait used her free time studying Crestyss notes on his experiments to look for any way to help her. The reading had left her with more than a few sleepless nights, but she waved off any concerns over herself.

Jayr had left to track down a few stubborn members of Theresa's support group, and detain them to prevent them from retaliating against Arion. He spent a week alone just trying to convince his fellow Drakens that Theresa was not what she seemed. He told them of the army, how she had used their people and tossed them like garbage, and of the dangerous potion she had taken without a care for the lives of anyone that could have gotten caught in the battle. Their leader announced their allegiance with Arion and his decision, and it had stifled any further discussion with those that remained on Mount Draken.

Cy had volunteered himself to repair the buildings that had been damaged from the fight. His demon form scared most people at first, but when they saw how helpful he was, they quickly seemed to forget what he was altogether. It helped that he preferred to appear human, but it was hard to keep it up on the more tiring days. Gil had seen him on his trips to Centric, and he seemed to be fitting in perfectly among the Mages.

Arion had set himself the task of restoring the tower, and it took all of his time and attention. Gil had offered to help on multiple occasions, but he was waved off with the excuse that it could really only be done with magic. Even when Gil suggested he get Cy, Arion argued that he was too busy helping everyone else, and not to bother him. Eventually, Gil gave up, accepting that it was something Arion just had to do himself.

Even though Gil had told him quite a few times, it didn't seem like Arion believed that he had gotten his memories back. He was less wary then he had been just after Theresa's death, and Gil told him too many times for Arion to have never heard him. But Arion still refused to look him in the eyes.

He just needs time, he told himself. *After how I treated him before, it could be a lot of time.*

Gil was shaken from his thoughts by someone running frantically across the docks. They stopped frequently, yelling for help from any worker.

Gil quickly ran after them, and recognized Kaitlyn once

he caught her. "Gil!" she gasped, her voice failing her as she struggled to catch her breath.

"What's going on? What's wrong?" Gil asked frantically. He noticed a small bag clutched in her hands.

"The ship...for Molanse...did it leave...already?" she asked between quick breaths.

"It was set to leave early this morning. Why?" Gil helped her stand up straight, and she finally got herself under control.

Kaitlyn thrust the bag against Gil's chest. "Arion forgot this. He *needs* it, Gil. You have to get it to him. I have to get back to the clinic. You know I can't leave Twila alone."

Gil took the bag carefully. He tried to calm Kaitlyn down, "He'll be all right, Kaitlyn. I'm sure he took everything he needs. Besides, he's only there for one night, for a proper introduction. And he's got Cy with him."

Kaitlyn glared at Gil. "That's exactly why he needs this, Gil."

Kaitlyn grabbed his arm and pulled him in closer. "It's for the nightmares. I know he doesn't like to take it. He thinks he's fooling me, but he's not. And if he has you believing he isn't having nightmares, then you're dumber than I thought."

Gil pulled away, tucking the bag under his arm. He couldn't deny that he had his suspicions, but what was he to do when Arion wouldn't tell him anything. He certainly looked better than Gil had ever seen him, but he didn't want to risk an argument when things were still tense between them.

Gil looked over at the passenger ship, now emptied and being cleaned for the day. "I'll take it to him."

* * *

CY WAS SHOCKED to find out there was a government building in the port town where he had woken up a month prior. He had only seen the run down part of the city, and couldn't believe that such a nice building could reside in the same place.

The request for a meeting with Arion came as a shock to everyone. Cy tried to convince Arion to stall, worried that relations between Molanse and Lontorra were still too tense. Arion argued that was exactly why he had to go now. He had to do as Molanse asked to prove he was willing to make things right between the two countries. Cy was just glad Arion hadn't pushed to go by himself when Cy offered to accompany him.

It was nearly as big as the castle, and they needed guides to lead them through the halls. The cold stone was covered with lush carpets, the walls holding endless tapestries. Upon arrival, they were taken promptly to a large common room filled with people. Cy was sure they were only meeting those in charge of the country, and was stunned to be put in front of a small army.

Arion had been the one to handle communication, and he insisted on teaching Cy what he had learned of Molanse's government, but it had been hard to wrap his head around. There was no single person in complete control, but it was not a council of equals like in Lorile. There was one person at the head of it all with their own assistant, and multiple councils of people below them that saw over different aspects of the country, like currency and laws. The person at the top— a strict woman with a motherly side, much like Jemmina— couldn't make any decisions on her own. Instead, her ideas were presented to the councils, and there was a vote. If most of them voted in favor, then there was a long process to implement said idea. It was one of the reasons it had taken so long before they could make a physical appearance before them. Arion had been dead set on doing things right this time, and it paid off in the end.

The day had been a long one filled with endless questions and show-and-tell games. They wanted demonstrations of their magic, and of Cy's demon form. It was exhausting. Cy and Arion could barely keep up with the man that was guiding them to their room.

Cy cast a sneaky glance at Arion. He drug his feet on the ground, nearly stumbling over the rug a few times. A yawn overtook him, and his eyes remained closed for a long moment. They opened with a start, and Arion shook himself.

Cy was glad to see Arion looking healthier. There was color in his cheeks, and he had put on weight. Cy thought he could still put on more, but he knew better than to pressure him. Arion was working hard, and trying to turn himself around, he could tell that much.

What worried him the most, though, was that Arion hadn't asked anyone else for help. It was like he was still living as though he were alone.

"Here is Master Arion's room," the butler said, gesturing into a room. The door was open to reveal soft light from a lamp— *electricity*, Cy reminded himself, *we need to get that*. The light spilled over an ornate bed large enough for four people to sleep comfortably in, as well as other oversized furniture, an armchair with curled, wooden armrests, an oval mirror sat atop a dresser, gold plating gleaming in the light, a wardrobe that almost touched the domed ceiling.

Arion trudged in sleepily, and collapsed in the

armchair. The butler gave him an odd look, but said nothing.

Cy stepped forward to curl up in the bed, but the butler stopped him. "The next room is yours."

"We can't stay together?" Cy thought. His stomach roiled with suspicion. He wasn't unaware of the enemies that Arion had made; Jayr had kept him well informed whenever he successfully caught another one. He couldn't help but be suspicious of anyone that wanted to separate them.

"It's only proper that you get your own accommodations," the butler said simply. It was a reasonable enough statement, but Cy felt it left no room for argument.

"You gonna be okay, kid?" Cy called into the room. Arion waved his hand dismissively, and it fell limp at his side. Cy watched Arion's features soften as he fell asleep. Feeling satisfied with Arion sleeping soundly, he nodded and followed the butler to his own room.

It truly was the next room, though the doors were a walk away. His room was a mirror image of Arion's, stuffed with the same giant furniture. He sighed and stepped into the room. The door clicked shut behind it, and Cy was relieved that there was no sound of a lock. From the hallway outside came the echo of Arion's door shutting as well.

Stepping in front of the mirror, Cy let his human form fall away. His skin turned pale, and small talons sprouted from his fingertips. Cy had gotten used to filing them down, and they rested on the dresser evenly without risk of scratching up the wood.

He ran his hand over his face, trying to wipe the exhaustion from him. His body was buzzing with worry, and he refused to go to sleep yet. They were leaving first thing in the morning, and he knew he needed rest, but something kept him awake.

Suddenly, screaming filled the hallway. Cy jumped and launched himself at the door. He barreled through it, possibly breaking the handle, but he didn't stop to check. The halls were empty, and the screaming was coming from Arion's room.

Cy turned to run to him, but was grabbed by two guards that had rounded the corner. Two more ran past them, and opened Arion's door. They barely had time to duck before bolts of magic flew from the room. Cy wrestled himself free and joined the other guards, staring into Arion's room. They held him back, but he could clearly see Arion suffering.

He was writhing on the floor, kicking and flailing his arms. Over and over, he dug his nails– no, *talons*— into his skin, scratching himself. Blood was dripping onto the floor while Arion thrashed. He was completely out of control, and magic was spewing from him in bolts that lodged themselves in whatever they touched. Tears streamed down his face, and Cy realized he was stuck in a nightmare, but this was worse than he had ever seen before.

Cy tried to push his way through the guards, but they were stronger than he expected. The other two were upon him, pulling him back, and it was four against one. *"Let go, I have to help him! Let. GO!"* Cy screamed.

"We can't let you get close. Something's obviously wrong, and he's too dangerous," one of them argued.

"I can help him," Cy growled, and for the moment, he regretted dulling his talons. He didn't care that attacking the guards would be bad for diplomacy. He needed to get to Arion.

"Arion! Wake up!" he yelled over the guards when he couldn't break free.

A sound came from down the hallway, and all the guards turned to see what it was. Someone was running down the halls, followed by two more guards.

"Gil?!" Cy yelled in disbelief. Gil raised his hand, and Cy saw a small vial filled with dark tablets. The medicine Kaitlyn had made for Arion to help him sleep.

Puffing his chest, Cy blew out a thick cloud of smoke that filled the guards lungs and they fell into a coughing fit. They held their grip on Cy, but he didn't need to get through. He laughed triumphantly as he felt a gust of wind blow past as Gil ran through the smoke into Arion's room.

"Arion. Arion!" he yelled, but Cy could hear him struggling to grab him. He winced as Arion struck him, and Cy had had enough.

He shook the guards off of him, and ran into the room. He grabbed Arion's arms and held them down, while Gil sat on his legs. He dropped two tablets into his mouth, and Arion's fighting slowly ceased. He blinked the tears from his eyes and looked around wildly. He found Gil leaning over him, and the tears started to flow again.

"You're alive," he whispered.

Gil nodded. "I'm fine, I'm here. It was just a dream. Everything's fine, Arion, I promise."

Cy leaned back and released Arion's arms. Arion glanced at him for a second, but as soon as he realized he was free, he wrapped his arm around Gil's neck and pulled him down to the floor with him. Arion kissed Gil, and Gil was frozen for a moment before kissing him back, his face flaring purple.

Gil hugged Arion back, and comforted him. Cy quietly left the room, and met with six dumbfounded guards. He chuckled at the absurdity of it all, exhaustion quickly washing back over him. He grabbed hold of the door and glanced back into the room. Gil had gotten Arion to his feet, and was guiding him to the bed, Arion refusing to release his hold on Gil.

"Time to go. Trust me, you don't want to stick around for this," Cy said as he ushered the guards away from the door. He shut it firmly behind him, and sneakily used his magic to lock the door until morning.

The guards followed as Cy returned to his room. "What happened? Will he be all right?" One of them asked what they all were thinking.

Cy paused just inside his room, thinking of the family Arion built for himself. *"He's going to be more than okay. We all are,"* Cy said simply, a smile resting easily on his face.

Without another word, he shut the door, looking forward to the future ahead of them.

THE END

Find more books by T. Ariyanna by visiting www. tariyannabooks.com

About the Author

T. Ariyanna is a newcomer to publishing, but a veteran at storycrafting. After being enchanted by the worlds within books during middle school, she spent her high school years creating her first novel-length story. A few years later she hit the scene with a magical debut, *The Mage's Son*.

Ariyanna's specializations run from realistic fantasy to dystopian steampunk. She juggles writing with being a stay at home mother to a daughter just as adventurous as any heroine. Her hobbies include reading, crafting, and playing video games.